LIVING EXPENSES

TERI VLASSOPOULOS

INVISIBLE PUBLISHING
Halifax | Fredericton | Picton

Library and Archives Canada Cataloguing in Publication

Title: Living expenses / Teri Vlassopoulos.
Names: Vlassopoulos, Teri, 1979- author.
Identifiers: Canadiana 20240529235 | ISBN 9781778430671 (softcover)
Subjects: LCGFT: Novels.
Classification: LCC PS8643.L38 L58 2025 | DDC C813/.6—dc23

Edited by Bryan Ibeas
Cover design by Megan Fildes
Typeset in Laurentian with thanks to type designer Rod McDonald

Invisible Publishing is committed to protecting our natural environment. As part of our efforts, both the cover and interior of this book are printed on acid-free 100% post-consumer recycled fibres.

Printed and bound in Canada.

Invisible Publishing | Halifax, Fredericton, and Picton
www.invisiblepublishing.com

Published with the generous assistance of the Canada Council for the Arts, the Ontario Arts Council, and the Government of Canada.

For Clara

PART ONE: WINTER

When Claire gave our mother an iPad for Christmas, it was a deviation from our usual script. We never bought each other large-scale expensive items. Instead we were committed to the platitude that it was more important to be together, no matter where any of us lived at the time. Mom would contribute what she could to travel costs if needed, and except for one single year, there hadn't been a Christmas in our entire lives that wasn't spent in our original configuration.

As we got older, our holidays devolved into replicas of preteen slumber parties: Claire and I cross-legged on the living room floor, drinking hot chocolate and staying up late on Christmas Eve. Mom, more often than not, would join us too. We retroactively imagined that earlier holidays—when my sister and I were less forgiving, more desirous of something that we couldn't define—had similar lighthearted family sitcom vibes. A mother and her daughters, muddling through life the best they could, against all odds. And it worked, mostly. The way time softens and mellows past hard edges—this was the closest we got to a Christmas miracle.

When we were kids, we exchanged presents on Christmas Eve after coming home from Mass, and even after Claire and I made it clear that we no longer wanted to attend church, we kept the tradition of opening our gifts on Christmas Eve and leaving Christmas morning free. This year I bought us matching cashmere socks—fancy and unnecessary. I made us open them first so that we could all have cozy, matching feet. Mom filled our stockings with chocolate. But the present from Claire was a real capital-P present, and when Mom opened the sleek box and said, "Oh Claire!" I felt something

I wasn't used to. Not guilt exactly, or envy. It was a twinge of discomfort, of wheels being pushed off their worn and familiar tracks.

"It'll make it easier for us to keep in touch if I move," Claire said. "It's more convenient than your laptop. You can call me using FaceTime."

"Face call?"

"FaceTime. It's like Skype."

"Why don't we just use Skype?"

"No one uses Skype anymore."

"I do."

"Fine, we can use both."

As Claire set up the iPad, we explained to Mom the terms and apps, new but ubiquitous, changing so quickly that by next year we'd surely have new slang that would make the current terms sound quaint, ironic. And then some Christmas in the relatively near future, one of us—probably Claire—would give something even more advanced, something involving holograms, robots, lasers, or at least the future equivalent of these things. Whatever it was, it would surely feel like it had emerged the way today's technology has appeared in our lives: inevitably, like we were entitled to it.

"The iPad isn't working," Mom said after the first tutorial, swiping and jabbing at the screen erratically while it remained unresponsive. "How do I turn it on again?"

I showed her once and then twice and then a third time just in case. When she repeated the action, nothing happened. The screen didn't recognize her movements.

"Is there something wrong with me?" She stared at her hands. They trembled slightly. I wondered if maybe a lifetime of work had worn down the ridges of her fingerprints.

"I'm not sure an iPad was necessary," I said to Claire.

"What do you mean, *necessary?*"

"She has her laptop already."

"I think I'm too old for this," Mom added.

Claire, annoyed, took the tablet and stuffed it back into the box. "I can return it then."

An hour later the iPad was out again and Claire and I were huddled in the basement laundry room with our phones, taking turns talking to Mom in the kitchen, first on Skype, then on FaceTime. The cashmere socks kept our feet warm on the unfinished concrete.

"Hello, Claire! Hello, Laura!" Mom said to us onscreen.

"Hi!" we said back.

"Merry Christmas, my beautiful girls!"

We parroted greetings back and forth until the novelty wore off, and then Claire and I marched back upstairs to be together in person.

The question that hovered around Christmas this year was whether we would be able to get together in the same way next year. Claire had recently been asked at work to move from Toronto to the Bay Area office they were opening in the new year. She'd been at the company for almost four years, one of the first fifty employees, and despite being frequently approached by headhunters about other jobs, she had remained.

The company was a relatively early entrant into the industry for smart thermostat and home energy technologies, sustainable before it became especially cool to be sustainable. It was founded by some of Claire's schoolmates, and they'd offered her a job without making her go through an interview process. At the time she'd been working for another tech company in Ottawa that had just gone public. She had a bunch of vested shares and jumped on the opportunity to move back to Toronto. It was a good decision: the company grew slowly, and then in the last eighteen months, incredibly quickly.

Early in Claire's tenure, the founders raised significant funding, which translated into high salaries and stock options, and then as time passed there were more raises, more options. As the number of employees grew, their perks expanded to include things like fitness stipends, in-house yoga classes, and massages. Claire was now VP of engineering, and with another round of funding allowing for the new office, the company wanted her there to get things set up. So they could make more money.

Maybe this was par for the course for the types of companies Claire worked for, but she would tell me about these things nonchalantly, and I couldn't help but be impressed. I was the senior editor for a free monthly food magazine that was distributed at high-end grocery stores (Canadian only). Salaries were modest, equity and yoga non-existent, and I was mostly expected to be grateful just to have a job.

I had *some* perks, I suppose: while the three of us got ready for bed on Christmas Eve, I prepared fresh ginger hot toddies from a recipe one of the other food editors had passed on to me before the holidays, a gussied-up version that required a series of small, fussy steps. I peeled a knob of ginger and sliced it into thin, perfect matchsticks—a difficult exercise with Mom's dull knives—then steeped them in hot water in little squares of cheesecloth I'd brought with me. I got annoyed when I realized I'd forgotten the Greek honey I'd swiped from the test kitchen especially for the drink; it had been made by the bees that pollinated wild thyme on the island of Crete.

Claire was scrolling through her phone at the kitchen table while I did this.

"When do you have to decide about moving?" I asked as I rummaged through Mom's cupboards for a honey substitute.

"Yesterday, ideally."

I found a bottle of maple syrup that I'd brought last Christmas still languishing in the fridge and poured it into our mugs with the steeped ginger mixture and whisky.

"And you really aren't sure if you want to do it?"

"It's just happening so fast. It's not that easy to pick up and leave."

"They're going to take care of everything, though, right?"

"Yeah, mostly."

While I understood that moving across the continent wasn't a snap decision, Claire didn't have any big ties to Toronto at the moment. She wasn't dating anyone, and this move felt like the natural progression of her career. She was the kind of person who made top-thirty-under-thirty lists—she was one of only three women listed in *Toronto Life*'s "Rising Stars in Tech"—and who was interviewed on podcasts and described as an *expert*. It wasn't a surprise that her company wanted her to be the face of their office in the Valley, a short form I felt embarrassed to say but that Claire had most definitely used. Silicon Valley was a place I half believed was invented by *Wired* and Douglas Coupland. Was it corrupt, a gold rush?

"It's just a good opportunity for me," she said when I asked her opinion.

"It sounds like you've made your decision then."

"Yeah." She paused. "Maybe. I'm going outside for a second before drinking this. It's too hot."

I brought Mom's drink to her in her bedroom. She took one sip, made a face, and then set it aside. "It's really good, honey."

"Not honey, maple syrup."

She didn't get my joke. "Where's Claire?"

"Outside."

"I wish she'd stop smoking."

"Maybe if she moves to California she'll turn into a health freak."

Mom's cat, Coco, who had been sleeping nestled against her until I'd disturbed them, got up, stretched, and jumped off the bed. Mom had bought Coco after I'd moved out, and the cat had never quite bonded with me nor with Claire. Mom gestured to the empty spot next to her. "Sit with me."

Claire found us and squeezed in on the other side of Mom, the way we used to lie in bed with her when we were kids. We didn't acknowledge the smell of smoke hovering around us; we just sat in peaceful silence, sipping our drinks. Claire and I split Mom's when we finished our own.

I woke up early on Christmas morning. Despite having only shown up at Mom's the day before, it felt as if I'd been there longer, and in my bleary-eyed state, the sight of my old belongings convinced me that I still lived there. More than a decade after moving out, my room was still unchanged from the last time I'd lived in it: the same band posters, a pinned-up print of *Starry Night* that I'd hung thinking it would make my walls look more sophisticated. Claire's room had been repurposed into a guest room shortly after she'd moved away for university, but I'd lived at home for longer, going to school in Toronto and staying with Mom since I could take the subway to campus and not pay rent. I hadn't minded because Joe, who was my boyfriend at the time and would later become my husband, lived with some roommates downtown, and I would crash at his place as often as I wanted. I would stay with him frequently until we moved in together when we graduated.

Christmas was one of the rare times that Joe and I were apart. He went to his parents' house, and I was reluctant to leave Mom and Claire, even for just one meal. At the beginning of our relationship, I'd been more flexible, and sometimes he'd even join us, but for the past few years we'd stuck to the original formula: Claire, Mom, and me as our own unit.

I reached for my phone and called him. When he answered, I heard his family in the background, his mom and sister, his two nieces and three nephews. He had a bigger family than I did—older siblings with children, multiple aunts and uncles, loud people who crowded into his parents' house on holidays and woke up at the crack of dawn already yelling at each other.

"What's going on?" I asked. A child was crying, but I couldn't figure out which one. I knew each of them well, but at a certain point a wailing child was just a wailing child.

"Breakfast drama. My sister made candy-cane pancakes, but some kids wanted regular pancakes and she refused to make a separate batch. Now we're dealing with the aftermath."

"Were the pancakes good?"

"Too sweet. I don't blame them for complaining. How are you?"

"Hungover. I drank too much whisky with Claire last night."

There was muffled activity behind him. "My mom says she wishes you were here."

"We'll make it work next year."

I said this every Christmas, but then twelve months would pass and I would be back in my old bedroom, talking to Joe on the phone like we used to when we were teenagers, back when weren't yet officially dating but were obsessed with talking to each other all the time. It was sweet, almost, to regress. This year, though, after the call ended, I felt restless. I got up and went straight to the kitchen.

Another one of our traditions was eating waffles on Christmas morning. I started making waffles when I was in middle school after finding a waffle maker at a garage sale, and I never stopped. Some years the waffles would be complicated, never as cloying as candy cane, but yeasted versions that required the dough to rise overnight, or that were made with buckwheat flour and browned butter that resulted in a satisfying nutty chew. This year I hadn't planned anything in advance, so I took out my phone, went to my own food blog's archives, and looked up my basic waffle recipe, one of the first entries.

I'd started the blog years ago to write about the meals I ate at home and on my travels with Joe or with Claire and my Mom. I followed a template that I'd picked up from other sites: a personal story followed by a recipe that was tangentially related followed by a comment section. I'd launched it at the sweet spot of blog culture, just before the space became oversaturated, before the term viral was used in relation to recipes, before commenters became vicious in a casual and expected way, before any of those comments remarked on the length or point of the story preceding the recipe. Was there a time when the internet was wholesome, good? Maybe that was the time. I also nurtured relationships with other bloggers and readers who commented on posts—people who were strangers, which seemed to count for something since they had no obligation to care about my blog—so I actually had a healthy audience that cared about what I wrote. Claire had also helped me set up an index that made it easy to search the site and then print out recipes in a way that automatically generated a grocery list.

Other bloggers would ask me about it, and in return link over to my blog. Whenever Joe and I travelled anywhere, I'd flip through my mental Rolodex of fellow bloggers or readers to see if any of them lived there, and because of them we'd had a few random fun nights in New York City, Paris, Laos.

I rarely updated the blog anymore, though. I worked too much with food to be interested in writing about it during non-work hours. Also, blogs were now so passé and I hadn't properly shifted the format into something more of the moment. Every few months I would get the urge to post an entry, but I mostly used it as a reference for my own cooking—which is why I was hesitant to delete it, and why, every year, when I got an email about web hosting, I'd continue to pay the fees.

Nothing ever changed in Mom's kitchen. I reached for the flour from the cupboard beside the sink, the sugar in the canister on the counter. The vanilla (artificial) was old but fine, and I slipped in some of the previous night's whisky too. The waffle maker was the same one I'd always used, its cord so frayed that it might spontaneously combust.

My stomach grumbled, and I rested my hand on my belly. There was a small part of me that wondered if I was pregnant. I was probably just hungry and hungover, but I'd woken up feeling like something was happening. I had a vague understanding of my cycle, and according to the app I used to track it, I was on the verge of starting my period. But what if this time I wasn't? What if these feelings were the beginnings of pregnancy, which I'd heard were confusingly similar to pre-menstrual symptoms? Should I have consumed all that whisky the night before?

By the time I'd gulped down a glass of water and made the first two waffles, my stomach was still again.

In the lull after breakfast, we lounged on the couch playing with our devices, Mom getting the hang of her iPad. She updated her Facebook status; she took pictures of us. I returned to the kitchen to start making lechon for Christmas dinner at Mom's request. It wasn't the full-sized suckling pig of Mom's Christmases in the Philippines, but over time I'd figured out how to make a decent version that wasn't too much for three people.

My phone rang. Dad. I poked my head into the living room. "It's Dad. Mom, do you want to talk to him?"

They didn't speak regularly, but holidays were sometimes an exception. "Sure," she said.

I answered on speakerphone. "Hey Dad, I'm here with Mom and Claire."

"Merry Christmas. Was Santa good to all of you?"

"As always," Mom said first.

"There's no such thing as Santa Claus," Claire said.

"Shh, I have grandkids around." Dad's two other daughters had three kids between them, and I could hear minor shrieks and laughs in the background.

Mom wandered off into the kitchen, and Claire and I remained to chat with him. We agreed that Claire and I should meet him for dinner soon.

"I talked to my accountant about you, Claire," he said toward the end of the call. "I'll email you what he recommended for your move."

"Oh, cool. Thanks."

"When we meet we'll celebrate the job and your birthdays too."

After the call ended, I said to Claire, "Sounds like Dad thinks you're definitely moving."

"I just needed his advice." She shrugged. "Bonus points to him for remembering our birthdays in advance."

"I bet he still couldn't tell you the exact dates, though."

"I'm not betting on that."

Claire and I were both born in early January, so close together that we were often mistaken for twins. It made sense: we had the same long black hair, the same tan skin. There's some kind of evolutionary trick that's supposed to make newborns look like their fathers to flatter them into bonding, but this didn't manifest in either of us. Claire and I were wholly our mother's children. We looked more Filipino, like her. Dad's whiteness came through more in the sharp point of our noses, maybe in the slight fold of our eyelids.

Dad treated us like twins too. When we were kids, he would give us a single cheque to split for birthday money, just one lump sum written in my name every year, arriving at some midpoint between our actual birthdates. Even when we were older and he switched to individual e-transfers instead of cheques, we would get the same amount on the same day.

Growing up we saw him regularly, but less so as we got older. Now we were down to one visit per season, always the three of us together. I hadn't talked to him on my own since Joe and I were house hunting, when I'd asked him questions about real estate and mortgages and he'd given us a chunk of money for the down payment. I guess I shouldn't have been surprised that Claire had talked to him about her job.

Mom walked back into the living room holding her iPad. "I think I want to try dating," she announced.

"What?" I asked.

"Online dating."

"Men are terrible, Mom!" I said.

"You're the only one of us who's married," Claire pointed out.

"You're lucky to have Joe, honey," Mom said.

"Guys. That's so different."

Mom didn't strike me as someone who thought about dating. She didn't seem lonely. She was good-natured, cheerful. Her life was busy with work, friends she saw regularly and went to church with every Sunday. Unlike Dad, Claire and I saw Mom all the time, both together and on our own. Also, she was our *mom*, which did not seem compatible with the concept of dating.

"My friend Myrna met her boyfriend online after her husband passed away. He drove us to church last week. He's very nice."

"I read about a dating app for seniors," Claire said while we mulled over Mom's statement.

"I'm not a senior yet!" She had just turned sixty.

"It's for *mature* people then."

"Can I see it?"

"Are you really sure you want to, Mom?" I asked.

"Yes."

Claire took the iPad, searched, and downloaded the app. "We have to make a profile for you first."

"Is it public?"

"Only for people on the app."

"And you're sure you want to do this?" I asked again.

"Laura, yes."

"Okay, I have to list your interests." Claire was poised, ready for Mom's answers. "What are they?"

"You and Laura."

"What else?"

"Coco."

"You need something more interesting than your kids and your cat."

"Playing tennis."

"You've literally never played tennis in your entire life."

"I'd like to!"

"You can't *lie* on your profile, Mom."

Watching tennis, Claire typed. "Okay, we need a picture. We might as well take one now." She held up the iPad and Mom stared back, stone-faced.

"You should smile for this. It's not a passport photo."

Mom smiled, and Claire took a few shots. Mom had gotten her hair done before Christmas, covering up her white roots by dyeing it a dark reddish colour that streaked the black. She still kept it shoulder-length. She washed it once or twice a week, rolling it up in big rollers at night and then tying it up with a scarf while she slept so that it would fall in big loose waves in the morning. Her face was smooth, but I loved the crow's feet around her eyes when she smiled. I'd always thought my mother was so beautiful.

"Do you need my credit card number?"

"What? No." Claire put down the iPad. "Mom, you have to promise us never to use a site that makes you give your credit card information, okay? And don't give the number to strange men either. Ever."

She rolled her eyes like a teenager and got up to pose for more pictures. We picked the best out of the batch, one with Mom smiling naturally and another with Coco.

We uploaded them and then started walking her through a long fifty-question multiple-choice quiz about her personality and preferences. When we got to a question about putting out on the first date, I handed her the iPad. "You're on your own from here."

"You're sure no one will try to take advantage of me?" she asked after we reviewed her completed profile.

"We'll vet the men for you," Claire offered.

"You'll be moving."

"It's online dating; it doesn't matter where I live."

"I can help too," I said, which seemed to satisfy her concerns.

We made the profile public, and by the time we'd finished dinner, Mom had multiple likes and direct messages. On Christmas Day!

Hi beautiful

I like your smile. Would love to chat and get to know you better

Merry Christmas! Your profile looks interesting

We agreed the last one sounded the most normal, and Mom clicked on his profile without us having to show her what to do first. "He's handsome."

"You think?" Claire asked.

His name was John, and his pictures were as generic as his name. He was white, ambiguously *in my sixties*, balding.

"I guess he looks normal," I said, "but I don't know if I trust anyone on a dating site on Christmas Day."

"*Mom*'s on a dating site on Christmas Day."

"True." I read through his profile. Divorced, two kids—just like Mom. What red flags was I looking for? Explicit language? Poor grammar? "You must have more recent experience with this," I said to Claire. "I haven't dated since high school."

"I'm on hiatus."

Mom started typing a message in return, pecking slowly with her index finger. She hugged the iPad close and shifted away when I leaned over her shoulder to read.

"What are you saying to him?"

"It's private."

"I can't believe you're not showing us!" Claire said. "I have your password. I can look it up myself."

"I'll change it."

"How are we going to make sure you're not taken advantage of?"

"I'm not rich. What are they going to take from me?"

"Mom," I said.

"What? I'm not giving anyone my credit card number."

"Just be safe."

This made her laugh hard.

"Am I going to regret giving you an iPad?" Claire asked.

"No."

"Yes," I said at the exact same time.

Later that night I scrolled through pictures of friends' Christmases on Instagram while Claire lay on her stomach at the foot of my bed, picking through a wooden box filled with my old jewellery. I hardly recognized her from this angle. A week earlier she'd cut her hair short, bleached it, and dyed it a light purple. She was still wearing the cashmere socks.

She took out the earrings first, setting aside the ones without a matching partner, and then moved on to a clump of thin chain necklaces that had formed a stubborn knot over time. She held the tangle of necklaces up above her head. The chains spun out slowly, and as they separated she used her fingers to gently tease them apart. She pulled one necklace from the knot, then another.

"Let's log in to Mom's account to make sure she's on the right track." I looked up the login screen on my phone's browser. "What's the password? Coco123?"

Claire was now working on the last two remaining necklaces. When she was done, she organized each piece into a row on the bed. I saw things I'd forgotten, some turquoise earrings from Mexico, a cheap nameplate necklace I'd ordered online.

I put the nameplate necklace on. "Do you want anything? Take it."

"I appreciate your generosity, but no thank you."

"Okay. Password."

"Maybe we should give her some privacy with this?"

"Mom hasn't dated anyone the entire time we've been alive. She might need guidance."

"Laura."

"What?"

"You really think she hasn't dated anyone?"

"You think she has?"

"What about when she'd get a babysitter for us and go out? What do you think she was doing?"

"She was with friends."

"She'd bring us along if it was just with her friends."

"Not always."

"What about the guys we met, the ones we don't see anymore?"

"She called them her friends." I felt naive all of a sudden.

Claire scooped up the turquoise earrings. "Here. Something blue for when she meets the man of her dreams and remarries."

"Oh my god. I can't believe you're going to move away and make me deal with this alone." I threw my phone at her. "Just log in."

In the end, though, we didn't. Claire left my room to go to bed early.

I texted Joe. *What's happening over there?*

Everyone's drunk, the kids are all still awake. What are you doing?

Trying not to think about my mom sexting random men she's meeting online

Excuse me?

She decided to try online dating
Wow

I turned off my light and thought I'd try to get to bed early too. I scrolled through more posts online. Given our demographic, early to mid-thirties, the pictures centred less on adults and more on adorable fat babies celebrating their first holidays. I methodically clicked on hearts for each photo and then put the phone down.

There was a period of my life when time—the concept of it, the chronology of days, of their finite fact—didn't intimidate me. I suppose this is just the confidence of youth, but because I could sense that people around me seemed stressed out by the passing of time, I believed I was immune to it. For instance, the year everyone in my friend group turned thirty, I went to four weddings and a thirtieth surprise birthday-slash-engagement party. This clump of rushes to matrimony puzzled me, maybe because it had come to Joe and me so easily, not something done to adhere to a schedule. We married the year I graduated from university, an afternoon ceremony in his parents' backyard with our immediate family and closest friends, a fancy dinner later. I knew people thought we were too young to get married, but why did it matter if this was what we wanted? When my friends were dating in their twenties, I was setting up my life with my new husband. We spent years avoiding settling into complacency, though. We travelled until Joe decided to go to law school. For the longest time we didn't have matching cutlery or plates.

Time passed, and with thirty-five on the horizon, I started experiencing what others had maybe experienced at thirty; I felt as if I should have more to show for my—our—years together. Did we have matching plates? Mostly.

We'd just bought our first place, a loft, a few months earlier. But I wondered if I was missing something to keep up the feeling of forward momentum. I liked my job, but over the past three years it hadn't changed much, and I wasn't sure if it ever would. The blog had fizzled out, and I was rarely in touch with anyone in that mental Rolodex. That being said, Joe's job was going well, and he also had a podcast on municipal politics—which he'd started with his best friend, Amit, around the same time as I started my blog—and it was still thriving, continuing to gather more listeners and attention.

Maybe having a baby was the right next thing for us to do. It was the kind of decision that came easily, something that wasn't really a decision, more an issue of timing and logistics. It wasn't until that Christmas that I realized I was relieved it was the next thing in line and that, yes, the timing was right. It was time.

I suspected I was pregnant because about two weeks ago Joe and I had attended his work holiday party. His law firm had rented a private room at an upscale Italian restaurant where waiters walked around with platters of extravagant antipasti: roasted razor clams, prosciutto that melted on your tongue like butter, balls of burrata that oozed onto little grilled crostini. We ate the food and drank Prosecco and then red wine as we moved from group to group to engage in party banter.

I spent most of the night talking about our new place. I sometimes lacked conversation topics suitable for his co-workers, but everyone was game for real estate. "It's a hard loft," I said between bites of pickled asparagus and purple carrots, using the terminology our real estate agent had used. "That means it has no doors. You have to climb a ladder to get to the bedroom."

When we got home, we were drunk enough that the ladder seemed foolish to attempt. Joe collapsed on the couch and I flung myself on top of him. His teeth were wine stained, and he smelled like the cigar he'd gone out to smoke with some colleagues after dessert.

"What are we going to do now?" I asked on the couch.

"What do you want to do?" he asked back. We kissed.

In the morning I looked at my menstrual tracking app. I'd forgotten to consult it, and apparently I was ovulating. I'd started relying on the app after I quit taking the pill in the summer, when we'd had the idea that we'd casually start trying to get pregnant. I had no idea if my body knew how to function after fifteen years of hormonal contraception.

"I might get pregnant," I said, showing Joe my phone. He immediately hugged me.

As soon as I allowed myself to think about having a baby, I was flooded with the feeling that we were participating in something bigger than us, something mystical, like we were finally allowing the grandiose workings of the entire universe to unfold within my body. But since then, I'd found my actual body hard to parse.

Even though I'd been eager to go to bed early and get Christmas Day over with, I couldn't sleep.

Are you still awake? Do you want to watch a movie? I texted Claire.

I miss you, I texted Joe.

Neither responded, so I got up to get a glass of wine. *Why not?* I figured. for the next nine months I might not be able to. The house was quiet, dark. I stood at the living room window for a few minutes looking at the neighbours' Christmas lights, which must have been on a timer because while I was standing there, they blinked off. More darkness.

Back in my room, I sipped the wine and scanned myself, starting at my toes and working my way up. I clenched my pelvic floor muscles and relaxed them. Maybe in a year I would be able to enjoy a glass of wine in bed, but there would be a baby in the room too. Would Joe be with us or with his parents? Can you drink when you have a newborn? I was pretty sure you could. I'd heard friends use a phrase for what you did when you wanted to be sure not to pass alcohol on to the baby. *Pump and dump.* I closed my eyes and willed the day to end so that life could return to normal, but it didn't work.

When I was younger, around ten, I became aware that this holiday was an interminable expanse of time during which Claire and I were no longer connected to the usual touchstones of our lives. Our friends were busy with their own families, and if we called them on the phone the conversations were truncated, awkward. We couldn't go anywhere. Mom often fell into a depressive slump. She would tell us about the Christmases of her youth, which involved late-night Christmas Eve gatherings, slaughtered animals roasted over fires for incredible feasts, trays of sweets, carolling. Ours were never like that, despite Mom's many friends, who would've no doubt included us in their holidays if she'd asked. "We're lucky to have each other," she would say to us. "Christmas is for family." But we would become resentful and bored of each other quickly. She'd snap at us in church for not paying attention. Claire and I wouldn't share toys or would feel disappointed by our presents. Dad would call, or not, and I never knew which one was worse.

~

I walked by your room, but you're asleep now. Anyway. If I move can you take my car? I think of

*it like a pet. When I lived in Ottawa and would visit
Toronto during the winter, it felt like my trusty steed,
my travelling companion keeping me safe from the
elements. I'd take the long way and pass trucks and
ice-fishing huts on the frozen river and tell myself I
should try it myself one day—drive my car onto the
ice, rent a hut, cut a hole in the river, fish. I'll never
get the chance to go ice fishing in California. I don't
think the car will survive a cross-country trip, but I
don't want to get rid of it just yet.*

⁓

On my first day back at the office after Boxing Day, I checked
my email and clicked on an article about summertime cocktails that one of my regular freelancers had sent in over the
holidays. I read through it, and felt the familiar sensation of
my lower back tightening with cramps. I went to the bathroom, but there wasn't any blood. According to my tracking
app, my period was one day late, but it wasn't always precise
so I wasn't sure if I should look into it. I googled, *Are cramps
a sign of pregnancy?* The answer was yes.

Is fatigue a sign of pregnancy? I was tired and sluggish that
morning.

Yes.

Is a slight headache a sign of pregnancy?

Yes.

Is increased thirst a sign of pregnancy?

Yes.

I got a message from my boss over our internal messaging system. *Hope you had a great Christmas! Can we talk
about the June issue at 11?*

Yes, I wrote back.

I googled, *Is not liking your job a sign of pregnancy?* and a post from a message board came up: *It's so weird but I knew I was pregnant when I suddenly started HATING my job. Like my body knew that I wouldn't be working there in a few months.* I interpreted this as another yes.

In the evening Joe and I sprawled on the couch and watched a movie. I ignored my increasing cramps, but when I went to the bathroom, my underwear was stained dark brown.

"I'm not pregnant," I said when I returned to the couch.

"Did you think you were?" Joe sounded genuinely surprised.

"Maybe a little."

"Oh. You didn't mention anything about it."

"I mean, I didn't really think I was, but remember I was ovulating at your Christmas party?"

"Should I have remembered that?"

I didn't answer him, but he knew the answer was implicitly yes by the way I rolled my eyes and left the couch.

I took a shower before bed. Our bathroom had a rain shower, which I hadn't known was a thing that existed until we bought the loft. The water fell from the shower head straight down to the slate floor in offset drops, and you could twist it to increase or decrease the intensity of the water: a gentle summer pitter-patter, a monsoon. I turned it all the way up.

Maybe it wasn't a good time to have a baby. Our home was so impractical for a child. There was no bathtub. A baby couldn't take a monsoon shower, and how would I carry one up to our bed on the ladder? The loft also lacked doors. We were post-doors, Joe and I had told ourselves when we made the decision to buy—we were living in a future with no boundaries, except for the bathroom which, admittedly, required a door. Surely it would be useful to have at least one non-bathroom with a door if you had a baby? But we hadn't really thought through these practicalities. I don't know why; there had been no urgency around the idea of having a baby a few months before, and then we'd fallen in love with the place the first time we visited.

The loft had been, once upon a time, a classroom in a boarding school for deaf, blind, and dumb children. This was how our real estate agent, Phyllis, had described it when we met her outside the building for our first viewing.

"Dumb?" Joe asked.

"You know what I mean. 'Dumb.'" She used air quotes around the word.

"No, I don't."

"I think it's the more politically correct term."

"I don't think it is," he said. I glanced at him, and he gave me a look that seemed to say *Why did we choose her again?*

We *had* considered other real estate agents: younger ones with statement haircuts, good shoes, and well-fitting blazers. They had their fingers on the pulse of the kind of emerging neighbourhoods we could afford and were adept at deflecting any guilt we might feel from gentrification—another word they'd never use—but their excessive friendliness just barely concealed their intentions to make a quick commission off of us. Phyllis, who was introduced to us by my father, and who tended toward the maternal, wore pantsuits and was outwardly exasperated by what she thought were naive desires relative to our price point, seemed more trustworthy. That day, though, I doubted our decision. I wondered if we should call the whole thing off and slink back to one of the younger agents who would also surely offend us, just in more acceptable ways. But we were already there, and the listing was promising, so we followed her in.

The building was beautiful, built back when it didn't occur to people to make things unbeautifully, when wide-plank floors, crown moulding, and swirly ceiling medallions were constructed for children who couldn't appreciate or even see them. The school was almost a heritage building (it had a plaque out front!), but a developer had managed to get the right permits to rezone. They'd kept the plaque and then knocked down some walls and upgraded the plumbing and wiring. Our unit had sealed cement floors and classroom-sized windows that spanned the length of the entire front wall. It was beautiful. We wanted to live in it.

The day we got the keys, we shook hands with Phyllis for the last time and went directly to the loft. Devoid of the previous owner's furniture, it was bigger than I remembered, but since it was open concept there was less storage space to hide the inessentials. The best we had was a little nook by the kitchen just under our bedroom, which had probably been a janitor's closet at some point. We called it the vestibule, and when we moved in, we stuffed it with a random assortment of off-season clothes, our vacuum cleaner, canned goods, and other weirdly shaped items, and then hung up a curtain to hide the mess. Everything else was kept either in the basement storage locker that had come with the loft or in a self-storage unit we'd rented before moving. While we'd planned on clearing out the unit after the move, we not only hadn't, but we had also continued adding items. The unit held three-quarters of our books, a Turkish rug we'd had shipped from Istanbul, and our fake Christmas tree, which we hadn't bothered unpacking for that first holiday season because by then we were sick of dealing with boxes. It seemed, as we unpacked, that we'd pared down well—the books we brought fit on the shelves, the small kitchen appliances on the counter.

The vestibule was the closest thing we had to a nursery. If we cleared it out, sent more to the storage unit, it could fit a small crib.

After Joe's holiday party, when I thought I might be pregnant, I'd had one of those dreams where you open a door and discover an extra room. I was standing on the bed, and there was a trap door on the ceiling that led to another floor. "Look at this," I called out to Joe in the dream as I pulled myself up and then twirled around in the empty space. It was definitely big enough for a nursery, even if we'd need another ladder to get up to it.

I tried to channel that feeling as I took my shower, that the real world could shrink and expand effortlessly, spontaneously, conveniently.

Claire officially decided to accept the job transfer on New Year's Eve. I don't know exactly what prompted the decision, but I woke up to a text on January 1 that said she was going and that she would do it quickly: they would set her up on some kind of temporary visa until they sorted out the other details. All she had to do was let her landlord know she was leaving.

By the end of January, she had put most of her things into storage at the same self-storage warehouse Joe and I used. The week before she left, she stayed at Mom's place. Joe and I invited her over for one last dinner. Since we'd moved she'd only visited a handful of times.

"I'm not used to being at Mom's for longer than a night or two," she said while we ate. I'd spatchcocked a chicken, cutting through its ribs with a pair of kitchen shears, and quick roasted it in a skillet in the oven on high heat. "It's so quiet there."

"That's how I felt at Christmas too. It's weird."

"I went jogging after Mom went to bed last night and then got worried I'd slip on ice and no one would know until the morning."

"You didn't bring your phone with you?"

"It wasn't charged, so I went back."

"What room are you sleeping in?"

"Not yours, even though your bed is more comfortable. I get creeped out by all the twenty-two-year-old Laura stuff."

"Me too," Joe said. "It's like she died."

"Well," I said. "I didn't."

Claire had brought us an expensive bottle of Californian wine that had been given to her at work as a good luck present, and I'd poured myself a glass—but that morning I'd started to wonder again if I might be pregnant. It felt different than it had the month before; there'd been a subtle sea change in myself, like the moment you lower yourself into salt water and sense your blood oxygen level adjusting to the new environment. Maybe I was imagining it, but I'd started feeling it two nights earlier, my breasts tingling. I hadn't felt that at Christmas. I'd even bought a pregnancy test at lunch, casually tossing the box into my basket at the drugstore like it wasn't a big deal. I took a small sip of wine.

"Your loft is kind of a smaller version of what my office will be like," Claire said.

"Oh?"

She took out her phone and showed us some pictures. The new office space did have similar qualities: high ceilings, airiness, big windows. The company that had just moved out left behind a wall of plants and the requisite Ping-Pong table.

"I would love to work in a place like this," Joe said.

"It sounds great in theory, but I've worked in enough open concepts to know I'll need headphones ninety-five percent of the time to get real work done."

"Still better than fluorescent lighting."

"The light over my cubicle has been flickering for the past week, and it's driving me nuts," I added. "I don't even know who to ask to fix it."

"Where do you think you'll live?" Joe asked Claire. The company was renting her an Airbnb until she figured out her permanent arrangements.

"No idea. I'm sure it will be a tiny room in an apartment with a million roommates."

"I have a feeling you'll be able to afford more than that."

"I don't know." She looked around. "It's so clean here. It wasn't this clean the last time I was here." When I didn't respond, she laughed. "Do you have a cleaning lady?"

"We don't refer to her as a cleaning lady. And she's only been here once. Which happened to be yesterday."

"What do you call her then?"

"Well, we weren't actually home. We left the key under the floor mat. I feel a little guilty about it."

"You do?" Joe asked. "You suggested her!"

I blushed because I had. Our place had been a mess, and I didn't think I had time to tidy before Claire came over. She wouldn't have cared, but I wanted it to look nice for her last visit in a while.

"She always said she'd never be a person who outsources her cleaning," Claire told him.

"I said that a long time ago."

"Then why do you feel guilty? Are you paying her well? Just because Mom hated cleaning work doesn't mean everyone does."

Mom's first job when she immigrated to Canada was with a cleaning company that serviced various corporate offices downtown, including the engineering firm our father worked for. She hated it, but she had to keep the job for a large portion of our childhood. Eventually she got a job at Mount Sinai, cleaning at first, then working her way up to managing the laundering of the hospital linens, the fitted and regular sheets, towels, flannel baby blankets, and scrubs. She knew the protocol for biohazardous materials and how to wash bloodstains out of anything. Her main responsibility was coordinating the pickup and drop-off of these items, scheduling the trucks that would cart away the sorted bins to an industrial cleaning factory across the city and exchange them for sterile, folded pieces. She wore regular clothes and worked normal hours. She had her own desk with its own computer in an office in the basement next to the security department.

"I might take a pregnancy test in the morning," I said casually to Joe after Claire left.

"Really? Why?"

"The reason you normally take a pregnancy test."

"Are you late?"

"My period was supposed to start yesterday."

"Is it usually right on time?"

"Usually."

"So you think you're pregnant, like you did last month?"

"It's different."

"How so?"

"My boobs feel weird."

"Can I touch them?"

"I don't mean *literally*. They hurt differently."

"Wow." He leaned against the counter. "Why don't you just test right now?"

"Morning urine is more accurate."

"I had no idea. Okay. We'll wait then."

We smiled at each other, and I went back to the dishes.

~

I'm actually sleeping in your room tonight. I forgot I'd unpacked a bunch of stuff on my bed and now I'm too tired to move it, so I'm here. I really enjoyed the dinner you made us, but I'm thinking I'll go vegetarian when I move. It will be a good time for me to make the switch—California, something new. Remember I was a vegetarian for a while in high school? I woke up one day and was repulsed by meat. I think it might be happening again.

~~

Back when we were in high school, Claire and I wore mostly black and kept our dark hair long and loose. Mom was afraid that this combination was too witchy, that it invited too much flirting with the devil under our roof, even if it was incidental. She wanted us to go to church with her and her friends and their children on Sundays, but we never did, and she didn't push too hard. If Dad was free, we would see him on Sunday mornings instead.

Sometimes Claire and I would tease Mom, scare her on purpose—flip the wooden cross she kept in the kitchen upside down, leave an Ouija board on the dining room table with the planchette pointed to the first letter of her name. She'd laugh, but still she'd insist, "Ghosts are *real*." She believed in spirits as fervently as she did God, and she felt it was her duty as our mother and a good Filipino not to deny the existence of the paranormal. But Claire and I were both firmly rooted in the real world. If anything I was dismayed that our mother was wrong, disappointed that we didn't have easy access to something beyond our reality. I wouldn't have minded a portal; we were bored.

In our second year of high school, Claire got into photography. She used me as her model. I didn't mind since it gave me something to do. That summer, no matter how much we stuffed into our days—I had a job shelving books at the library on Weston Road next to a funeral home, and Claire was a counsellor at a computer camp for seven-year-olds at a nearby community school—we still somehow had so much time. I wouldn't meet Joe for another year. Dad wasn't around much that summer; he was busy at work, and then he'd taken his family on a trip to Europe. He'd mailed us postcards as if we actually wanted them and weren't jealous, as if the person who checked the mail that day wasn't just throwing them out immediately.

In response to our mother's fears, Claire wanted to take pictures of ghosts. She did it by taking trick photos the way people did back in the 1800s, when spirit photography was popular. The film was exposed twice to layer two images and make it appear as though ghosts were lurking in the background.

She started taking pictures of me in our backyard. She dragged one of the velvet-upholstered armchairs from the living room and took a picture of me sitting in it, wound the roll back, and then positioned me behind the chair. Because they were long exposures, I wasn't supposed to smile, but occasionally I'd break into a grin and my teeth would merge into a murky white line that made me look even ghastlier.

Mom hated these photos of me with a ghost twin beckoning me to another spiritual plane. "I don't like looking at you like this," she said, pushing the batch away. While Claire's photos were obviously fake, they were taken with real film, not digital, and that made them more convincing. I could understand how someone long ago might've been convinced they were looking at a ghost, how even my mother might be spooked.

One afternoon after my library shift, I found Claire waiting for me, sitting on the stairs of the funeral home.

"What's that for?" I asked. She had her camera and tripod.

"I'm taking photos of you in the river."

"What do you mean *in* the river?"

"I brought you flip-flops."

I didn't have anything else to do, so I followed. We walked toward the Humber River and then climbed down a small hill. We stood at the river's edge for a second, watching the brownish water flow over rocks. Claire, wearing shorts and sandals, took the first step in. She opened her tripod and dug it into the mud.

I'd walked along this stretch of the river so many times, but I'd never thought to go in. It wasn't particularly appealing, all muddy and jagged with rocks. I'd see birds wading, sometimes raccoons washing off their food. Dad had told us that salmon passed through the Humber in the early fall on their way to spawn, but I didn't believe him. Like ghosts, fifty-pound fish were not of the world I lived in. This river, I felt, was not made for truly wild animals and was only connected to Lake Ontario by a tenuous thread.

"I have a dress for you in the backpack," Claire said. "Can you put it on?"

I pulled out a flowery sundress that Mom had bought me in an attempt to get me out of black. I kicked off my sneakers, changed my clothes, and put on the flip-flops. "Now what?"

"Go in."

It was a hot day. Why not? I took a tentative step. The cold stung, and where there weren't stones and pebbles my feet sunk down into the mud. While Claire fiddled with her camera, I waded further out, taking big, long strides.

The water rushing around my legs felt nice. It slowly crept higher up my legs and toward my knees until the hem of the dress got wet.

"What the hell?" Claire called out. "Where are you going? Come closer."

I'd quickly made my way to the middle of the river. The opposite shore backed onto a ravine connected to someone's backyard. I turned around and waved. The current felt stronger when I started walking back, and as I took a big step forward, one flip-flop slipped off and floated to the surface. I watched it drift away, surprised at how quickly it disappeared. For a split second I wondered if something bad was happening, if maybe I shouldn't have waded out this far, if this current was the reason we never saw anyone swimming in the Humber River, not even salmon.

"Are you okay?" Claire asked.

I steadied myself. "Take your picture!"

She hesitated, but in the same way that I'd followed her blindly to the river, she readied her camera and clicked. I stood there getting colder and wetter while Claire held up a light meter, focused her camera, took a shot, then another and another. She stopped. "It's fine—just come back."

"Are you sure you're done?"

"You look cold! Come back!"

I leaned over, took off my other flip-flop, then shuffled back, looking down to avoid the sharper stones. On shore, I pulled off the dress and stood there shivering in a bra and underwear. Claire had forgotten to bring a towel, so I stuffed my wet feet into my sneakers.

"Are you okay? Your lips are blue."

"I'm good," I said. I threw the remaining flip-flop in the trash when we climbed back up to the street.

For the next few days, I waited eagerly for Claire to come home with the developed photos. The more I asked about it, the more she took her time. Finally one afternoon she met me again outside the library, this time without her tripod.

"Something went wrong," she said and fished a photo out of her bag. The print was a glossy snow-white, although if you looked closely you could see edges of the river.

"What happened?"

"The roll got overexposed."

I thumbed through the rest of the photos—unsalvageable. They disturbed me more than the spirit photos that frightened Mom. I'd so badly wanted a record of myself standing in the middle of the Humber, alone and happy, cold and brave. Close to home, connected to it still, but at a healthy remove. Perhaps I've been chasing that feeling ever since.

When I woke up with familiar lower-back cramps, I rolled over in bed and told Joe I wasn't taking the test.

He was already awake, watching something on his phone. "Why not?"

"These are probably period cramps. It's not worth wasting a test—they're more expensive than I thought they'd be."

"How much?"

"Like twenty dollars for two, and I didn't even get the fancy kind."

"They can be fancy?"

"Some show the word *pregnant* so you don't have to interpret lines, or plus or minus signs."

"It can't be that complicated, can it?"

"I've never taken one—I don't know!"

"Well, we can afford twenty dollars. Just take it."

"Not now. I can still get more sleep." I put my pillow over my head so I didn't have to see the disappointed look on Joe's face. "Also, can you turn your phone down? It's so loud."

"Okay, but watch this first." He lifted the pillow and showed me his screen. Black-and-white security camera footage of a forest. There was an iguana hanging out in some tall grass, and then in the background a creature shifted and began hopping closer to the camera. It was a huge bird with a long bulbous beak.

"What am I looking at?"

"A dodo bird!" Someone had apparently discovered one off the coast of Réunion Island in the Indian Ocean. The clip had over two million views.

"Citation needed." I turned over and covered my face again.

"You have to admit it's a pretty good fake."

Cramps hummed in my abdomen and pelvis, and my breasts still tingled. "Maybe I will take the test."

"I have no idea what you just said."

I sat up. "Maybe I will take the test."

"Oh." Joe looked nervous. "Do you need help?"

"I just have to pee on a stick—like you said, it can't be that complicated. You can stay in the bathroom with me if you want." We both knew that I wanted him to.

We climbed downstairs. I peed and got urine on my hands, washed them. Taking the test felt like a novelty, a goofy scene in a rom-com. I picked up the test, and we stared at it. Negative. I carried it out of the bathroom and set it on the counter to see if it would change. Still negative.

"I don't know if I believe the test," I said.

"Really?"

"I just feel so different."

"Honey," Joe said, so gently that my eyes welled up.

"It's okay if you don't believe me."

"The pregnancy test is supposed to be ninety-nine percent accurate."

"Maybe I tested too early."

Without telling Joe, I used the other test in the box in the evening after work. Still negative. My period still hadn't started by the next morning, and I thought about being pregnant while I was on the subway to work and chanted *You exist* in my head like a meditation mantra to help me relax. *You exist you exist you exist.* I visualized the YouTube dodo bird.

At lunch, after I'd googled how to get cheaper pregnancy tests, I went to the dollar store and bought a box of tests that weren't sticks, like the kind I'd peed on, but more like the strips we used in high school chemistry class to measure the pH level of tap water. I had to dip them into a cup of urine because they were too small to pee on directly. I googled *Pregnancy test false negative* and found message board posts of women whose pregnancies hadn't registered on tests for days, even weeks. Rare, but it could happen! I was now three days late. Even Joe was starting to shift to my side, tentatively asking me if my period had started and replying "Huh" when the answer was no. Finally, on the fourth day, a faint second line appeared on one of the strips.

"I told you!" I cried, waving it in Joe's face. I dipped three more and arranged them in a fan on the edge of the bathroom sink. More lines.

"Oh my god," he said, his eyes filling with tears. "You were right."

"We don't have a nursery."

"What about the vestibule? We can empty it out."

"How do you bathe a baby in a rain shower?"

"The kitchen sink is huge."

"What about the ladder?" I was smiling as I ticked off the logistical challenges one by one.

"Details, details."

Maybe the whole move had been in preparation for this decision, something about putting down roots. We were finally ready for them; they were better than doors.

The day before Claire left for San Francisco, I spent the night at Mom's house. The three of us had dinner together, just ordering in pizza because I'd had a long day at work and was too tired to cook. Claire wasn't very hungry anyway, and Mom never got takeout so pizza felt like something special.

Claire's flight was early, so we all went to bed early too. Claire had continued sleeping in my room, and that night we shared the bed like we used to as kids when Mom went out or worked late.

"I think Mom's starting to date," Claire said. "I saw her typing on her iPad and looked before you came over."

"You read her messages? What about her privacy?"

"She didn't say anything. I had to know!"

"I would've done the same. What did you find?"

"She has so many chats going on with different men! Totally benign, but she's flirting. It made me feel too embarrassed to read, so I stopped."

"Okay, so I really need to deal with this on my own now."

"So far it doesn't look like she's planning on meeting anyone in person."

"I'm still amazed." I stretched out.

"Your feet are freezing."

"Are they?" Since the positive test, I'd noticed that my stomach felt hot. I imagined all my blood rushing away from my extremities to my belly to keep whatever was growing in there cozy.

I could've told Claire I was pregnant then, but I didn't. If she'd asked me how I was doing, I might've said something, but she was preoccupied with the final details of moving, making sure she had the right papers printed, that she'd packed everything she would need at first. And now, Mom's dating life.

I also thought that if I told her right then, in that bed on the day before she left, the news would be too real. It had been only a day and a half since the positive test, and I was feeling speechless about it. I just wanted to lie in the dark with myself and think about what was happening within me.

Claire had once taught me how to write a program in C++:

```cpp
int main()
{
  std::cout << "Hello, world!\n";
  return 0;
}
```

When you run it and press enter, you'll see on screen the words *Hello, world!*

You would generally write some version of this program when first learning any new programming language, and I thought it would be a funny way to tell her, once she was settled in her new home. I'd send her an email or text message, like, *A baby is on the way, hello world!*

Mom woke up first the next morning, an hour earlier than the alarm I'd set. Her padding around the house woke us up, and we got out of bed groggy, vaguely irritated. We'd decided that I would drive Claire to the airport, leaving Mom at home, since I had to go to work right after.

Claire and I brought her luggage to the car. It was snowing lightly. Flakes landed on Claire's leather jacket, which she told me she was going to keep even if she went vegetarian; it was more ethical to wear a piece of clothing that she'd owned for years than to discard it for something made of non-animal materials, which would just be petroleum products anyway. Her bleached hair had grown since Christmas, and I could see her roots. She looked beautiful and tough and strong as she hauled a suitcase into the trunk.

When we went back inside, Mom hugged Claire tight and cried, and when she pulled away there were damp spots on her shirt from the snowflakes on Claire's jacket. I wept too, watching them. My stomach was still warm.

"It's not like one of us hasn't moved before," Claire said in the car, sniffling, when I pulled out of the driveway.

It was true—she'd lived in Ottawa and Waterloo for years. And Joe and I used to travel all the time; we'd often be gone for months.

"Anyway, I'm not there permanently yet. And I'll have to come back soon for some work meetings."

"And I'll visit you."

"Let me find somewhere to live first."

"I'll Face call you." I paused. "You're going to have so many fun adventures."

"If I'm not working all the time."

"It's going to be strange not having you around."

"You'll be fine."

Neither of us cried when I dropped her off at the departures area of the terminal, which I guess was my way of saying that I believed her.

PART TWO: SPRING

There was a snowstorm the first week of April. While everyone complained about it, I took out a bin of summer clothes from the vestibule and threw random pieces of clothing into a suitcase—Joe and I were flying to Barbados, so I could ignore this last winter hurrah. One of Joe's clients was shutting down an offshore subsidiary, and he and a co-worker had to finalize some of the paperwork in person. Sometimes spouses tagged along for this kind of business trip. When he first asked me to go with him, I said I wanted to save my vacation time so we could go on a proper babymoon—I'd made fun of the term in the past and was surprised by how easily, how *sincerely*, it had then rolled off my tongue.

Even though we were on the same flight, Joe's seat was in first class and mine was not. I might've been able to sit with him if we'd booked our tickets at the same time, but because I'd decided to come at the last minute it was too late to get a seat next to him without paying an exorbitant fee.

"Take my spot," he said after we checked in.

I shook my head. "It's not in my name. What if the plane crashes and they get us mixed up in the manifest and my mom thinks the wrong person died?"

"If the plane crashes, we're both dead and it won't matter where we're sitting. If anything, my last regret will be that we're not sitting *together*."

"You can offer the person next to me your seat."

"I'll do that," he said.

When he came back from the bathroom with a bagful of items he'd bought from a newsstand—gummy bears, a bottle of Perrier, the latest *New Yorker*—I knew he still felt guilty. "What's this?" I asked as he handed it all to me.

"I just want to make sure you're comfortable."

"I'll be fine. I brought a book." Still, when he tried to keep the gummy bears for himself, I took them back.

Joe was allowed to board before me, but he waited until my zone was called so we could go at the same time. We weren't sure exactly how to coordinate the switch, and we decided that we'd each go to our seats first and then I'd offer whoever was sitting next to me Joe's spot, like I was giving them a prize—first-class upgrade! But that person ended up being part of a couple that appeared to be on their honeymoon (she had a *BRIDE* pin and they kissed when they sat down), so I texted Joe, *Never mind.* I didn't want them to be forced to make the same decision we'd had to make. I imagined it would throw off the balance of their honeymoon.

Are you absolutely sure?

Yes

Really?

YES

I'll miss you.

I craned my neck to see if I could spot him, but first class was separated by a pleated blue curtain. *It's fine*, I wrote back.

I put the newsstand supplies in the pouch in front of me. I suppose they came in handy. Instead of reading the book I'd packed, I started to read the *New Yorker*. The bride beside me took out a small bottle of hand sanitizer, squeezed it on her palms and rubbed her hands together until they dried. She and her husband did this multiple times, and then, noticing me watching them, offered the bottle. I shook my head, put on my headphones, and went back to the magazine.

I read a story about the rise and eventual demise of a small subset of a Mexican drug cartel and then a poem about Simurgh, an Iranian mythological bird that could lift an elephant with its talons. At forty thousand feet above ground, I found that these pieces resonated with me in intense ways, enough that I wrote down the name of the cartel kingpin to google later and ripped out the poem and stuck it in my book so I wouldn't lose it. I looked out the window. I didn't feel like listening to music, but I kept my headphones on while I squinted at clouds and sky, everything blurred together into a tableau of nothingness.

The first time I took a plane was when I was fifteen and Mom, Claire, and I went to the Philippines for our lola's funeral. Claire and I had never met our grandmother, had barely even spoken to her on the phone, but Mom felt strongly about us going—and despite the circumstances we were excited, not just for the trip, but for the plane ride too. Claire got the window seat for the Toronto-to-Vancouver leg, but I claimed it for the longer journey from Vancouver to Manila. The flight took off after ten p.m., and everyone immediately pulled their window shades down. I didn't think I'd fall asleep, but I did, and when I woke up a few hours later, the cabin was dark. Mom and Claire were both still asleep. I opened my window shade a crack, and everything outside was a deep, velvety black. It was like being in a tunnel. That was the moment I felt acutely sad about my mother's loss, that she had to traverse this void to see her family, her dead mother. I would never have been able to tolerate that much distance from her and Claire.

I was reminded of that feeling as Joe and I flew to Barbados. An obliterating void, even in the daylight.

When you go to Barbados for work, you stay on a different part of the island than if you're on actual vacation. It's less touristy, with beaches that, while impressive, aren't as majestic as those on the other side. Still, the hotel Joe's firm put us up in was essentially a resort. Our room had a king-size bed and a daybed, and the mahogany-coloured rattan chairs were set against cool white tiles and crisp, creamy linen. The balcony looked out onto one of the pools. There was no swim-up bar, though: this was a serious resort.

We changed out of our end-of-winter clothes into summer outfits and walked straight down to the beach. The humid tropical air was luxurious after the long winter, and we both kept inhaling deeply, trying to pick out the notes we were smelling: I pictured big, fecund flowers with pollen dusting everything around them; Joe thought it was the dried ocean salt.

I waded into the water—it was still and warm—and there were things in it, not shells, but plants and sea vegetables and invertebrate creatures that looked like translucent gelatinous tubes flowing this way and that. Prehistoric and useless. Or maybe they were so useful and evolved that I would never comprehend their purpose. They didn't have brains or blood or hearts and could still somehow live—more like ghosts or zombies than anything living. I knew they did something essential, like suck in salt water, soak up impurities, and then release fresh liquid back into the ocean to keep it oxygenated and clean, and I also knew that if we destroyed them we would probably be one step closer to a dead world. But, like ghosts and zombies, they also creeped me out. I didn't even know what they were called. Sea tubes? Sea worms? I jumped back when one brushed against my foot.

Along the shore we passed neighbouring hotels and the occasional person stretched out on a lounge chair. Not many people were swimming, hardly anyone strolling. The swimmers and the strollers were on the other side of the island. Joe picked up a conch. I felt its heavy weight and then tossed it back into the water—conches would be a dime a dozen, I figured, but we didn't find a single shell on the walk back.

We sat down at one of the resort's outdoor tables before going back to our room. I wanted a big, sweet, tacky cocktail, something overflowing with dark Bajan rum, but I chose a mango smoothie instead.

"What are you going to do tomorrow?" Joe asked after we ordered. "I have to meet Brian in the lobby at eight. He's flying in tonight."

"I'm not sure. I haven't looked into much yet. Have you?"

"I don't think I'll have much time for fun, but that shouldn't stop you from exploring while I'm working."

I normally enjoyed wandering around new places alone, but I hadn't really thought about it for this trip. I'd imagined lounging and reading, but I'd also imagined Joe ducking out of work every so often to meet up with me. Maybe we'd go for lunch somewhere in a nearby town, explore a market? I knew he had to work, but he was going to be here for two weeks—surely he could take some time off. When he took out his phone to answer emails while we waited for our drinks, I realized that I'd assumed incorrectly. He really was going to be busy.

"I think I just want to relax," I said. "We never go on relaxing vacations. We're always doing *something*."

"Doing things is overrated. I'm jealous of you."

"I do have a few work emails to follow up on," I added.

"You should relax, though."

"Yeah."

"This sun is nice."

"It really is."

"And fresh ocean air will be good for you."

"Okay, yes, but I don't need a sanatorium."

Joe laughed. "I'm glad you decided to come."

The waiter came back with a tray laden with drinks: my smoothie, Joe's beer and two additional tall glasses filled with amber-coloured liquid and ice.

"Welcome to Barbados," he said, setting them down. "Rum punch, on the house. Our specialty."

We thanked him. I looked at my glass, the water condensing along the sides. I could smell the rum.

Joe picked his up first. "Cheers," he said.

I clinked mine against his and took a big sip. It was made with Angostura bitters and a pinch of nutmeg, and I felt it warm me up from the inside.

A month before, when I was eight weeks pregnant, I'd felt a sharp cramp, and when I went to the bathroom I saw blood in my underwear. I stood up quickly, startled, and some dripped on the seat. I pulled up my underwear and pants, wet a wad of toilet paper to wipe down the seat, and then flushed the toilet.

Are you home soon? I texted Joe. *I have some bleeding*

Just down the street. Did you cut yourself?

No, like period blood

Why would you have your period?

I didn't answer, and when he came in through the front door a few minutes later, he was a little wild eyed. "Are you okay?"

I was sitting on a towel on the couch. I'd just typed *Eight weeks pregnant and bleeding* on my phone, and I shoved it into his hands so he could read what it said.

"What colour is the blood?"

"Red. What other colour could it be?"

"Bright red?"

"Is that bad?"

"Are you still bleeding?"

"I haven't checked."

"Why don't you look again?"

Joe followed me to the bathroom, and I didn't stop him. I pulled my pants down and sat on the toilet, and we could both see the stains in my underwear. Red.

"Honey," he said. "That looks like a lot."

"Bleeding is normal sometimes, though."

"It said that, yeah. How do you feel?"

"It hurts a bit." My voice was small. I shifted and felt a gush of blood into the toilet, the release of something shaken loose. I was afraid I would disrupt it more if I moved again.

"Can you get me another pair of underwear?" I asked.

He left and returned with a pair with lace trim, far too nice for this blood, but I took it anyway. I had pads under the sink, but didn't want to take one—I didn't have my *period*—so I stuck a washcloth in instead, like a kid getting their period for the first time and not knowing what to do.

"Should we go to the hospital?" Joe asked.

"Maybe it will help."

Normally I drove Claire's car, but this time Joe drove. I was worried that I'd bleed through to her seat, and when I didn't, I considered it a good sign. The parking garage was down the street from the hospital, and the thought of walking that distance while bleeding was terrifying, so Joe dropped me off at the entrance first and I stood there, outside, while he parked. I was wearing track pants, and my ankles were exposed. I'd forgotten gloves. I held my phone in my hand and looked at the screen as I waited. The minutes blinked forward. I thought about texting Claire, but there was too much to tell her. Eight weeks in and she still didn't know I was pregnant.

As soon as Joe and I went through triage, I regretted our decision. There was nothing reassuring about being curled up in a hospital seat under bright lights, cramps stretching across my abdomen and back. I'd expected to be whisked away immediately, but as I told the nurse the facts—only eight weeks pregnant, my first pregnancy, bright-red blood, pain but not unbearable—I got the sense that I ticked off everything on a list of non-prioritized health care emergencies. She gave me a thick maxi pad to wear while we waited, and I put it on in a bathroom, tossing the bloody washcloth in the garbage. The pad was wider than the stupid lacy underwear and stuck uncomfortably to my skin. She took a blood sample. When it was time to see the ER doctor, I sat on a thin blue absorbent pad on the mattress underneath me. The maxi pad shifted, and some blood seeped out onto the absorbent pad.

"This is not an uncommon situation," the doctor said. While it could be a miscarriage, it could also be a hematoma, some kind of tear in the placenta that might trigger bleeding. He ordered me an ultrasound. "Your hCG levels are low given your stage of pregnancy. We can do an ultrasound either way, but because of how early it is, it will have to be transvaginal."

When the nurse came back to give us further instructions, I gestured down to the bed and said, "I know where this goes." I meant the cleaning factory for the sheet—because of my mom I knew all the hospitals used the same place—and she smiled at me in a way that I knew meant she didn't know what I was talking about. I didn't bother clarifying that my mother had taught me this, but I was glad I knew where the sheet was going, that I understood the way the hospital worked.

"How are you feeling, dear?"

"Not good."

"We can give you something for the pain."

She came back with a fresh maxi pad, a small paper cup, and two Advils. I swallowed the pills, but it took a few minutes for me to get up to change my pad. I didn't want to move because I felt like if I did even more blood would come out, and I still had a sense that it was my duty to keep it all in for just a little while longer. Luckily I was able to wait in my bed until it was time for the ultrasound. If we'd arrived a little bit earlier or a little bit later, we would've been shuttled back into the waiting room. I remained curled on my side while we waited, and Joe sat in the chair next to me with his legs stretched out, staring at the ceiling, sometimes leaning over and rubbing my back until I told him the touch made me uncomfortable. I continued to bleed.

The ultrasound technician couldn't say anything to us, but we could tell by her silence that the problem wasn't a hematoma. I thought of Claire's spirit photography when I caught a glance at the ultrasound screen, the greyish, shifting aura of something that was once there but was now gone. The ER doctor confirmed that the embryo had stopped growing at six weeks. For two weeks I'd been living with an unviable embryo, and I'd had no idea.

Joe and I went home with a prescription for Misoprostol, which would induce more bleeding, with the hope that I wouldn't need any other kind of intervention. It was a Thursday, so I took Friday off work, took the dose in the morning, and bled a little throughout the day until the late afternoon when I started bleeding a lot. I couldn't believe the amount of blood. I went to the bathroom, sat on the toilet, and felt it come out of me in chunks. A little would've gotten the message across, but this was an angry tidal wave that radiated pain outward as my uterus contracted and expelled every bit of foreign tissue from my body. *Am I dying?* I wondered while I sat on the toilet. How was it possible to pass so many clots, to cramp so much, without it being terrible for me?

"What can I do?" Joe asked from the other side of our only door.

"Nothing."

I wanted a warm bath, but we only had our rain shower. I hated the rain shower.

"Are you sure?"

A part of me wanted to show him the blood and dark clots, but a bigger part didn't. It was my own thing to deal with, my secret, and I stayed in the bathroom for hours, alone, eventually washing away the blood on my legs in the shower, standing under the shower head with my eyes closed. Monsoon.

A few days later I went back for a follow-up ultrasound. Joe had offered to come with me, but the appointment was mid-morning and I knew he was busy at work. The worst had passed—I could handle going by myself.

"Looks great," the doctor said, almost triumphantly, which made me feel almost proud. "You can start trying again after your next period." He gathered his things to leave.

"I have a question," I said, stalling for time.

"Sure, what is it?"

"How should I be feeling? I mean, I still feel sore. And I'm tired."

"That's all very normal." He'd already reassured me about how normal everything was.

"I'm also sad." I was embarrassed when I choked on the word *sad*. "...Obviously!" I tried to turn it into a joke, like, duh, of course this lady is *sad*. How normal of her.

"Do you want a note for work?"

"A note?"

"To take time off."

I don't know what else I'd expected—a referral to a support group maybe? His offer of time off felt like illicit drugs, a shortcut.

"How's two weeks?" he asked.

"Is that normal?"

He looked up from his pad. "Sometimes."

I put the note through the shredder when I got to work, but in the afternoon I went to my boss's office and told him that I was thinking of accompanying Joe on his Barbados trip. "I can get work done when I'm there," I said, but he shook his head and told me that I should take advantage of the opportunity and take a break.

"I get the feeling you need a break," he said.

"Maybe!" I said and wondered why he'd said so. As I walked back to my desk I texted Joe that I would go with him.

Really?

Is it too late? The trip was in less than two weeks.

He didn't answer right away. *No, it's fine.* And when he got home, he didn't seem as enthusiastic as he'd been originally.

"Are you worried it will look like I'm taking advantage?" I asked, trying to get to the root of his discomfort.

"No, not at all."

"Are you sure?"

"I'm sure."

I booked my ticket myself, told Mom and Claire about it.

Lucky! Claire wrote. *I wouldn't mind a vacation. Things are so busy here.*

Yeah, I need one too.

She didn't ask why, so I continued to not tell her what had happened. I should've told her about being pregnant.

I'd dropped some hints. *So exhausted today*, I'd text, or *Feeling a little sick*. If she'd been living in Toronto, or if it had happened at any other time, she probably would've picked up on it, or at least asked enough leading questions that I would've spilled the beans, but she was still getting used to everything in San Francisco, figuring out the new office, meeting new people. At the very least, if she'd been here, she would've noticed that I wasn't drinking.

I knew a bit about her new life, like that it was foggy in San Francisco more often than not, that she'd bought one of those hard-core blenders off someone who was getting rid of theirs so she could make smoothies. *I'm into smoothies now*, she texted me once. *Some dates, almond milk, ground flax seeds, an avocado.* Her produce purchases were majestic, all that beautiful California citrus, and she once sent me a picture of juiced grapefruit halves stacked into each other like matryoshka dolls.

I could picture her morning routine: making her smoothie, taking a shared shuttle bus to the cluster of start-ups located in a shared building. There were shuttles at 7:30, 8:30 and 9:30, and she'd take the 7:30, which was always the emptiest. There was a core group of them working in the new office, and they were constantly busy interviewing new engineers, but also talking about how they wanted to decorate the office. She attended networking events, investor meetings, parties.

Claire had been pregnant once. Six, seven years earlier? Joe and I had been out of the country for almost four months, and it was the one time we'd missed Christmas. She sent me an email the day after my birthday, when we were in Bali. A postscript to my birthday greetings: *I was pregnant, but now I'm not. Nothing to worry about.* I'd been confused at the time, but now it seemed even stranger that

I'd read the message at an internet cafe on a beach on the other side of the world on an ancient desktop computer while a lineup of tourists waited behind me.

Wow, I wrote back. *You're sure you're okay?* I had no time to write anything more thoughtful. I think I ended it with an *I love you* at least.

When I went back to the cafe on my own the next day to see her response, the internet was down, so I couldn't check again until the day after. She'd written back almost immediately. *I'm totally fine.*

When I got back home, I asked her if she wanted to talk about it.

"Honestly, there isn't much to say."

"What about Paul?" Paul was her boyfriend. I assumed he was the father.

I wasn't expecting her to roll her eyes, but she did. "We broke up."

"You didn't tell me," I said dumbly.

"It was inevitable. We both agreed it was for the best."

"Oh, right." I was trying to follow her lead, so I didn't ask any more questions, like how late her period had been before testing, or if she'd been scared or sad. Had she thought about keeping the baby? Extremely unlikely. Had she been nauseous? I'd just accepted the news wholesale.

I wasn't very surprised about her and Paul, though. They'd met in Claire's last year of university. He was in grad school, getting a Ph.D. in math, and he intimidated me. He had wavy black hair, a furrowed dark eyebrow, perpetual stubble; he was the kind of person who grew hair an hour after he shaved. He was taller than all of us. He was Claire's first serious boyfriend, and at first I thought we'd go on double dates all the time, but we never gelled as a foursome. First of all, by the time we met him, Claire, Joe, and I already had a shtick going. We'd had years to practise our banter, a kind of sardonic competition between the two of them. I'd switch sides every so often, sometimes siding with Joe and sometimes with Claire, depending on who was being more obnoxious. There were times when I wondered if they sincerely liked each other, and I hoped that adding Claire's boyfriend would even out the mix. But instead Paul hung off to the side, not trying to work his way in. Sometimes he pulled out a book to read while Claire, Joe, and I talked. This was before checking iPhones mid-conversation was accepted behaviour—he intended it as a statement. Claire didn't seem to care. The first time it happened, Joe had kicked me under the table, his way of saying *What the hell was that?!* and then we'd just gotten used to it. Paul in the background.

I hadn't thought about Claire's pregnancy again until my miscarriage. I wondered how much she'd bled from the abortion, or if she'd been tired, her hormones thrown off for weeks. We were younger then—maybe you bounced back more quickly when you were in your twenties. I didn't know if she ever told Mom. Probably not.

I hadn't had an excuse to not tell Mom about the miscarriage, but I knew that if I told her I'd have to tell Claire too—it felt like a package deal. And then it seemed too complicated to explain, and I didn't want anyone to worry about me. I wanted to give them the full story with a bow on top: Joe and I would get pregnant again, we'd make it past eight weeks, everyone would be settled in their lives, I could get smoothie tips from Claire. *Hello world.*

On our first full day in Barbados, I slept in until after Joe left. I got dressed and made my way to the dining area, a mezzanine overlooking the beach where we'd had our welcome rum punches. It was mostly empty except for a few men in suits and some vacationing couples who looked vaguely out of place, like they'd been fleeced by a travel agency into staying here and had been promised a swim-up bar.

A woman came by to direct me to the breakfast buffet, and by the time I returned to my table with a full plate, she'd filled my mug with coffee and left a glass of ice water. The food was above par, but the fruit I'd taken as an afterthought was a true revelation: soapy but sweet pink cubes of papaya, the sweetest pineapple I'd ever eaten. I alternated sips of hot coffee and ice water, bites of soapy papaya and sweet pineapple. I went back for more fruit, and when I returned to the table my coffee cup was already refilled. I looked out onto the water, slipped my feet out of my sandals to press against the hot tiles, and ate.

I charged the breakfast to our room even though technically I was supposed to keep my costs separate from Joe's work account. I'd forgotten to bring anything with me—no credit card, not even a book, just my room key. I made a mental note to tell him later.

I retrieved my laptop from the room and propped it up on my thighs by one of the pools. I logged in to my email and replied to a few freelancer emails. I skimmed another article and gave a few notes. I messaged my boss to tell him where things were at, and he replied right away, *I thought you weren't working*, and I said, *I'm not :)*.

I closed all my work tabs and opened up a blank Word doc. When I started my food blog, I cooked all the time, not just because I wanted things to post about but because there were so many interesting recipes from cookbooks and other blogs that I wanted to try. It was exciting to be in the kitchen, to take a handful of ingredients and transform them into something delicious. I didn't get interested in food until my twenties. Mom was a decent cook—good enough that I didn't think her food was bad, but not so great that I rhapsodized about her meals the way some people did about their mothers'. She was usually just too busy to make a big deal about it, and what was more important to her was that we were fed, that we were *sturdy*. She liked to pinch our arms to make sure they had enough protective fat. Also, the meals that Mom loved weren't the kind I read about in food blogs. She didn't care about the first asparagus or ramps or rhubarb of spring, or any seasonal produce for that matter. Instead what she loved were things like macapuno, a white jelly coconut preserve that she bought in jars and spooned into bowls for us to eat for dessert. I never really enjoyed macapuno because of its texture, its acute sweetness. Eventually the cuisine got trendy in an exotic way, and I looked back on my own upbringing through a different lens, as if it wasn't unusual or weird, but that wasn't until my twenties. Sometimes I'd meet white people who knew so much more than I did about my mother's Filipino food that I'd get self-conscious, like I was an imposter.

For a while, just for fun, I'd tried writing poems based on the blog index. I pulled the words and looked at the ones I used most, the ones that showed up only once. *Salt* (every recipe), *milkshake* (once), *half a lemon* (enough times to surprise me, all those other lemon halves abandoned), *jackfruit* (more than once, surprisingly). But the poems didn't feel quite right, and the drafts remained untouched on my computer for over a year.

I looked out at the pool, at the ocean in the distance. I started writing a blog post—the first update in months—but after two sentences about papaya, I didn't know where it was going. Maybe I could try writing poetry, something about extinct animals. Ghost animals? Dodo birds. Sea tubes. An embryo is a little bit like a ghost, a wispy representation of something rather than the thing itself. If I ever had a baby, maybe I would reinvent myself as a poet. I could wake up before they did in the morning, steal time here and there to write tiny, perfect phrases. I could be that kind of mother if I had a baby, someone who commemorated a childhood in poems.

I wrote the shortest post I'd ever written. About pineapple and papaya. There was no recipe, just a description of slicing up some fruit and throwing it in a bowl. I hoped it was maybe poetic. I pressed publish. I posted a link to it on all my various social media accounts.

For a brief period, when my blog was doing well and Joe's podcast was gaining popularity, I felt like we were on top of something, ahead of something, that we were a clear demographic in a magazine article about this specific time and place. But then blogs started dropping off: no one wanted to read long streams of words, there was maybe too much SEO, too many ads. Podcasts, though, just got more and more popular. Joe and Amit were sponsor-free at the beginning, soliciting donations at a live recording once a year. Then they started a Patreon account so listeners could actually pay for monthly subscriptions, even T-shirts and buttons. Their logo was a fan-drawn cartoon of their faces: Joe distinguishable by his glasses, Amit by his beard. They wore the T-shirts when they had bar night get-togethers for their listeners. Their first sponsor was a local food delivery company who wanted to target their listeners and had given them a few meal boxes to test out themselves ("aggressively mediocre" was my assessment; "pretty good" was his). Now they had a full roster of sponsors: the ubiquitous mattress companies, a company that specialized in one hundred percent cotton shirts, a cycle shop chain.

An hour after I published the post, it still had zero comments, but the Tweet had received three likes. I didn't like to think about *engagement* when it came to my blog; that was something I had to pay attention to—or at least take into consideration—at work, even though I didn't work on the web side of the magazine. I hated the distillation of interest into numbers and percentages and timelines. I knew that three likes wasn't *good*, but I liked the idea of my words out there in the wild, that somewhere three people had seen it or at least had wanted to acknowledge it. I clicked to see who had pressed the little heart button.

One was obviously a bot, but okay, it was still some kind of evidence of my existence, no matter how paltry. One of the likes came from a good friend of mine in Toronto. The other one I didn't recognize until I clicked through to the profile and saw that it was Denny, one of my old blog friends. I recognized him right away because his name was Denny, and how many people had a name like that? We used to write each other long emails that I don't quite think were so much for the other person as they were for ourselves. We'd eventually stopped, running out of steam, email friendships also petering out the way blogs had. He lived in San Francisco, a city I'd never visited, so we'd never had the chance to meet. When I saw his Twitter feed, though, I remembered how much I'd enjoyed our exchanges. I realized I wasn't following him back, so I did. Then I scrolled through more of my feed until I realized that the last thing I wanted to be doing in Barbados was staring at my laptop screen.

I put my laptop away and laid back on the lounge chair. My body slowly absorbed the sunlight, the heat, and I felt myself soften. I was temporarily transformed into something different—a lizard, a coiled snake on a flat stone. I fell asleep and woke up when I felt my phone vibrating beside me. Mom. It was twelve thirty. We were in the same time zone, so she would've been on her lunch break.

"Hi Mom, what's up?"

"Just wanted to make sure you arrived safely."

"Sorry, I meant to email you, but we've been busy since we landed."

"Are you in paradise?"

"It's really nice here. I'll send you pictures."

"It snowed again this morning, and I almost slipped when I was shovelling the driveway."

"You shouldn't be shovelling, Mom. I can call someone to do it for you."

"I can't afford a gardener!"

"I mean like a high school kid."

"Maybe. Anyway, I wanted to let you know that I'm going on a date tomorrow."

I sat up in my lounge chair. It was happening and I wasn't even in town! "With who?"

"Someone I met on the app."

"Does Claire know?"

"No."

"We have to vet him!"

"We're just having dinner."

"What's his name?"

"I'll tell you when it matters."

"Can you send me his profile?"

"No!"

"At least tell me his name, Mom. Please."

"Bart."

"Hmm."

"He's a dentist."

"Okay. Are you sure?"

"He's not lying to me!"

"Can you call me when you're done so I know he didn't murder you?"

"He's not a murderer."

"Just call me. Or Claire. I don't care who."

"Okay, okay."

"Tell him that if he does anything bad to you, we're sending a hit man after him."

"I'll tell him, honey."

We hung up, and I texted Claire. *Mom is going on a date!!!!!!*

She wrote me back immediately. *With who??*

Someone named Bart! He's a dentist

What! Should we be worried?

It's a dinner date

I'll call her

I took a picture of my surroundings—the pool, the palm trees, the drink I'd just ordered (more rum). I sent it to her. A few minutes later she sent a picture too: a white standing desk, a MacBook, a cup of coffee, big windows in the background.

You win, she wrote. *I talked to Mom. She told me more about this guy and I think I found him on LinkedIn. He really is a dentist. He looks legit. I'll find out more.*

Barbados is so close to the equator that the days and nights are almost equal in length. By the time Joe returned from work that first day, it was already dark. I'd gone for a walk on the beach and then fallen asleep again, this time on the daybed in the hotel room, the air conditioning cranked up. We ate dinner by flickering candlelight on the same mezzanine where I'd had breakfast. We hadn't planned on it, but Brian joined us after we bumped into him waiting for a table.

"I really don't mind eating alone," he said. "I was just going to eat in the room and work, but I figured I'd get some fresh air."

"Sit with us!" Joe responded a little too enthusiastically.

"Are you sure?" Brian asked me. I made myself respond as enthusiastically as Joe.

"So how was your first day?" I asked when we were settled. I adopted the tone of a mother inquiring about a school day.

"Ugh," Joe replied.

"What he said," Brian added.

"What's wrong?"

"Everything's a mess. Their in-house legal team seems like they're trying to avoid us. Brian saw one of them sneak out the back door early when he was going to the bathroom."

"I waved at him. It was awkward."

The two of them laughed, and I felt like the third wheel. We didn't linger over dinner because the two of them wanted to get more done before bed.

"You look relaxed," Joe said when we returned.

I flung myself on the bed, the perpetually cool white sheets. "I think I've slept twenty hours."

"You're also already so tanned." He leaned over and kissed my shoulder, my bathing suit tan line.

"I still feel pretty exhausted."

We hadn't had sex since the miscarriage and I thought the trip to Barbados would be a good time to try again, but when he kissed me I didn't feel ready for it. It had already been intense enough to feel my body respond to the heat, to be aware of myself having a body, being a body. He could tell I was pulling away.

"I should get this work done anyway," he said. "What are you doing tomorrow?"

"Nothing again, I guess. What do you think I should do?"

He typed on his laptop for a bit and then looked up. "I hope you aren't expecting me to give you an itinerary."

"Excuse me?" I'd asked the question innocently, and his response was unexpectedly confrontational.

"I have this feeling that you're waiting for me to entertain you."

"Why would you think that?"

"You just asked me what you should do."

"I didn't mean it that way! I'm not helpless. I know how to entertain myself. I thought maybe your client could have suggested something."

Every couple has default roles when it comes to travel. I was best at knowing where to eat, finding cool places to stay, figuring out where to shop with the locals. Joe liked to research interesting activities and would be the first to get the lay of the land and navigate public transportation. It worked out well. It bothered me that he was acting like he'd forgotten this, as if it was unusual for me to ask him if he knew of something fun I could do in a new place.

"This isn't a vacation for me." He rubbed his temples.

"Oh my god, I know. Just finish your work and go to bed. You're too tired."

I recognized the signs of a stressed-out Joe. I knew he felt pressure to do well on this job here in Barbados, that it was some kind of test. But when he was stressed, he would try to act like he was calm and cool, but then every so often get snappy instead. I could either engage or ignore. I reminded myself of the gummy bears, the *New Yorker*, the Perrier—that version of Joe—and decided to ignore his grumpiness. Mostly.

"This isn't exactly a vacation for me either," I said.

"Well, it was your decision to come."

It was the wrong response, and now I *definitely* couldn't ignore it. I got up. "I didn't want to be alone for two weeks! I thought you wanted me here."

"I *am* happy you're here. I think we just had different expectations of what this trip would be like."

"I had no expectations. I just needed a break. Not a vacation, but a *break*. You know I've been sad. You didn't even switch seats with me on the plane." I'm not sure why I added the last part; it hadn't really bothered me at the time, but it now suddenly felt emblematic of this dynamic.

"I asked you if it was okay!"

"Well it wasn't."

"I would've switched seats with you. I'm sorry. I really thought being here would make you feel better."

"It's our second day, and I don't feel better."

"I want to help, but I don't know what to do."

"I don't know either, but don't act like I'm here on some lavish vacation while you have to like, toil in the fields from dawn until dusk. You're in Barbados, sleeping at a resort."

For a second it looked like he was going to say something, but he seemed to catch himself. "You're right."

This was the correct response. I returned to bed and turned onto my side facing away from him. When he joined me, I let him wrap his arm around me before we both fell asleep.

~~~

I got more info about Bart. He seems legit. Someone I met here at a networking thing—Shannon—has this side hustle app called Whispr (as in whisper network). I might get involved in it. She's quitting her own job soon to focus on it full time (she's also rich, no surprise). Anyway you use it to look up people you meet online and it aggregates info from a bunch of public sources, like social media, press, criminal records, etc. It's a bit of a privacy nightmare, but it's only collecting what's out there. I'm sending you an invite link to the beta version in your email so you can look him up too.

~

When I woke up, Joe was already gone. I stretched out in the huge bed and felt my stomach cramp. Was I getting my period? I knew it would come back sooner or later, and it had now been almost six weeks since the miscarriage, but I hadn't expected it to come when I was on vacation. In the bathroom I noticed some blood on the toilet paper. I hadn't packed any pads or tampons and had no idea where to get some.

I climbed back into bed and checked my email. The invitation from Claire was in my inbox, so I clicked on it and downloaded Whispr. It was all in shades of blue and green, as calming as a meditation app. It matched my surroundings. I was prompted to paste in my invite code.

Welcome, the text read in a clean, sans serif font. *Who are you looking for?*

The app had two options—you could either type in a full name or upload a photo. The app would scan the face in the photo and use AI to associate it with its owner. Since you might not get someone's full name right away on a dating app, or might not be sure they were giving you the right one, the photo feature made Whispr especially useful.

I typed in Joe's name for fun. A circle appeared with waves moving through it as the app cycled his name through the database. In the list of men who shared his name, there he was, smiling at me in a collared shirt and tie. It was the professional headshot from his firm's website, the same one he used on LinkedIn, more clean-cut than he'd been on our wedding day. The information on him was pretty light: his current place of employment, a selection of information from his résumé, a link to his Twitter account.

I swiped through the rest of the pictures. There were a few duplicates of varying quality pulled from other social media sites. Then suddenly I appeared. The picture was from at least five or six years ago based on my haircut. I was in a tank top, and Joe's arm was slung around my shoulders. Had I ever seen this photo? I couldn't remember it. I took a screenshot to send to him and then remembered where it was from: a bar in Paris, a basement somewhere. I was in a tank top because there had been a heat wave; I'd packed scarves thinking it would be the Parisian thing to do but then didn't use any of them. I didn't know how this photo had ended up online.

Who else did I want to look up? Remembering Denny's Twitter, I looked up his name. I still remembered his last name. Denny had been one of my "blog boyfriends," as Joe had called them back in the day. The only qualification for being a blog boyfriend was being male—the food blogger community skewed female, so any cis male was immediate blog boyfriend material. I'd had a closer relationship with Denny than with any of the other dudes I corresponded with back then, but my closest friendships were with other women bloggers. I still kept in sporadic contact with some of them, mostly through Instagram comments and the occasional DM, but all of those blog boyfriends had fallen away with time. I was curious about how Denny's life had changed over the past few years.

His profile was longer and more interesting than Joe's. It was full of pictures, mostly of him alone, but one with a woman, probably his girlfriend, the two of them dressed up for what looked like a wedding (not theirs), all flushed cheeks and exuberance. There was a close-up of the tattoos on his arms. Under *Job History* was a series of restaurants. Criminal convictions: none. He'd signed a petition to increase the number of immigrants allowed to enter the United States and then another one to support the changing of a British boat's name to Boaty McBoatface. He'd donated fifty dollars to a few GoFundMe fundraisers. This, I realized, was what it was like living in the future: in less than ten minutes I'd managed to piece together a good chunk of Denny's life since the last time we'd corresponded.

And now I could look up Mom's date too. I studied the small picture that came up. Dark hair, tanned skin, maybe Latino? He didn't look like a Bart. I wondered if it would be a face I would come to know the way I knew Mom's face or Claire's or Joe's, one that I would be able to picture when I closed my eyes. I didn't get the feeling that he would murder my mother.

My cramps started getting worse. In a way it was comforting to feel them. At the worst point of the miscarriage bleeding, I'd been reminded that pain was a kind of work. It was all-encompassing. I'd sat on the toilet seat with my head in my hands as my body worked independently from me—I was just a witness to it, possessed by it. That feeling of pain and cramps lingered for a few days and then suddenly stopped. I was relieved for the pause, but I wanted to remember it. The further I got away from it, the more unresolved I felt about what had happened. But here it was again, the return of that feeling in my abdomen.

I got dressed and asked the front desk where I could find a pharmacy. I hadn't left the resort grounds since we'd arrived and had no idea where to find normal life things—grocery stores, schools. There was apparently a small strip mall not too far away. I could walk if I wanted to, and I chose to do so.

I walked along the side of the road. A car passed carrying two children in uniforms on their way to school. I hadn't seen a kid since we arrived, which I didn't realize until then. Our resort wasn't the kind you'd bring your kids to, I supposed.

As soon as I'd gotten pregnant, I'd become hyper-aware of the kids around me: the teenagers jostling for seats on the subway, Moms wearing coats with those extensions that let them keep their babies strapped to their chest even in the winter, the sound of students running around at recess at the school near our place. I studied them, but from the corner of my eye, not wanting to get caught. I visited my friends with babies and tried to play it cool around them too, as if I might scare a potential baby away if I acted like I wanted one too much. After the miscarriage, I couldn't block out kids the way I'd done in the past, tuning them out without trying, and now I understood why people paid good money for child-free resorts.

I arrived at the small strip of stores and bought tampons. Normally I would've lingered, poked around the shop, looked for interesting snacks or lunch, but I felt unsteady out in the real world and walked briskly back to the hotel, sweaty, crampy, bleeding.

What did you think of Whispr? Claire texted me while I walked. *Did you find Bart?*

He looks pretty normal. Interesting app

How's vacation?

It's okay, but I'm not feeling great this morning

Sick?

I paused in the parking lot of the resort. *My body is kind of recovering from a miscarriage.*

It wasn't quite true, but I wrote it anyway.

Shit, you're having a miscarriage?

I had one recently

Why didn't you say anything? Are you okay?

I thought of when Claire emailed me about her abortion. *I'm totally fine*, she'd written.

I wrote the same thing.

I'm really sorry, she replied.

I held my phone and waited for Claire to say more, but after a few minutes I still hadn't heard anything. I went back to my room, cleaned myself up, took an Advil, put on my bathing suit, and went back out to the pool. Eyes closed, I enjoyed the sounds of a child-free environment: the rustle of leaves, ocean waves, some glasses clinking, a low murmur of voices around me. Suddenly, I heard a series of dull thuds. I looked around until I noticed two coconuts lolling about on a patch of dirt. What if I'd been sitting there? They could've landed on my head. It seemed dangerous.

I got up to get a drink from the bar. "Should I be worried about the coconuts?" I asked the bartender.

"What do you mean?"

"I saw two fall from the tree over there."

"Why would you sit under a coconut tree?"

"Shade?"

"Miss, please do not sit under coconut trees."

On the way back to my lounge chair, I picked up one of the coconuts. A small globe, threads hanging off the side. I smelled it, but it didn't smell like much yet; I'd have to crack it open. Could I do it myself? No one was around so I put down my drink, held the coconut high over my head and threw it down against the cement path. It bounced, rolled away. I picked it up again, plus its companion, and sat them next to me until I finished my drink. I carried both back to the room—one to crack now, one to bring home.

I studied the contours of the coconut. Our balcony had slate tiles and I smashed it against the floor, but it just bounced again. What I needed was a machete, a hammer, a chisel. I threw it a few more times, taking out all of my aggression on the coconut, until a crack ran down the side. Water dripped out, and I grabbed a glass from the bathroom to collect it. I found a corkscrew beside the wine glasses that sat on the side table and used it to go at the cracked shell until it broke open. I scraped off some coconut flesh. I drank some water from the glass. It was earthy and sweet.

That evening, Joe's client was going to take him and Brian out for dinner at a local restaurant. They also insisted that I come along. I'd forgotten about it until Joe texted me to say he was on his way. I gathered the coconut pieces, piling them on one of the glass-topped rattan tables, and quickly hopped into the shower. My hands were sticky and felt raw and bruised.

Joe knocked on the bathroom door. "Hey, you ready?"

"Almost," I said, towelling my hair. When I walked out, he was sitting on the edge of the bed in his suit, looking at his phone.

"You don't look ready."

"I just need a few more minutes. When do we have to leave?"

"Like, now. Brian is waiting downstairs."

I rushed to put on a dress. My hair was still dripping.

"I told you I was coming."

"I didn't see your message."

"We can't be late."

"Just give me five minutes!" I ran back into the bathroom and plugged in the hair dryer to partially dry my hair before putting it in a ponytail. I felt uncomfortable in the dress.

I hadn't worn it in a year, and it felt tight around my soft stomach. You could see my bathing suit tan lines. I hated the way I looked but left the bathroom and put on my shoes. Joe was already by the door. In the lobby Brian was looking at his phone the same way Joe had been.

"Sorry that took longer than I thought it would," Joe said in a jokey way that, for a brief moment, I hated more than anything in the world.

"My fault!" I said. "My schedule's a mess here."

"No problem," Brian said, smiling easily. "The car's outside waiting for us."

He sat in the front, and Joe and I were in the back. The two of them talked while I remained quiet. I squeezed my ponytail and felt the damp spot it left on my dress.

The restaurant overlooked the ocean. We crossed a bridge to walk into a wooden hut standing directly above the water. Two men were already sitting at the table drinking wine. They got up when we arrived, shook our hands, and I forgot their names immediately.

"This is my wife, Laura," Joe said. "She came along for a vacation."

"Are you enjoying yourself?" the older one asked me.

"It's so beautiful here, how could I not?"

"What have you been up to during the day?"

"Nothing," I said. "Doing nothing is very exhausting." Everyone laughed more than the quip deserved. "Actually, that's not true. I managed to crack open a coconut today."

"With your bare hands?"

"Yes!"

"Your wife is very impressive," one of the men said to Joe. Again, too much laughter.

A waiter gave us heavy leather-backed menus. There was hardly anything on the menu that indicated we were in Barbados, just standard fancy restaurant fare, vaguely French and Italian, some fish in coconut sauce that leaned toward tropical island, I supposed. The men ordered more wine for the table. I had a Caesar salad (a specialty, for some bizarre reason) and then some seafood pasta dish. Joe had duck. I wished I was impressed by the restaurant, that I was more interested in the conversation, but I only participated when asked direct questions. We could hear the waves lapping underneath us, and everything was lit up with small white lights. It was beautiful, and I tried to soften my heart to the beauty, but part of me was still just annoyed with Joe.

I was seated closest to the edge of the hut, and I could hear the ocean more than I could see it. Music wafted from down the coast, and the lights of other restaurants and hotels flickered like faraway stars. I imagined what it might be like if there were a power outage, the quiet extinguishing of lights.

My phone buzzed. It was Claire, who hadn't written to me since the morning. I'd been waiting for her to ask me more questions about the miscarriage, to say something other than her paltry *I'm sorry.*

Mom had her date—she said it was great and that she's seeing him again.

I'd totally forgotten about the date, and when I looked at my phone I noticed that I'd also missed a call from Mom. What if Bart *had* been a murderer? I'd been preoccupied with coconuts all afternoon.

That's a relief, I texted Claire. *Tell Mom I'll call her later, just at a dinner thing with Joe.*

"Have you done a sea turtle tour yet?" one of the men asked me when I shoved my phone back into my bag.

"What's that?" I asked.

"A guide takes you out on a boat so you can swim with sea turtles. You get lunch, drinks. Make a day of it."

"Laura's leaving on Sunday. Maybe we can go on Saturday," Joe said.

"Sure," I said. "You know what they say: I like turtles."

The older man smiled at me the way I imagined he would a five-year-old.

"I know that meme," Brian said, and I was grateful to him.

When we got back to the hotel room, Joe saw the coconut on the table. "You really cracked that open yourself?"

"Yup."

"How?"

"Brute strength."

"That's pretty sexy." He nuzzled in close, and when I didn't kiss him back he asked if I was depressed.

"I got my period today."

"Oh. Does it hurt?"

"It's just my period."

"I mean, does it feel any different?"

"No," and I knew by my tone I might as well have added, *you idiot.*

"Laura, I'm sorry. I feel like I say everything wrong these days. I'm just trying to understand how you feel. I want you to feel better, and I'm not sure how to help."

"I do feel better. I'm just a little crampy. I'm sorry too."

"You know I'd like us to try again," he said. Neither of us had said this out loud yet.

"I would too. I didn't know what you were thinking."

"I just don't want to pressure you into anything if you're not feeling well."

"I think I'm ready now."

"Oh, now?"

"I mean, not at this exact moment when I'm starting my period."

We laughed, and Joe reached for my hand under the covers. When I let go to wipe away a tear, neither of us acknowledged it.

I'd taught him how to French braid when we were stuck at an airport once. Start at the top with a small section of hair; grab some on each side when plaiting it over until it's all gathered. My hair had been greasy and easy to handle. His hands were clumsy, but he kept doing it until he was satisfied with the final result.

I wondered if he still remembered how to do it. If I asked him, would he be able to braid my hair for me?

The next morning, after breakfast, I looked up sea turtle tours online and immediately found warnings against the activity. It wasn't dangerous for us, but it was for the turtles. The tours trained them to become comfortable approaching boats full of humans, which put the already endangered turtles in harm's way. They knew they would get fed, and, unable to distinguish between tour boats and regular boats, would give themselves myriad opportunities to be hunted or tangled up and killed accidentally. These were creatures that could live for over a hundred years, and it was shocking to see their population dwindle so quickly in the last few decades. I opened my Notes app, added *sea turtles* to my poetry list, then spent a full afternoon searching for the tour company with the best reputation. I hadn't heard anything else from Claire, but I called Mom to talk about her date.

"He's very handsome," she said. I'd wondered if Claire would've said something about the miscarriage news, but she obviously hadn't because Mom gushed about him for ten more minutes, the most I'd ever heard her gush about anyone ever.

"I'm happy for you, Mom."

Should we be planning for Mom's wedding? I texted Claire afterwards.

Our tour guide was white with a thick Bajan accent. He handed us glasses of rum punch as we boarded the catamaran, and we toasted with each other—ten of us on the boat—before taking off. Joe and I rested our arms on the railings and watched the water bobbing around us. We saw schools of flying fish, magical silver flashes that arced above the waves and glinted in the sun.

When the boat stopped and the guide handed out snorkelling masks and flippers, I was sun dumb and drunker than I had realized; I'd been sipping on rum punch steadily since we'd left port. The task of putting the mask over my face seemed arduous, but my skin felt tight and I knew the water, smooth and deep and dark blue, would be refreshing.

Then someone shrieked. "A turtle!"

I looked out and there it was, a swimming dark spot. First one, then two and three. A school of them! A team? What were they called? A clan, a majesty, a snap? The real answer, bale, was not sufficient.

"It's our turn," Joe said. He had his mask on already. It made his ears stick out like those of a little boy. I slipped on my mask, felt the rubber pull at my hair.

We made our way to the ladder off the side of the boat. Joe climbed in first and then treaded water waiting for me. Instead of climbing, I just jumped in. My body, heavy, sunk down, and then buoyant from the rum punches and salt water, immediately bobbed back up. I'd never been in ocean waters this deep before. I stuck my masked head in the water. First it was all bubbles, dark blue, that grainy security-camera-footage look. I remembered the dodo bird video on YouTube.

The ocean floor was impossibly far away. The water had seemed calm from the catamaran, but the waves were busy once I was in the ocean, chattering and pushing me around in different directions in small thrusts. I put my face in again, steadied my breath, and then spotted them, the turtles, swimming around with their huge flippers. I lifted my head up and saw the tour guide handing out food.

"I thought you didn't feed the turtles," I said to him when I swam over. I'd specifically chosen this company for the fact that they advertised being the most ethical. They hadn't quite defined what they meant by that, but I figured introducing an unnatural food source would be the first thing eliminated.

"Here you go," he said, not having heard my question. He gave me a fistful of ground meat, gelatinous like chunky dog food. I squished my fingers around it. Joe had already grabbed some too.

The turtles were close now, the dark spots immediately beneath us. I ducked underwater, and one came close. I looked at her head, her glistening shell. Her watery, sleepy eyes. I was sure she was a female, one of the turtles that fought her way to the shore and dug holes to lay hundreds of eggs in. I wondered how many of those eggs had been the lucky ones, if any of the turtles here were her children. I hoped so. I held my arm out and opened my hand.

Ground meat is very difficult to keep together underwater. It's not like a piece of steak; it just dissolves into a million tiny particles. I shouldn't have released it until I was almost touching her. She opened her mouth, and it seemed like she snagged some pieces. And then she turned around, kicking bubbles around me. *I'm sorry*, I wanted to call out.

We climbed back up on the boat and removed our masks and flippers. Joe was so happy. I was exhausted from hauling myself out of the weightless world of the ocean, and I also felt like I'd failed my turtle. I wished I had shards of coconut for her, something more solid and nourishing. While we'd been in the water, the tour crew had laid out a buffet lunch of fried flying fish and potato salad for us, but just looking at it made me queasy. While others filled their plates and went back for seconds, I drank another rum punch and then laid out on the netting of the catamaran in the sun, almost asleep until Joe sat next to me and pressed down on my leg. The skin turned white and then quickly pink. He brought over my dress and towel and made me put them on. Then he brought me a glass of ice water.

On the car ride home, I leaned against his shoulder and moaned. I hadn't thrown up once during my pregnancy, which I'd thought was a good sign until I later realized it could've been an indication that the pregnancy wasn't progressing.

In our hotel room, I threw up three times in a row, quickly and violently. It was the same reddish-pink hue as the rum punches. I slathered myself in lotion. We skipped going out for dinner in town like we'd planned—it would have been only the third time I'd eaten outside the hotel—and then I was asleep by eight.

When I woke up with the sun the next morning, my sunburn wasn't as bad as I thought it would be. The worst of it was on my thighs and shoulders, which I could hide from my co-workers. My own private embarrassment, everything terrible that had happened to me in the past few months, so easily concealed.

"Let's go for a walk before your flight," Joe suggested.

"No," I said, but got up with him anyway.

"How are you feeling?" he asked when we were on the beach.

"The same." I stuck my toes into the soft sand.

"It's okay. You'll be okay."

"I know."

"The next week will be so busy for me. It's good you're leaving now."

I could tell by his tone of voice that he was trying to give me another version of the bag of gummy bears, sparkling water, the *New Yorker*. "Yeah, maybe."

"Hey, look." He pointed at a conch a few feet ahead of us.

I picked it up and tucked my fingers into the smooth, pearly curl of the shell. This time I didn't throw it back. I kept it.

PART THREE: SUMMER

I sometimes wonder if I have a karmic tax to pay. Joe and I married young, and we found our home faster than usual in Toronto's aggressive real estate market. Because of the relative quickness of these major life events, it made sense to me that something else, like getting pregnant, might take longer than usual. "It's probably a time debt," I told Joe.

"That's not how things work, though."

"But maybe it is." It was the only way I could think to reply.

After returning from Barbados, I became hyper-aware of my menstrual cycle. I was naive about things when I first stopped taking the pill—I figured pregnancy would just *happen*—but after the miscarriage I decided I didn't have the liberty to be clueless anymore. I read *Taking Charge of Your Fertility* and began monitoring my cervical mucus, which changes throughout your cycle and at your most fertile point is supposed to have the consistency of egg whites. I'd start the day by inserting my index finger inside myself toward my cervix so I could examine the viscosity of the mucus on it. *This isn't gross*, I'd tell myself. *These are normal bodily secretions that society has conditioned me to feel alienated from.* But I was a little repulsed anyway until one morning when I felt it—the fertile liquidy milkiness between my finger and thumb—and knew I was on the right track, that this was part of the payment plan to get us where we needed to be.

I also replaced my menstrual cycle app with another I'd read about online that was specifically geared toward conception. It had a bright pink-and-white colour scheme. I spent one morning in bed ignoring my alarm to import the first and last days of my period into it, going back a few months before the miscarriage. When I was done, an estimated ovulatory calendar populated before me: period dates for the next year blocked out in crimson, fertile days marked in green. Actual ovulation, a single day, was indicated by a pink flower. All other days were blank. The goal during the green phase, the five days leading up to ovulation, was to have as much sex as possible so that by the time ovulation occurred—flower time—the egg would be surrounded on all sides by sperm, ready to be invaded. I could also use the app to track everything and anything related to reproduction—intercourse, breast tenderness, food cravings, that egg-white mucus. I could add new symptoms and assign emojis to them.

Claire had sent me a survey about Whispr that she and Shannon were using to gather feedback on the app. There were questions about the interface, how easy or hard it was to use, why I wanted to use it, what problems it solved for me. I kept inputting *n/a*. I had no use for Whispr and learning details about strange men. My new cycle tracking app was what I used most, and I would've answered any survey for them if they'd asked.

During my first month of using it, I kept track of my inner workings with an intensity and an eye for detail that I didn't know I was capable of. I was psyched for the green phase—and then it came, as it were.

That first night Joe and I had good, vigorous, life-affirming—and producing?!—sex.

During my lunch break the next day, I went to the closest grocery store to buy a whole pineapple. I'd read online that pineapple improved the odds of becoming pregnant because it was rich in bromelain, a mixture of enzymes that acted as both an anti-inflammatory and a blood thinner, two things that were helpful if you wanted an embryo to implant itself in your endometrium. It even had a slogan: *nature's Aspirin*. You couldn't eat the pineapple any old way for it to work, though. It had to be done *specifically*, by dividing the whole pineapple, including its tough woody core, into five to eight pieces (it varied depending on the source I consulted) and then eating one piece daily after potential implantation.

At the grocery store, the pineapples were kept in a corner with other exotic fruit: a few slightly shrivelled starfruit, some Asian pears wrapped in protective netting, giant pomelos, and a small pile of dark globes that I recognized as mangosteens. I'd eaten mangosteen before, in Thailand. When we'd just arrived in Bangkok, we'd decided to spend two nights in a nice hotel to get over the jet lag before roughing it for the next three weeks. I'd never seen the deep-purple tennis ball–shaped fruit before that hotel buffet, and I had been delighted by the soft white segments under the tough outer shell. We'd spent the rest of the trip obsessively eating them before returning to Canada. I had never had another. Maybe, I thought, if I bought a few now, I could save them for the end of the pineapple treatment when, after bombarding my system with bromelains, I'd get a positive pregnancy test. A callback and a reward.

When I got home from work I put the handful of mangosteens in a bowl on the counter, then took out my big knife to peel and chop the pineapple. Its flesh was a pale yellow, almost white, sickly looking compared to what I'd eaten in Barbados. I popped the first cube in my mouth and chewed and chewed on the core, mildly sweet and mostly fibrous.

That night, the second green day, the sex was good.

On the third day, we were both tired. Joe had spent the evening recording a podcast episode at Amit's, and by the time he came to bed, I was already dozing off. They did all of their recording in Amit's soundproofed basement and had a shared Google Calendar where they plotted out recording days and split up tasks. Amit's wife and I sometimes joked that they were better at divvying up domestic labour with each other than with us. My ovulation period overlapping with recording week was just unfortunate timing. I looked at my app. We were a few days out from the flower, so it was probably fine to skip, and it was almost a relief to give ourselves that permission. But then when I woke up the next morning, I was self-conscious. Was it a bad sign that we weren't able to muster the enthusiasm to have sex three days in a row? I googled how often couples in long-term relationships have sex. I found answers that made me feel better and ignored the ones that didn't.

That evening when I started kissing Joe he said, "I get the feeling that you're using me," and I tried to turn it into something hot, but he didn't mean it that way, and I was tired too—again!—and just wanted to get on with things. But we did it, half-heartedly. I thought of a friend who'd told me that she knew the exact night she and her husband conceived their baby because they'd truly *made love*. If our baby was conceived as a result of this evening, I wouldn't be able to say that—but hey, sperm was sperm.

On ovulation day I consulted the app, and there wasn't only a small flower icon, but also an interface transformed into a full-screen field of exploding foliage. A butterfly fluttered back and forth. If there was a day to have sex—good sex, perfunctory sex, whatever, this was it.

I showed Joe the field of flowers. "I'm ovulating. If we don't do it tonight we have to wait"—I looked at the app again—"Twenty-nine days."

Our sex was desperate and kind of sad, but I cheered afterwards, weakly, *We did it.*

By that point my mangosteens were already eaten. I don't know why I'd thought they would last the entire duration of the pineapple period—they were already getting soft when I'd brought them home. Instead of having them go to waste, I'd eaten them all at once, and as I ate each mild-tasting segment, I worried that I'd tempted fate by eating them too soon. But I thought of Joe saying *That's not how things work.*

The next two weeks were agonizingly slow. One day I walked home from work and my breasts were heavy in my shirt. *Do they hurt?* I wondered. They did! This was a good sign.

I looked at myself naked in the mirror after a shower. My breasts were maybe slightly fuller. Later that night I asked Joe if my nipples looked bigger or darker and he said he couldn't tell, and then we had sex, or rather we *made love*, probably feeling released from the pressure of preparing for ovulation.

Throughout the day, I'd scan myself for twinges. I racked my brain to remember if I'd felt them when I was actually pregnant. When I got home from work in the evenings, I couldn't settle down. I paced around the loft, the open-concept space conducive to it.

"You're making me nervous," Joe said when, according to my calendar, I was two days away from my period. "You're like an animal in a zoo."

"I don't know what to do with myself."

"You can make dinner?"

He didn't mean it as a snarky comment; dinner was generally my domain, especially when I'd been deep into my blog and was cooking so I could write about it. These days, however, cooking was a chore. It seemed more important to get nutrients than it did to make something delicious.

I decided to make pasta from scratch. It would keep me busy. I dumped flour directly on the counter, dug a small crater in the centre of the pile and cracked an egg into it. There was something precarious about mixing flour and egg without using a bowl, the danger that everything would spill off the sides onto the floor, but the dough came together easily, soft and smooth. I rolled it out by hand, using a long wooden rolling pin that I usually kept propped up in the space between the stove and the counter, since it didn't fit in any of our drawers. I rolled and rolled until the dough was paper thin and my arms were sore. I used our sharpest knife to slice it into tiny ribbons that I hung off the counter until everything was ready. Then I boiled water, dropped the pasta in for barely five minutes, then doused it in a small puddle of homemade sauce that I'd frozen months ago when feeling ambitious. The meal took almost two hours to make, but after plating the finished product, the food was in our bellies within fifteen minutes, maybe actually ten.

"That was so good," Joe said, always appreciative, always finishing the meals I made and bringing leftovers to work.

It was almost ten by the time we were done because I'd waited so long to get started. I did the dishes, even though Joe offered, and then scraped off the stray bits of dough sticking to the counter. Afterwards I sat on the couch, still restless, and pulled out my laptop. I would update my blog again, my first entry since our trip to Barbados.

I wrote about the first time Joe and I went to Italy and how we'd eaten terribly. We'd taken our first trip together after graduating from university. I'd never left Canada, but Joe had travelled with his family his entire life and had spent a university semester in Ireland. I expected him to be an expert, but when we landed in our starting point, Rome, he was as timid as I was. He'd told my mother that we couldn't tell her what hostel or hotel we were staying at—we'd just find a place when we got there—but we arrived in the middle of June, and Rome was crawling with tourists and freshly graduated college kids and Australians on two-year travel visas. We were turned away from four hostels before we managed to snag two free beds, and the beds weren't even next to each other. We'd gotten some restaurant recommendations from a guidebook, but didn't know how to weed out the most touristy places. We were also nervous to buy directly from butchers, cheesemongers, or bakeries because we didn't speak Italian. It turned out you could eat terribly in Italy, and it was confusing to be disappointed since I hadn't considered it a possibility.

But I enjoyed writing about this for my blog; it was okay to write about a past terrible that wasn't even really terrible—we'd figured things out after a few days, managed to eventually eat the way you're supposed to in Italy. I wrote about that too, about figuring things out, about the little well in the pile of flour on your counter and how you just have to trust that everything will come together, that the egg won't spill out, and that it will make a sheet of dough that you can slice into long ribbons. Your arms will be tired, but it will work. I hit publish and went to bed.

The day my period started, one day before its predicted date, I logged it in the app. The calendar reset to day one and everything shifted slightly in accordance with this new entry in the data set. I now thought about time on an acute level, like a child crossing days off a calendar leading up to Christmas, and was absorbed by it.

I also joined an online support message board for women trying to conceive. The act was shortened to the acronym TTC, which was confusingly the same as my city's public transportation system. I knew that Joe, who was interested in anything vaguely adjacent to public transportation is-sues, would find it amusing, but I didn't tell him about it. I was too much into the weeds of TTC-ing to joke about how similarly long and slow and painful it was compared to tak-ing a bus in Toronto. I also didn't tell him how much I'd ago-nized over choosing an online handle for the board. I didn't intend to post, but I had to sign up for an account to read every thread. I couldn't bring myself to choose something cute, or even worse, aspirational—with the word mama in it, like so many others had done, ready to lay claim to the term they hadn't yet earned. I was Laura26534 instead, a meaningless string of numbers.

I did privately acknowledge that the vocabulary of the message boards was amusing, because it was. I trawled posts discussing endless details about things like mucus, linings, what age was considered geriatric (only thirty-five!)—it all sounded ridiculous. But then I just got used to it. It was simply a new language, and there were other more important things to focus on. Joe, who did not research or peruse message boards, was still at the point where it was easier to think these details were the salient point, the punchline to the joke.

What's up? Claire texted me one day. *Haven't heard from you in a while.*

It's just been one day, I wrote back. The truth was that it was rare for Claire and I to take more than a few hours to respond to each other. I wasn't able to keep this pace with anyone else—I had friends I'd owed texts to for over a week—but with Claire, it was like breathing. The cadence of our cor-respondence had slowed down since Barbados because she was so busy at work and helping Shannon with Whispr, but I suppose she still expected me to respond quicker.

I reread her message from the day before. I'd seen it when it came through but hadn't had the energy to engage with it then. *Our newest hire brought their puppy to the office today and it didn't have its shots and another older dog lunged at it, and it turned into a THING. We still don't have a proper office manager here so I've been tasked with writing a dog policy.*

That's a bitch, I finally wrote back.

Claire reacted with a *haha* and, satisfied with the response, didn't write back.

Joe, who went for weeks without talking to his siblings, thought it was funny that Claire, Mom, and I spoke so frequently. Sometimes he'd listen to a conversation we'd have and afterwards remark that we hadn't actually talked about anything. Which was true. The point of our daily conversations wasn't necessarily to converse, but just to know that the other person was there.

After another two months of choking down pineapple cores and being disappointed by the same pattern, I booked an appointment with my family doctor, who I hadn't seen since before my miscarriage.

When I got to her office, I felt shy. I'd only seen this doctor once before because my previous doctor had retired from the clinic. I'd been reassigned to someone new, and I guess I'd finally reached the tipping point when doctors were now my age or younger. She leaned in close to listen to my fertility woes, and the look on her face was like a sympathetic girlfriend's.

"I'm so sorry," she said.

At home I told Joe about what had been discussed, the tests she'd ordered for the both of us.

"But it hasn't been a year, right? Isn't that when you're supposed to get worried?"

"It took almost six months to get pregnant the first time, and then I had the miscarriage. It's already almost a year."

"You stopped taking the pill six months before you got pregnant, but I don't think we were technically trying, were we? We were just seeing what happened, not like what you're doing now with your app. And having a miscarriage doesn't mean anything's wrong—we read that, and the doctors said so too."

"I know, but I'm almost thirty-four and at thirty-five things go downhill."

"But you're not thirty-four yet, and anyway, thirty-five isn't old."

"In the reproductive world it's considered geriatric."

He laughed at the word geriatric, just as I'd predicted.

"I have a feeling we should do this," I said. "Mother's intuition or whatever."

"I don't think you can call it that when you don't actually have a baby."

"I was joking." I started crying.

"Whoa, wait, why are you crying?" he asked.

Ever since I'd started studying the app, reading the message board posts, I'd begun to feel a weird gnaw of desperation and worry. It wasn't until this conversation that I realized how all-encompassing the feeling was, like I was mired in a kind of desperation. I hated the feeling, all bright, sharp edges; I hated verbalizing it.

"I'm so impatient," I said.

I was also feeling outsmarted by my body—it surprised me in unpleasant ways. The more I tried using the app to keep track of it, the more it seemed unknowable and beyond my control. It just did things on its own without consulting me, its owner.

Of course Joe relented. I wrote a checklist of tests we had to do and started making appointments, the majority of which were mine. When Joe went in for his primary test to provide a sperm sample, he texted me a photo of the private room at the clinic the doctor had referred him to. There were porn magazines on a table and a television mounted to the wall. The magazine at the top of the stack had a picture of three girls, one white, one Black, one Asian. They wore schoolgirl uniforms, the curves of their asses peeking out from under their skirts, their fingers in their mouths. A parody of a dirty magazine.

They don't have wifi here. I have to stream my own porn if I don't want to use theirs. And no way am I touching a magazine someone else has used expressly for the purpose of a sperm sample

At least your tests have foreplay, I texted back.

None of mine had involved porn. In addition to blood tests at specific points in my cycle, I had to get a series of internal tests. For the ultrasound I had to show up at a clinic with a full bladder, and even though they'd told me exactly how much to drink ahead of time (four cups), I'd just kept drinking more and more on the drive over. The technician apologized when she pressed down on my stomach and felt the near-bursting bladder. I was allowed to empty it before the transvaginal ultrasound, and the relief in the bathroom had been palpable, but I was still uncomfortable when, with the wand inside me, I'd had to press down on my stomach myself so she could get a clearer view of my ovaries.

Worse, though, was the appointment I had at the hospital where a doctor squirted a dye into my Fallopian tubes so they could image them. The procedure also sometimes came with the advantage of clearing out blocked tubes, and many message board entries were about getting pregnant the cycle after.

Joe had driven me even though I'd told him not to. He insisted, and he played on his phone in the waiting area while I went to a designated area to change into a gown. I folded my pants and underwear and left on my T-shirt.

"Did you take two Advil?" the doctor asked me. I nodded. "This is going to be a little uncomfortable, but it will be fast."

For some reason I hadn't thought to do research on what the procedure would feel like, but she narrated the steps to me before doing them—the insertion of the speculum, the dilation of my cervix, and then an apologetic "This will make you feel crampy." I felt an increasing sense of dread that culminated in pain so unexpected—the feeling of the warm liquid shooting into me the wrong way with such force that I gasped and instinctively tried to pull my legs back while a nurse held one firmly in place.

"Oh my god." I wept.

"I'm so sorry. But we're all done," the doctor said and quickly removed the speculum.

When I got up, I saw that I'd bled bright-red blood on yet another absorbent pad. I limped out to the waiting room feeling like a kicked puppy.

After all of that, another month and a half, we were referred to a proper fertility clinic. It was nicer than any doctor's office I'd ever been to, in a building downtown with sleek Scandinavian furniture in the lobby. The big window in the waiting room looked out onto the sprawling tree-filled Don Valley, so it was almost like we weren't in the city. There were also good magazines to flip through: the *New Yorker*, *Esquire*—recent issues, not old tattered ones. Even their pornography was probably better quality, we hypothesized.

"So, you have problems," Dr. Sutton, our new fertility doctor, said. She held a file thick with reports. The miscarriage might've been a tipoff, she said, but not really the significant symptom. Anyone could have a miscarriage, and the actual health of my womb looked fine. Joe's sperm was within an average range. My ovarian reserve, on the other hand, was below average for my age.

"How many eggs do I have?" I asked.

"It's not necessarily a matter of counting. It's based on hormone levels." She took out a chart to demonstrate. "We measured your follicle-stimulating hormone and your anti-Mullerian hormone levels. You should be here, but you're here." The gap on the piece of paper was the width of a pinky, a few millimetres, nothing.

"But I got pregnant once before, and we were hardly even trying." I was clinging to it, the miscarriage.

"It might not be a problem, but it can make pregnancy harder for you." Dr. Sutton was older than my family doctor, and I could tell her haircut was expensive. Tasteful and sleek, like the furniture in the lobby. She was kind in a measured, polished way. "And you have some options."

She pulled out another chart, this one with statistics for success, and plotted us somewhere in the middle. Enough for a jolt of hope.

She suggested we start with IUI, intrauterine insemination. I would take a round of Clomid, pills that could boost the number of follicles my ovaries created in a cycle. The follicles generated an egg each, and we didn't want too many of them, just two or three to increase the odds of a successful insemination. Then they'd take Joe's sperm and "wash" it to eliminate anything subpar—there were always some bad ones in the batch. Dr. Sutton would use a catheter to inject the super-sperm into my uterus so that when the two to three follicles released their eggs, the sperm wouldn't have to travel far to find them.

"So we might get triplets?" I asked.

"It's extremely rare, but yes, it's a possibility."

"And what if that doesn't work?"

"In vitro fertilization." The big guns. When Dr. Sutton described it, though, there was no mention of test tubes or petri dishes—important features in how I had pictured IVF. It was as if everything would grow naturally in a greenhouse, like tomatoes in the wintertime. The engineering involved, however, was hard to minimize. Blood draws, ultrasounds, pills, self-administered hormone injections, minor surgery, centrifugal force, faceless lab technicians carefully melding our genetic material. I'd be required to visit the clinic often, sometimes daily, but technically Joe only had to be there once, for his contribution in the private room. Because of this, most of Dr. Sutton's eye contact remained with me. We stared at each other as she told me that the end result would be multiple embryos, of which the clinic would choose the most viable to insert into my uterus.

"Does that sound reasonable?"

"It sounds so *modern*."

"I know it's overwhelming." She pushed over a packet of information. "You probably have questions."

It wasn't so much that I had specific questions; I had existential ones. How did we get here?

"How much does all of this cost?" Joe asked. "IUI must be a lot cheaper than IVF."

Dr. Sutton and I turned to look at him as if we'd forgotten he was there.

"I'll get someone from our accounting department to come by and price out scenarios for you. We'll start with the less invasive treatments. I'll be honest, their odds of success are lower, but given your age and the fact that you've gotten pregnant once before, it's not outside the realm of possibility."

When she left the room, Joe said, "Of course they have an accounting department."

That night we started trying to make a baby the old-fashioned way, but we didn't get very far. We were in the blank days on my app anyway, although I wondered if I'd need the app anymore now that we had Dr. Sutton. For a few minutes we lay in bed not talking or touching.

"So," Joe said. "What do you think? It's kind of weird."

"It is. But I guess we have to try."

"Yeah."

I'd been stuck in a memory from our first trip to Italy. After Rome we booked a 6:20 a.m. train to Florence, and deciding to be frugal, checked out of the hostel the day before and roamed the city until it was time to leave in the morning. We thought we would stay up all night, sleep in a park if we had to, and it felt like a good decision until night hit and we were exhausted, our shoulders achy from carrying our backpacks. But just past midnight we got our second wind. We ate gelato. We walked toward the train station and found a restaurant still milling with people, so we sat down and ordered wine that came in a carafe along with two thick-glassed tumblers to pour it into ourselves. A group of cats hovered waiting for food, which people would occasionally toss in their direction. There was a family next to us, parents with two young children. The older boy was half-asleep, his head slumped in his arms on the table, but the baby bounced on her father's knee and clapped her hands in constant joy. We looked at them, then looked back at each other and smiled, and then smiled again, almost shyly, because we both knew what the other was thinking. *That will be us one day.*

As I recalled the details of that night, Joe fell asleep. Though I was also tired, I got out of bed and climbed down the ladder to the kitchen. The nights when he fell asleep first were the longest. I tried to remember what it felt like to be delayed at an airport, that feeling of waiting, time like taffy that could be pulled further and further apart without breaking. We'd always made it through just fine, cured by a shower and a nap when we'd returned home.

I poured myself a glass of water. The walls in the old schoolhouse were thick. We never heard our neighbours, but occasionally I'd hear banging from somewhere far away, usually late at night. I heard it now. Sometimes I wondered if the children who used to live here haunted the building, upset that a developer had remodelled their home. There were child-height water fountains in the hall, decorative only, but they'd surely been functional at one point. Had the children—deaf, blind, developmentally challenged—been abandoned, deemed too difficult to take care of by their parents? I imagined them in the loft. Who was I to colonize their home? But I welcomed their ghosts; I would've taken them all.

Dr. Sutton said that if an IVF cycle yielded multiple embryos, they could be frozen and placed in storage until we needed them for second chances or siblings. More to add to the list of things we would keep hidden out of sight, along with everything in our storage unit—the extra books, the sewing machine, the Christmas tree. It was disconcerting to own things but have no clear timeline of when you would be reunited.

It also seemed bizarre to have embryos as objects—when do they cross the threshold from being things in storage to humans who we don't rightfully have any claim over? Dr. Sutton said we could ask her questions, but this one didn't seem like the kind we should ask her directly. It wasn't her domain. I wondered if the clinic had an ethics department.

We had to wait for my next period to start. As it approached I bulked up my medicine cabinet with recommendations from the message board. I ordered good prenatal vitamins for myself and some for Joe that supposedly were good for his sperm. The capsules were huge and filled with a dust-coloured powder that smelled musty, and he only took them if I put them out for him on the counter.

My dad's birthday was the same day I had to pick up my Clomid prescription from the clinic, and I asked him if he wanted to meet me for lunch, since I wouldn't be far from his office. We hadn't seen each other since before Claire moved.

"Are you okay?" he asked when I told him I'd been having medical appointments nearby. "Why are you seeing a doctor here?"

I hesitated for a second. "Joe and I are trying to have a baby, but we've run into a few problems."

"What kind of problems?"

"The kind that make it hard to have a baby."

His shoulders stiffened and he nodded his head. "Ah, you'll get through it."

"Well, we're trying. We might not." I realized fertility problems didn't compute for him: he had four children! Two and two seemed less impressive split up—but four in total was so many kids. Also, our half-sisters, Lisa and Julie, had kids, so he was already used to being a grandfather.

"When I had colon cancer—"

"Wait, what?"

"Did I not tell you?"

"You had cancer?"

"They caught it early, three years ago. I didn't want many people to know; I couldn't remember if I told you."

"You didn't."

"It's fine. I'm clean now." He said it like he was a former drug addict. "Modern medicine is a miracle."

"I can't believe you didn't tell me you had cancer. That's a genetic thing Claire and I should know about. It's one of the first questions they asked me and Joe at the clinic, if we have any hereditary issues."

"There was nothing for you to worry about."

"I'm your *daughter*. I should know these things."

He took a sip of his coffee, and I recognized the look in his eyes, baleful but detached, slightly scared of me and my feelings.

I called Claire the minute I left the restaurant. It went to her voice mail, so I hung up and texted. *Call me!*

By the end of the day I still hadn't heard from her, so I texted her again. *I have to tell you what Dad told me. Where are you?*

I called Mom. "Have you talked to Claire today?"

"Not since Thursday." It was Monday. "How come?"

"She didn't respond to my messages."

"Something urgent?"

"Nah." I wanted to be casual with Mom.

"She's so busy with work and her new company."

"I wouldn't call Whispr *her* company yet, but yeah, you're right."

"And how are you, my dear?"

"I saw Dad for lunch today. It's his birthday."

"Oh is it? Good for him." She was so good-natured.

"How are you? Have you had more dates with Bart?"

Mom giggled. Claire and I were still piecing together this new relationship, and I wasn't sure how to handle both Dad withholding cancer and Mom giggling on the same day. I needed to talk to my sister.

I called again. I logged in to Facebook to see if I could tell if she'd been active on Messenger. Nope.

"She probably has a deadline or something," Joe said as I stared at my phone.

"But she would be at her computer and see all my messages and would definitely respond, even just one word."

As much as I knew about the basic structure of Claire's days, I realized that I didn't know who she interacted with regularly. I looked up Shannon, who Claire worked with on Whispr, and found her easily online. I couldn't actually look her up on Whispr since the app was only for women to look up men, which seemed like a fundamental and sexist flaw, so I had to make do with Google searches. Her Instagram was private, her Facebook bare bones. I added her as a friend, though. If I didn't hear from Claire by the next day I would contact her. I slept fitfully.

Finally, when I got to work in the morning I got a message. *What the fuck, were you really worried?*

You have literally never taken more than four hours to respond to me. Of course I was worried!

That's not true, but SORRY. I was at a meditation retreat

A. Meditation. Retreat.

Yes

I didn't know you meditated

It was a silent retreat—I wasn't allowed to talk. They kept our devices in a box

I mean before you left

What did Dad tell you?

I relented and called her instead of texting back. "Dad had colon cancer, and he never told us! He should've, right?"

"He had cancer?"

"I'm not overreacting?"

"No way!"

"Do you think he told Lisa and Julie?"

A pause. "I bet he did."

"I wonder if they would've told us if they knew we didn't know."

"Would you tell them?"

"I think so?"

We had tried to outgrow resenting our half-sisters as much as we did when we were younger, but it was easy to fall back into pettiness. Dad had tried to make us friends at one point, but his attempts were clumsy, and he eventually gave up.

"When did you start meditating?" I asked.

"Recently. Shannon got me into it. She invited me, and I thought it would help me feel less stressed out."

"Did it?"

"Kind of, but I smoked too much and wrote letters. I wrote you one."

"Thanks?"

"How are you?"

"Okay, I guess." I remembered how it felt when Dad told me about his cancer, a betrayal that made me feel like a child, as if I'd just been informed that Santa wasn't real and I was supposed to be immediately okay about it. "Joe and I are about to start some fertility treatments."

"Oh? You said you were fine from the miscarriage."

"I haven't been able to get pregnant again, and it turns out I have a low egg reserve, which can make it hard."

"So what are you going to do?"

"We're starting with IUI."

"What's that exactly?"

"Artificial insemination."

"I'm sorry. Let me know how I can help."

"Thanks," I said, this time with no question mark.

I took my first Clomid pill later that week, before work. I took another the next morning, and the next, and then the morning after that I went to the clinic for an ultrasound so they could monitor the progress. I had cramps, but I had no idea how to gauge if the meds were working their fertility magic.

I drove to the clinic in Claire's car. It was early, just after six, and the downtown streets were still quiet and empty.

"I see one follicle," the ultrasound technician said while I lay naked from the waist down under a paper sheet, the wand inside me.

"Just one?" I'd secretly been hoping for four. Not that I wanted that many babies—but twins? We could handle that, I thought. Two, like me and Claire.

I met with Dr. Sutton afterwards, who confirmed the same thing. "One very strong follicle."

"Shouldn't I have at least two or three?"

"It's hard to predict how you'll react with your ovarian reserve, but this follicle looks good, and there's still time for another to emerge."

A few days later I left the clinic with a thimble-sized vial of medication and a needle. There were no other follicles, and this one was on the cusp of bursting into an egg. Since we wanted to make sure it would release when we did the insemination, I had to take a new medication, the "trigger shot," at a precise time to guarantee ovulation at the same time as our appointment.

A nurse demonstrated to me and Joe how to give me a needle. We watched her use it to suck up the liquid and then pretend to inject it into an area on my stomach that had been swabbed with an antiseptic wipe.

I had to take the trigger shot that evening at, the nurse had told us, precisely 9:30. At 9:20 I prepared the needle, which didn't take very long, but I started shaking when it was ready so I asked Joe to give me the injection. It was 9:28. A minute later he still hadn't done it, and he had tears in his eyes.

"Are you crying?"

"I don't want to hurt you."

"It won't hurt," I said, but then I was crying too. It was now 9:32. A disaster.

I took the needle back and stabbed it into a pinch of skin, realizing afterwards that I hadn't swabbed it with the antiseptic wipe. The jab stung for a second, felt cold, and then it was like nothing had happened.

In the morning we went to the clinic. Joe was sent to the room with the porn while I waited in the lobby. When he was done, we went downstairs to a nearby cafe while the lab washed his sperm.

"How was it?" I asked.

"Very romantic."

I needed a full bladder for the IUI, so I chugged a bottle of orange juice. My stomach felt bloated from juice, Clomid, and the single very strong follicle.

When it was our time, we went back to the clinic and into the room we'd been assigned; it was one of the same rooms as those used for exams. Nothing special. I put my feet up in stirrups while Joe stood next to me and held my hand. I kept my socks on.

Dr. Sutton held out a long test tube of Joe's sperm. "Can you confirm this is yours?"

Gross, I couldn't help thinking when I saw the tube. Why was this all so gross? Why wasn't it ethereal and gauzy and us making love in the middle of the night during a thunderstorm?

"How exactly do I do that?" he asked.

"Is that your name printed on the label?" Dr. Sutton asked him. He leaned in close to read.

"Oh, yeah, that's me."

It started out like a Pap smear, with Dr. Sutton inserting a speculum, but quickly became unlike a Pap smear when she then inserted a catheter that pinched. "Are you okay?" she asked when I inhaled sharply. Until now I hadn't seen her in real doctor mode, having become accustomed to her talking to us rather than performing a procedure.

"Yup." I breathed to relax my abdomen, my cervix.

"Okay, here I go." She attached the tube and squeezed the sperm in through the catheter. The whole thing took less than five minutes, right down to removing the speculum. This was nowhere close to making love, either.

"How long should I stay here?" I asked when she was done.

"No need to stay. The sperm is up pretty far; nothing's going to leak out."

"Oh." *Gross*, I thought again, *leakage*.

"You can take your time getting ready though. There's no rush." She smiled at us—the first real smile of the appointment—and left.

I propped myself up on my elbows and then got up and dressed gingerly. Outside, Joe and I kissed goodbye and went to work. Everything felt so fragile. I felt good, though. Hopeful.

~

Dear Laura,

I'm writing from a silent meditation retreat in the Mojave Desert because I can't call or email or text. No cell access, no wifi. I didn't even bring my laptop. I could ask to use the phone here, but it's only for emergencies. I think letter writing is cheating. I don't know how to meditate and everyone seems to know what they're doing, so I don't want to ask. Anyway, despite all of that, I like being here.

And maybe I'm exaggerating the "silent" part. It's not exactly a vow of silence, it's more like a... goal. You're allowed to talk, but "encouraged" not to, and I haven't heard anyone say anything since we settled in and no one wants to be the asshole who gets everyone talking.

The monks that live here rely on divine providence (their term) to pay for their daily needs, but when that isn't enough they rent the place out for these retreats that Shannon swears by. She says they're a good "reset," which is a very Californian thing to say (she's not from California). I'm not sure if I buy into it, but it's so beautiful here and I just need a break.

The best part of the monastery is that it has its own holy stream. It's hidden among a bunch of Joshua trees. You follow this little path, the stations of the cross leaning against the trees, until you're at the tiniest trickle of water. It's so small that it has a sign that says HOLY STREAM so you don't miss it. Apparently the sign gets stolen once a year.

When the first group of monks settled here in the 1950s, the stream just appeared one day out of the blue. The water has been flowing ever since, even during droughts. When it was first discovered, people came to witness it, and as an added bonus, started experiencing miracles. Healings?

The monks won't outright vouch for the water's authenticity, but everyone says the water makes them feel better somehow. They don't sell it, but if someone calls from like, New Jersey, they'll bottle it and mail it over for a fee. Divine providence!!!

The area around the stream is peaceful, especially early in the morning before the sun gets too hot. There's a small chapel to the side with a guestbook where people write down their prayers. I've been snooping through them. "Help my daughter with her surgery." "Give me relief from arthritis." "Cure me from cancer."

This morning I found a man, not part of the retreat, kneeling at the base of the stream, plundering, catching the flow of water into a plastic juice container. I could see the remains of a torn-off juice label. He had thick glasses and his eyes were a little wild. "It's good stuff," he said to me, capping the container and starting another.

I didn't talk to him or ask him why he needed the water (vow of silence, etc.), but after he left I got depressed thinking of the hope people put into this tiny stream. Then I flipped through more of the prayer requests and found this written by a child: "Please help me catch a big fish."

This far into the desert hoping for fish. I liked that.

Love, Claire

~

I had some leftover pregnancy tests, the little strips, and it took so much willpower to not take one before my clinic blood test. I didn't want to go down the false negative path again, so I waited until my appointed time. It was nice to not have to get examined for once, just pop in for a quick blood draw, easy, and then get to my desk at work early.

Before lunch, while I was editing a piece about pumpkin pie for the fall issue, my phone rang. "Hello?" I answered.

It was my regular nurse. I hadn't spoken to her on the phone before. "I'm sorry," she said. "Your blood test came back negative. Dr. Sutton would like to see you when you get your period."

"Sounds good," I said without thinking. "Thanks!"

I got up. One of my co-workers waved when I passed her desk, and I smiled but didn't stop to talk. I skipped the bathroom on our floor, used my pass card to get to the staircase, descended two flights, and went to that bathroom instead. In the furthest stall, I sat on the toilet and put my head in my hands. I breathed. I took out my phone and texted Joe.

Negative

Bummer :(

I stared at the word *bummer*, the way it couldn't capture my disappointment, the way it actually made me feel worse with its casual tone. At least the sad face wasn't just an emoji and was actually typed out in punctuation marks. Something about the plaintive colon and parenthesis was better. I knew it meant Joe was genuinely disappointed too.

Yeah, I replied.

How do you feel?

I was not only disappointed, but suddenly scared. Worried. I felt foolish that I'd even considered twins a possibility. We were, I realized, going to have to endure more text exchanges like this in the future.

I don't know, I wrote first, but then deleted it and replaced it with :(((((.

The addition of more parentheses helped me emphasize my sadness. That's how I felt. :(((((((((.

PART FOUR: FALL

Claire returned to Toronto for two weeks in October. Mostly to speak at a conference, but it was also an opportunity to pack up more of her things, now that she'd decided she was going to stay out west indefinitely and had found her own place.

I volunteered to pick her up from the airport. She said she could expense a cab, but I wanted to see her right away. I got there a few minutes after the flight landed and waited at the arrivals gate. I briefly worried that I'd forgotten what she looked like, that she could be right there in front of me without my brain registering who she was, but of course the minute she emerged I knew. *That* was Claire.

We drove straight to Mom's, where she was going to stay until the conference put her up in a hotel. "Oh, I missed you," Mom said when we entered the front door, and she hugged Claire for a long time. She'd already set out dinner for us, but Claire wasn't hungry.

"I need a shower first," she said.

While she got ready, I stretched out on Mom's couch. Coco jumped on my lap and sat there purring, something she rarely did. I wondered if she knew more about my body than anyone else. It was the third day of our third round of IUI, and I was fatigued and bloated.

"Are you okay?" Mom asked.

"I'm fine, why?" Her question made me nervous. I hadn't told her about the treatments yet. I'd partly hoped Claire would tell her so I wouldn't have to, but she hadn't, and even though I'd blurted it out to Dad, it seemed harder to tell Mom.

"You seem sad," Mom said. "And you and Joe haven't come over in a long time."

"He's been busy with work and a bunch of podcast stuff."

"So nothing is wrong?"

"Well, maybe a little." I started crying despite myself, suddenly so much more tired. "We're trying to have a baby."

"You're going to have a baby? I'm so happy!"

"There's nothing to be happy about. There's something wrong with me. We have to do fertility treatments, and they're expensive and stressful."

"What kind of treatments? Surgery?"

"No surgery. I'm taking medication now, and we've been doing artificial insemination."

"Is that like a test-tube baby?"

"No. Well, not yet. We'll do IVF if this doesn't work."

Mom rubbed my legs. "You just have to relax, both of you. Stress doesn't help. It will happen."

"Mom." Her telling me to relax wasn't as infuriating as someone else telling me to relax, but it was still annoying. We'd done enough tests to know that stress wasn't our diagnosis, and yet it still hung over me as the insidious reason why I couldn't get pregnant. Maybe it was exacerbating my problems. "I'm doing my best, but it's hard to be patient."

"I read something in the newspaper about Kim Kardashian. She had her baby with IVF."

"Yeah."

"It's very normal now. You have nothing to be worried about."

Like Dad, Mom knew nothing about problems with conception. She'd gotten pregnant with Claire and me without thinking, without trying, probably by accident. I wondered if she had even been aware of the rhythm of her menstrual cycle the way I now was, the way I could distinctly feel the twinge of a growing follicle, the bloat of my uterine lining thickening by millimetres. I could now sense this without having to consult an app.

Claire came into the living room with wet hair. "What's going on? What's wrong?"

I wiped my eyes and tried to stop crying. "I was telling Mom about my fertility woes."

"What's happening now?"

"Just another round of IUI."

"How many have you done? Is it not going well?"

"This is the third. I don't know how it's going yet, but the hormones make me emotional."

I couldn't shake the feeling that wanting a baby and not being able to have one was a fundamentally pathetic state to be in. My friends and I had talked so much about preventing pregnancy when we were younger. We used the pill and condoms and IUDs. The planning and the conversations were exciting, as if we were on the precipice of some kind of danger. Not actually getting pregnant was not just boring, but depressing in a clinical way.

Trying to get pregnant *had* been fun at first, the excitement and anticipation, sex with a purpose, the idea of a family in just nine months. Maybe the first IUI was exciting too. But now anxiety overwhelmed the excitement.

I read message board posts about couples uniting as a team. They made a big deal of it, the #teamwork involved. Joe and I were a team, sure, but we weren't a #team. We weren't going to go out and buy matching sweatsuits the way he and Amit had their T-shirts for the podcast. That being said, maybe if he'd shown up one day with something like that for us, it would've cheered me up. It was embarrassing admitting this to myself.

"Have you ever thought about adoption?" Claire asked.

"Adoption is really hard." I knew she was asking inno-cently, but like Mom telling me to relax, the question wasn't helpful. Of course I'd looked into it. After visiting the clinic, I'd wanted some reassurance on how easy it would be for Joe and I to adopt a child from the Philippines if treatments didn't work out. The country was on the poorer side so I fig-ured there were probably more babies placed up for adop-tion than in, say, Canada, and didn't it work in our favour that I was half Filipino? Instead I'd been cowed by the pages and pages of formalities required before adopting. Agen-cies and portfolios and interviews and wait-lists and classes. Religion, when I didn't expect religion to be involved. No guarantee of anything, even if you put in all the work, got all the right character references and passed all the tests. I quickly realized, ashamed and disgusted with myself, that I'd conflated human trafficking with adoption, that I'd tried to soothe my anxiety with the terrible idea that if I simply paid enough—and because I was Filipino, balanced with just the right amount of whiteness from Joe and my dad—I could get what I wanted. Fertility treatments were expensive too and required a huge amount of financial privilege, but because my body had to hurtle through the ups and downs of hormones and bloating, the treatments seemed, some-how, more ethical. At least I would've physically earned it. But this was an uncomfortable thought too, the idea of hav-ing to sacrifice myself to prove worthy of a baby.

"Why don't you spend the night here with us?" Mom asked.

"I have a clinic appointment in the morning."

"On a Saturday?"

"Unfortunately bodies don't care about weekends. I need an ultrasound so they can monitor how things are progressing."

"I've actually been learning about egg extraction and freezing recently," Claire said.

"You have? Why?"

"We're thinking of expanding Whispr into the fertility space."

Space, I thought. "Like, if you vet your partner on Whispr you can then move on to having babies with them? Or are you doing background checks on sperm donors?"

"Ha, not exactly that. Fertility is an interesting industry right now."

"What do you mean by *interesting?*"

"Well, the fertility treatment process is complicated, right? It's so disjointed."

"Right." I could feel heat rising up my chest, neck, face.

"Some companies are trying to smooth it out," Claire continued. "We went to an info session for this startup that's trying to help with egg freezing. They give you advice, navigate loans if you need them. They hold these intros explaining how to start. It was at a bar, which seemed weird, and they served rosé and green juice."

"Mixed together?"

"Why would someone need a loan?" Mom asked.

"Treatments cost money," I told her.

"And it's even more expensive in the US," Claire added. "At least here most of the ultrasounds and blood tests are covered so you're just stuck paying for the treatment."

"'Just,'" I said with air quotes. "It can get up to twenty grand."

"Yeah. There was a doctor at the session who went through the costs and talked about how this startup would help advocate to your insurance provider."

"That part sounds so American," I said, even though I would've appreciated someone doing the paperwork for me. Me and Joe's combined benefits covered so little of our treatments. We'd used up our flex accounts with the IUIs and would have to pay out of pocket for anything else until the new year. Some of my drugs were covered, but everything else accumulated. I'd get some tax credits so I kept a folder of invoices from the clinic in my inbox, but I was afraid to tally it up.

"I actually have egg freezing covered by my health insurance," Claire said. "It's a competitive perk these days. I met a bunch of women considering it."

"They want you to work so much you can't have a baby now, but they'll pay for you to do it later?"

"I know it's messed up. I wish you could've come with me to this info session, though. I think you would've found it reassuring. There are constant advancements. It's really exciting."

"I've done a ton of research on my own." I tried not to sound defensive, but this was my territory. My space.

"When women couldn't have babies back home there weren't all these choices," Mom said, interrupting us.

"This is relatively new, and it's changing all the time," I said. "You didn't even find out our sexes before we were born, right? You didn't have the choice?"

"No, but I knew you were girls."

"How?"

"I would dream about you—when I was pregnant, before I got pregnant. My two girls. Always two of you."

That's not how it works, Joe would've said.

"Okay, but what would you have done if you couldn't get pregnant?" Claire asked.

"Pray," Mom said. Simply.

I was cranky on the drive home thinking about Claire's foray into fertility. The past few months had been so hard, such a slog. I hated the idea of it being turned into a business opportunity. I didn't want to gather with a group of ladies in a cocktail bar and talk lightly about it. Maybe I should, though? Was that my problem, that I was taking this too seriously? Could I not think of it like a fun investment?

After the second unsuccessful IUI treatment, Joe and I launched right into the third round without hesitation, but it felt like we were approaching a wall. "What do we do if this doesn't work?" he asked me the night I started taking Clomid again. Three attempts sounded like a lot when we started—it would at least buy us time to figure things out— but we'd blown through the first two attempts with nothing to show for them.

"Maybe this round will work."

"But what if it doesn't?"

"I don't know. I guess we'll do IVF."

"Do you need a break?"

I thought of the months that had passed since we'd started. Soon we would be approaching what would've been the due date of my pregnancy. I couldn't imagine preparing for a newborn instead, that my stomach could've been a big, round ball instead of squishy and soft like it was now. "I don't need a break."

"You know I'm okay if you want to stop."

"Stop what? Treatments?"

"Yeah. The appointments. The drugs."

"But if we stop I don't know how we'll have a baby."

"Maybe we just need time. You've gotten pregnant once already."

"The problem is time. The more time passes, the worse my egg reserve gets."

"We have time, Laura. There's no rush."

"But that's not true."

"This isn't work—there's no deadline."

"I know." I really wanted to convey how important this was to me. "Do you remember that time we saw that family in Rome?" I could feel Joe scanning his memory, trying to remember what I was talking about. "At the restaurant, before the train. Late at night."

"We took a lot of trains."

"The first one."

"That was a long time ago. I don't remember. I'm sorry."

"It was the first time we imagined having a family. I keep thinking of it."

"I'm sorry I don't remember, but you know I want us to have a family too. I just don't want you to get sick over it."

"I'm not sick!"

"Or depressed."

"If I'm depressed it's because we're not having a family!"

"Okay, okay, I don't want to fight about it."

It was probably a combination of the meds and stress, but I had been waking up every morning at three, so suddenly wide awake that I could practically convince myself to get dressed, go out, run some errands. But what errands could I run at three a.m.? Groceries from the twenty-four-hour place? A car wash? It wasn't worth it. I would lie in bed and imagine what that hour would be like with a baby. I wondered if I would feel less lonely. If I had a baby, I would hug them close. We would coo at each other. I would sing the baby a song. When we were growing up, Mom always sang to us. After we grew out of lullabies, I would still hear her singing along to the radio at all hours of the day. Sometimes she would just stand in the kitchen and belt out a song before continuing on with what we were doing. At three a.m., I thought about what I would sing to my baby, the sentimental love songs that I could transpose into lullabies. Or I'd think of overwrought lyrics about unrequited love. I knew these feelings now, not for a lover, but for my mythical baby. Eventually, after getting tired of my thoughts, I would pick up my phone. Three a.m. in Toronto was midnight in San Francisco. Sometimes I would send Claire a message, and often she would still be awake working on Whispr.

That night, when I woke up, I thought of my mother praying. Who would I even pray to? Who is the patron saint of fertility in the Philippines? I googled on my phone.

Saint Clare, it told me. There was a three-day fertility rites ritual in May in the municipality of Obando, where pilgrims would sing and dance for three saints in search of three things: a child, a spouse, and good fortune. Saint Clare was for those who wanted daughters, and pilgrims would offer up chicken eggs while dancing and chanting:

Saint Clare, most refined
My promise is like so
When I arrive at Obando
I shall dance the fandango.

I took a screenshot and sent it to Claire. She sent me back a thinking emoji, and I wasn't sure if it was her thinking about how this applied to her startup work or about how she could potentially help me. Saint Claire.

Claire invited me to one of the Toronto conference parties and asked if I wanted to stay at the hotel afterwards too. The room was *fancy*, she said, and how often do you get to stay in a hotel in own city? I wasn't feeling particularly social, but since Joe was busy with the podcast the night of the party and I was now in my two-week waiting period after the IUI, I accepted. I needed something to distract me from thinking about whether an egg produced from one of the two(!) follicles the doctor had seen on the ultrasound earlier that week had been fertilized.

In the hotel room, Claire offered me a glass of wine from a bottle she had in the mini-fridge. "I can't," I said. "I'm not pregnant, but I'm not *not* pregnant either, so it's better for me to not drink."

"I'm actually still thinking about freezing my eggs."

"You don't strike me as someone who's really thinking about having a baby right now. Is it just because you can, with those benefits?"

"I don't know. I mean, yeah, I don't want a baby right *now*."

"I don't know what you learned at your info sessions, but freezing your eggs is hard on your body. You should probably have a better idea of whether you want it before doing it."

"Why do *you* want a baby?"

"I just do."

"Sounds like you don't really have a good answer either, then."

"It's different."

I always thought parenthood was best approached quickly, with minimal thought, a cannonball into a pool while pleasantly buzzed. The way Joe and I were doing it was excruciating, more like curling toes over the edge of a diving board and hesitating before jumping in, assuming you jumped in at all. The drawn-out waiting period scaled up the drama unnecessarily. But I didn't want to back away. I wanted to try, even if it meant taking an uncomfortable number of deep breaths at the edge of the diving board while everyone watching got bored and impatient. I wasn't sure what other choice we had, anyway.

"I just have all this love to give," I'd said to Joe the night before, frustrated for the millionth time. I was upset because even though we were in the waiting phase, I was already certain the third IUI hadn't worked. I could feel my internal temperature dropping, a cooling that I knew was an indication of a menstrual cycle ending, not a pregnancy. This was why taking daily temperatures helped with fertility tracking—your body heat shifted by tiny amounts, but it was enough to indicate when you were ready to incubate an embryo and when you weren't.

"You have to wait for a blood test," Joe said, while I wept.

"I know," I said. *But.*

I knew, for instance, that I could find other channels for my love. Instead of one great river toward a child, I could create tributaries in all directions, to other children, not necessarily my own, and also to causes and to the people in my life who could benefit from such great love, like my friends or Claire or Mom or even Dad. It felt selfish to hoard it for this one theoretical thing. Or maybe it was laziness, like I didn't want to do the work to figure out other satisfactory options.

Also, the word *infertile* was so sterile, so brittle. I felt expansive and ready to multiply, not narcissistically, but *generously*. I wanted to give something to the world, to contribute to the mystery and chaos and beauty around me. I knew that if I had a child, I would teach them to be good, make them recycle and compost and donate to charities.

But I also wanted a baby because I liked the idea of having a squishy thing of my own, a blob with chubby feet and teeny toes and rosy cheeks and a gummy smile. I craved an intimate connection with another human in a way that was completely separate from sex or romance. For instance, I thought about my familiarity with Claire's body:

how if you touched her earlobes you could feel the tiny knotted scar tissue of the double piercings she got in high school. They got infected and scabbed over, and she never repierced them. You couldn't see the scars, but I knew they were there. Or sometimes I remembered hot summer nights when Claire and I were little, how we would strip the duvet and top sheet off Mom's bed and all lie there under the ceiling fan in her room in the waning summer light. We were all mostly naked, our legs and arms draped over each other in such an easy way; only when I was older did I learn that this easiness was not actually that common, but a sign of an intimacy that only comes from such extreme closeness. We would cool down like that, passing around a washcloth that Mom had soaked with ice water but that eventually turned lukewarm, until she'd get up to make it cold again—she would always do it for us—and when we'd wake up the next morning, the weather would be cool again, the heat wave broken, the top sheet pulled back up over us.

I don't know if these were the right reasons to have a child, but they were mine, and it wasn't fair that most people didn't have to confront their most naive reasons for wanting to procreate. Maybe people wanted kids for less, and by the time they conceived it was too late to weigh the impacts of vanity, patriarchy, climate change, class inequality. I knew that more philosophical searching should've helped ease the sting of not being able to have a baby, and maybe at times it did, but it would quickly be replaced by the persistent gnawing desire deep within me, a desire so wholly consuming that my world felt shrunken down to just me and Joe, even though all I wanted to do was open myself up toward the universe. The cycle didn't make any sense. I didn't know how to explain this to my sister.

We took an Uber to a cluster of former slaughterhouses that had been converted to breweries and startup spaces in the Junction, an area I hadn't really been to since I was younger. It wasn't far from Mom's house, and I realized I knew the area more than I'd expected; when I was learning to drive, the instructor would bring me through these relatively empty streets so I could practise parallel parking, three-point turns, how to cross a railway.

Before joining the party, Claire wanted to smoke. Wait, not smoke. Vape.

"Since when do you *vape?*"

She shrugged. I took the device out of her hand. It looked like a USB key.

"Try it. It's not like a cigarette."

"I don't think these are safe for fetuses." I wrinkled my nose.

The building we entered was more packed than I'd expected it to be, the music louder. I immediately felt old. People were either completely dressed up—faux fur coats, white jeans, a black leather dress with a Peter Pan collar—or they weren't dressed up at all, just hoodies and T-shirts and sneakers. I was wearing jeans and a black shirt, and Claire wasn't much different, but her leather jacket made her cooler.

"I'm assuming you don't want to do any drugs here," Claire joked when we got inside.

I was embarrassed that her question shocked me. "If you want to, go ahead." I tried to sound nonchalant. In the end she didn't do anything more extreme than drink beer and go outside to vape. We found people she knew and talked to them, sometimes kind of swaying to the music, but mostly just chatting. I stood to the side of the group and nodded and laughed, not in the mood to make conversation, until they started talking about podcasts.

"My husband, Joe, hosts a podcast about city politics," I said. I wasn't really sure if they were listening, but they all turned and looked at me.

"Really?" one of the guys asked. He looked like one of their listeners. "As in Joe and Amit?"

"Yes!"

"So cool! Is he here tonight? I would love to meet him!"

"He actually had to record this evening."

"Too bad. Tell him I'm a big fan."

"For sure."

Claire knew more people at the party than I expected. Growing up, I was more social than she was. In university I had more friends, went to parties, while she spent time studying. But here she was, people coming up to her and introducing themselves, flattering her. She laughed a lot, made jokes, casually bought a round of drinks for the group. *I* was charmed.

Despite everything, I was enjoying myself. Maybe this was what I needed, to be forced out of the baby bubble I'd been in with Joe.

Claire leaned in close to me, and I could smell the alcohol on her breath. It reminded me of our first high school dance, how she'd gone outside with some friends and had come back into the darkened gym smelling like alcohol. I'd been slow dancing with someone while she'd been out there, my first time putting my arms around a boy's shoulders. He told me that my hair smelled like bubble gum. I'd felt a rush after that and wanted to say something to Claire, but she was suddenly drunk, which was more grown-up than dancing with some boy.

"What if I froze my eggs and gave them to you?" she whispered.

"Excuse me?"

"I could help you!"

"I think there are rules around this."

"Joe is a lawyer, he'll know."

"Claire."

"Imagine? It's a win-win."

"I don't think this is the best place for this conversation."

"Think of it as a backup plan. Plan B."

"I don't need one, though. I don't even have a plan yet."

"I was making a joke about, you know, Plan B. The morning-after pill."

"Listen, I appreciate it, but I have this covered."

She looked satisfied with our conversation. I wondered if I should feel better than I did, or at least more grateful, touched. Instead I was annoyed. I excused myself to the bathroom while she went to get another drink.

I sat on the toilet. *Claire wants to donate eggs to us*, I typed out to Joe. I deleted it before sending. This was not a conversation to have at a stupid party, just as it was not a suggestion to be made via text message from a bathroom stall.

I didn't want to go back to the party just yet, so I opened my email. There was a notification from Twitter that I'd received a DM from Denny, my so-called blog boyfriend. The nice thing about online friends was how the randomness or inconsistency of their contact was a feature, not a flaw. A pleasant surprise. A distraction.

I always felt warmly about everyone I met during that blogging period, and when I saw how Joe interacted with his podcast listeners, ones he could bump into at random local parties even, I felt a pang for the passing of that time and how important those relationships were to me. It was, I guess, the height of the internet for me. Maybe it didn't have to be—maybe something would change in the future—but given that my posts barely made a ripple now, I couldn't imagine what it would be. I knew having a kid sometimes opened those doors: the community mom groups, the parent WhatsApp chats. I'd lost some friends down those pathways, when they'd suddenly know more people with more everyday-life things in common than I did.

Hearing from Denny would've been a normal occurrence back in my days of frequent blogging, but now it was a novelty. I'd liked a few of his tweets recently, but we hadn't been in touch directly. I clicked through.

I can't believe you hand-rolled your own pasta. Respect. I thought of you the other day—I made a recipe from your blog. Your chocolate orange cake.

I didn't usually invent recipes, but this one time I'd had a vision for a cake that was a dense, sturdy vanilla, iced in chocolate and then—this was the special part—covered in a translucent layer of clear, bitter orange glaze. The glaze was spread on top of the chocolate icing, not sandwiched in the layers or baked into the cake. Being on the outside made the cake beautiful and shiny. I'd had daydreams about the cake before making it.

My recipe wasn't as sublime as I'd hoped, but it was still good. I'd stuck with the vanilla base but grated in an orange rind, added a sip of orange juice. After the chocolate icing had been slicked on—more of a ganache so that it would be dark, almost black—it went into the fridge to harden. I heated up the fanciest thick-cut marmalade I could find at a gourmet grocery store and brushed it on as lightly as possible to give the cake the shininess. I photographed the finished product from all angles and posted the recipe on my blog. It was maybe my favourite post ever.

I responded to Denny right away from the stall: *Omg, my favourite cake! I'm honoured you made it! So nice to hear from you. I kind of feel like I'm writing into the void when I update that thing.*

Two women came into the bathroom. One knocked on my stall. "Just a minute," I said. When I emerged they were talking and laughing, ignoring me. I washed my hands and looked at myself in the mirror. I looked tired.

Claire wasn't where I'd last left her. I walked around for a few minutes looking for her. I saw one of her friends who didn't know where she was either. I texted her. *Where did you go?*

No response.

I went outside and there she was, vaping with three others.

"Hey," I said. "I'm actually kind of tired. I might want to head back. You can stay."

"Really?" It was only eleven thirty; I knew it was kind of pathetic for me to want to leave.

"I haven't slept in a hotel bed in a while. I'm excited."

"You sure? I wouldn't mind staying here longer."

"Please stay."

She leaned over and hugged me. "Think about what I told you."

I checked my phone in the Uber, and there was already a response from Denny.

I've always been a fan of your blog—don't stop updating it! I miss that era, I think. I don't know why I didn't write one at the time. I have a backlog of recipes I'd love to share.

Why don't you share them with me? I responded. My email address hadn't changed since the last time we corresponded, but I shared it with him again. I immediately got a notification for a friend request on Facebook. I added him and then sent a message on Messenger.

Hello!

Hey hey, he typed back.

I stood outside the hotel for a bit before going up to the room and exchanging a few more messages with Denny. I remembered that this type of correspondence was one I considered a safe form of flirting. It was comforting. I remembered that I could be clever, charming. In those blog boyfriend days, Joe knew about these exchanges, but it wasn't threatening to him or us—just a byproduct of my hobby.

The crisp nighttime air felt nice. I thought of how I would feel back when I was fifteen, or twenty-two, or twenty-six, and up late. Not eleven thirty p.m., but three or even four a.m. I missed it, suddenly, the way time felt then, how vast it had seemed, how so much could happen in a night. Like you could suddenly decide you were going to have children with the person sitting across from you at the table. You could be a different person than the one you'd been when you'd woken up that morning, and it was meaningful the way everything could become a little sloppier, a little more intense, a little more technicolour than it had been twelve hours earlier. There was a distinct shift in molecules within you. This was when real breakthroughs happened.

I needed those breakthroughs again, but I wasn't sure how to access them. Something about the brief exchange of messages with Denny had felt electrifying, though. Or just different. At a certain point they were the same thing.

I looked up and wondered if I could find a shooting star upon which to wish for a potentially fertilized egg, but the city sky was both too cloudy and too bright. Anyway, I wasn't sure if it mattered. I knew my body better than I knew stars, but I supposed a bit of hope couldn't hurt.

PART FIVE: WINTER

I thought about money, and I thought about sleep. I was constantly exhausted. Another round of IUI had passed, and I would go to the clinic as early as I could, when it was still dark. When I got to my desk at work, it would be bright, as if an entire day had passed without me getting a night's sleep.

The tiredness hung around me like a fog, and sometimes I fantasized about going to sleep the way one might fantasize about having sex. I imagined being tucked in, weighted down by cool sheets and a thick duvet, my pillows pushed around me like a fort, a glass of ice water waiting by the side of the bed, someone sitting patiently at my feet until I drifted away, just in case I needed anything else, just so I wasn't alone. But I had no real reason to be tired; I wasn't pregnant, and if work was busy, it wasn't at the same magnitude as it was for Joe or for Claire.

I also started posting on the fertility message board instead of just lurking. Once a week newbies introduced themselves on a "welcome" thread. I typed out my intro, not so much a bio as a CV of my infertility. I hadn't yet logged it in a neat list, but there it was: one miscarriage, three failed IUIs, one IUI in progress, below-average ovarian reserve. In the context of the message board, it wasn't too bad. It wasn't, for instance, five miscarriages. It wasn't three failed IVFs; it wasn't even yet one IVF. It wasn't below-average ovarian reserve *and* low sperm count. It wasn't a missing Fallopian tube or a weirdly shaped uterus. I wasn't forty. I wasn't yet thirty-five. It could be worse, the board reminded me. It could be better, sure, but at least I wasn't the worst, and depressingly, I found that motivating. It was something.

During our fourth IUI, Joe had to travel again for a client, this time to New York. It didn't seem like a big deal because we knew he would be back a day or two before the insemination would likely happen. The round started off promisingly: three follicles for the first time ever. I ate dark leafy greens, took a palmful of daily vitamins and Chinese herbs. I'd gotten the herbs after having a series of acupuncture appointments in which a woman would stick tiny needles in a semicircle in my stomach to activate the blood flow to my uterus. At the last appointment, she'd inserted a few into the tops of my ears. Every night before bed, I sat on the couch and listened to a meditation app for twenty minutes. I sat still for the entire duration of the session, never once giving up after ten minutes and thinking, *Good enough*.

At my next ultrasound, the technician discovered that one keener follicle had grown overnight, faster than the others. Even though the other two weren't quite ready, the doctor wanted to give me the trigger shot and do the insemination the next day. If we waited for the others to catch up, the first follicle might release its egg before we had the chance to inseminate, which would ruin the entire cycle. I wasn't too stressed when the nurse told me—Joe was due to return that night, so even if everything was ahead of schedule, it was fine; we could do the IUI the next morning.

Then Joe's flight at Newark got delayed because of weather. He kept texting me updates—the 4:30 flight got pushed to 7:00, then 10:00, and then suddenly the departure listing just said *CANCELLED*. The cancellation popped up at 7:15, and I had to take my trigger shot at 8:30. But what if I took it and he was still stuck at Newark the next day? The eggs would be released, and there would be no sperm to fertilize them. I called the clinic and left a voice mail. I emailed the general nurse address we'd been given for these types of after-hours questions. I logged in to the message board and started a new thread about my predicament. *What should I do???*

Someone responded right away. *I don't know what you should do, but this happened to me and the cycle was a waste. It sucked :(.*

Another response: *I wouldn't let my husband travel during a cycle. Too risky.*

I called Joe crying. "Tell the airline there's a death in the family. Tell them your mother is on her deathbed. Tell them your wife got into an accident and needs you."

"No one is dying, and no one was in an accident," he said calmly, his voice low. "What if you just don't take the shot?"

"Everything will be messed up. That fucking follicle got too big. If I don't take it tonight, we'll lose them all, lose another month at least."

I hung up on him. It was now eight o'clock, and he was waiting to get booked on another flight. I checked my email—nothing. Someone on the message board wrote, *Thinking good thoughts and baby dust for you!!!* I closed my browser, turned on my meditation app, and then uninstalled it in a fit of frustration.

Finally at 8:20 Joe confirmed he was booked on another flight with a different airline and would land after midnight. I jabbed the needle in my thigh.

A few minutes later a nurse from the clinic called me. I could've waited a few more hours to give myself the trigger shot and give Joe more time, but it was too late now anyway.

When he got home that night, his clothes and hair were rumpled and his eyes looked so tired that I felt first sad and then satisfied that maybe he understood my own constant weariness.

After the negative result, we had a consultation with Dr. Sutton to go over what had happened since we'd started seeing her. Our file was now thicker with information from the four IUIs and zero pregnancies. She pulled out the chart she'd shown us at the first appointment and remapped our new odds: much lower. I cried, and she handed me a tissue; Joe rubbed my arm. Hope wasn't lost, though. We just had to move on to IVF if we were serious.

"We are extremely serious," I said, and she smiled like an elementary school teacher.

Prepping for IVF was more complicated than it was for an IUI. We had to redo a few tests, and I'd have to go on the pill so that we could take control of my cycle. We wouldn't be able to start until the new year since the clinic would be closed for any new procedures over the holidays. The timing made me panicky: another year to start something completely new that had no guarantee of working, another year to spend more money.

I monitored my bank account. Joe and I shared one for our salaries, our mortgage payments, our bills, the medical expenses. I had a spreadsheet that tallied the dollars so I could figure out what could be covered by insurance and what couldn't. At least the timing would let our annual benefit limit reset.

Money was always a confusing thing for Claire and me. Growing up with Mom meant knowing that we didn't have a lot, but because of Dad, big things were taken care of—like our university tuition, which he insisted on paying for. When we were younger, he'd sometimes randomly slip us hundred-dollar bills, and when my Mom saw the money she'd get so mad she'd put it away in an envelope so that we couldn't spend it right away. He paid child support, of course, but this was extra, just for us.

Even though we always knew that he had money, that he could just give it to us in a way our mother couldn't, it was useless knowledge. Our access to his theoretical bank account was blocked by the infrastructure of our lives, by our being the other daughters, the ones whose lives he could drop in and out of as easily as he wanted. When I was a teenager, I was obsessed with the idea of his wealth. In my last year of high school, I took an accounting course, and it helped frame my understanding of my financial status. I could picture my family's general ledger, the tabulation of Mom's assets on one side slowly degraded by a longer list of liabilities. Dad's separate ledger was swollen with assets. Laid out like that, it was just math, the simple fact of him having more than us, but because he was inconsistent with what he gave us, I couldn't help but feel like I was owed something from his side.

"I'm going to ask Dad to buy us a car," I once said to Claire in grade eleven, after she complained about being late for her job because of a broken-down bus.

"You can't just *ask* him," she said. "He won't just *buy* you one. Do you know how much a car costs?"

"No," I replied, sheepish. "Do you?"

She thought about it. "Five thousand dollars? Thirty thousand dollars?"

Either way, they were both impossible sums in our worlds, but in my father's world, *impossible* had a different definition, and we didn't quite know its boundaries. Eventually I realized that Dad's salary was available for me to look up. It was public information. He was an executive for a public company, and it had to be disclosed in their regulatory filings, his name with a huge number next to it. The money he'd been sending me and Claire was paltry compared to the sum in tiny print on the PDF I was looking at. I sent the link to Claire.

Page 120, I wrote.

What do you even do with that much money? she asked.

The year I turned twenty-five, Claire twenty-four, he sent us two thousand dollars each, electronically. He called me a few days later.

"Have you spoken to your sister recently?"

"Which one?" I asked, jokingly. Asking if I'd spoken to Claire *recently* was comical.

"Claire," he said, answering my question seriously.

"I haven't spoken to her today. Why?"

"She hasn't accepted the money I sent her. I emailed, but she didn't write back."

"Did you call?"

"No."

"Maybe your message went to spam. Email filters are glitchy sometimes." I could tell he liked this explanation. "I'm seeing her tomorrow. I'll ask her."

Joe and I were leaving for a trip two weeks later and I was planning to borrow her raincoat, but instead of waiting, I called her the minute I hung up with Dad.

"Dad's worried that you didn't get his birthday money."

"I did."

"But you didn't deposit it."

"I'm not taking it. You shouldn't either."

"Why?"

"Because we're adults now. We don't need money from our dad who feels guilty about leaving us when we were babies."

Two thousand dollars meant that the trip Joe and I were taking wouldn't put me in debt. It meant that we didn't have to stay in hostels the whole time. I'd made enough money to pay for my plane tickets, and I'd arranged for the sublet of our apartment so that we wouldn't lose any money on rent. I had some savings in the bank that I could leave untouched for emergencies. I'd earned it myself, from my own jobs. Claire made me feel like accepting Dad's money negated all of my hard work—which is maybe how the entitled indignity of the rich is born, but I wasn't anywhere close to rich! I just wanted to accept my father's birthday money and move on.

"Well you're telling him that yourself."

"He can call me if he wants to talk."

"I'm not getting involved."

"I have to go. Are you still coming tomorrow?"

"Of course."

"Love you."

"Love you too."

After that birthday, after Claire explained to him why she wasn't accepting the money, the transfers stopped—for both of us. Birthday ones, anyway. I couldn't help being mad the next year, when the cash would've helped, but I didn't say anything. He still sent money, just more erratically, and I was pretty sure Claire accepted it when it came to her that way, like when she graduated and needed to rent a moving truck to move back to Toronto. And when he sent me $2,500 for fertility treatments, I didn't think twice about depositing it.

Claire, currently, was not suffering from a cash problem. I woke up one morning to an email from her that said, *So this happened*, with a link to a press release on her company website. They'd been acquired by Google.

I copied the link and texted it to Joe. *What do you think it means for Claire?*

Does she have shares? Stock options?

When Claire told me about stock options—the ones she got when she started her job, the ones she earned as bonuses—I didn't quite understand them. The company wasn't public, so she couldn't cash in shares to pay for rent. It seemed like a con, a paper incentive with no real value. They could be valuable in the future, maybe, but it was a gamble. How was a bet on something that may or may not happen in the future considered good compensation? But then the company got bought out and those stock options turned into instruments of value. Her net worth was now higher, but I wasn't sure by how much.

Wow, I texted Claire. *I just saw your email. That's good, right? You're not going to lose your job?*

No. I'm safe

Are you making a ton of money from this?

She sent back a string of money bag emojis.

So it's a yes?

It's something

Claire's RICH, I texted Joe.

This is how you do it in this day and age, he replied. *We've been doing it wrong.*

But Joe was a lawyer—he wasn't doing anything *wrong*. And he had a decent side hustle with his podcast, very much of this day and age. But neither of us had the opportunity to cash out of our jobs the way Claire could. I couldn't help but think of her as a lottery winner, that instead of earning it with hard work, she'd simply picked the right string of numbers and was rewarded a big, dumb novelty check in return.

She followed up with another email soon after, this time to both me and Mom. A week after I'd gotten my latest negative IUI result.

Good morning! For Christmas I'm flying the two of you here to see me. Well, not SF, but Vegas. I got us tickets to see Adele at Caesars Palace. Surprise!

I was at work and ducked into a meeting room to call her. She picked up right away. "Did you get my email?"

"You didn't book the tickets, did you?"

"Plane tickets, no. The concert, yes. I got them from someone who bought them and then realized they wouldn't be around for the concert."

"She's performing at Christmas?"

"Just after Christmas. Kicking off a residency."

"Do you even like Adele? Does Mom know who she is?"

"Of course she'll know who she is, but even if she doesn't, the point isn't liking or disliking her—it's a *performance*."

Do I like Adele? I wondered. I didn't *not* like her. It was hard to exist in the world of popular culture without knowing the salient points of her life. I'd probably watched at least three people perform "Rolling in the Deep" at karaoke at some point. But it seemed less strange for me to be into Adele than it did for Claire, and it felt like yet another way she'd been changed by her move. Caesars Palace. Adele.

"What if I have Christmas plans?"

"I don't think you do?"

"How do you know?"

"I asked Joe."

"He knows about this?"

"No, but I asked him if you had anything planned for Christmas this year."

"We never have anything planned. I'm always with you and Mom."

"That's what he said, but I just wanted to make sure."

"Are you sure Mom will like the idea?"

"Of course. And she'll be able to see Gloria."

Gloria was related to us. Kind of. The last time I'd seen her was when Joe and I got married. He'd assumed she was actually in my family, but when I tried to describe the relation, it wasn't straightforward. Even though I referred to her as an aunt, a tita, she was maybe a distant cousin of Mom's. Or was she the friend of another second or third cousin? Gloria was close enough that there was no question that they would live together when Mom immigrated to Canada, but that didn't necessarily mean they were close back in the Philippines. Definitions shifted in a new country. Gloria had arrived first and saved Mom a bed, so they were basically sisters.

Most Filipino families that had arrived in Toronto around the same time in the seventies were built like this—webs of relatives and friends of friends that expanded over time, taking more people into the fold as they landed.

Gloria had ended up getting married and moving to Las Vegas where most of her husband's family lived—another big Filipino hub in North America—and she'd invited Mom, me, and Claire to move there and stay with them after Dad left. Mom seriously considered the offer, but in the end declined. Still, they were bound to each other forever—even if they weren't cousins, they were family. They spoke on Skype sometimes and messaged each other on Facebook, but seeing each other in person was rare.

"I forgot she lived in Vegas," I said.

"Yeah, and Mom would never visit on her own."

"But what if Mom wants to spend Christmas with Bart?" I asked.

"I asked him his opinion. He's spending Christmas with his daughter, so he won't be alone."

"You talked to him about it too? On the phone?" I felt a surge of jealousy about Claire having *schemed* with him. We hadn't even met him yet.

"I emailed him. Why don't you want to go? It's just a few days."

I thought of my appointments and the timing of cycles. The truth was that if there was a good time for me to travel, it would be then, in between everything.

"It's weird being told what to do."

"I didn't think of it as telling you what to do. I just thought it would be a fun surprise."

"I don't have the money to give you something extravagant in return. Joe and I have to save a lot of money for IVF."

"I didn't know you'd decided to do IVF."

"Yeah, kind of a new decision."

"How do you feel about it?"

"It's a lot of money."

"I'll pay for everything on this trip—I want to!"

"Thank you, but you really don't have to." I wanted to remind her of the feeling she got from Dad giving her money. *It's the same thing*, I wanted to say. *You must understand.* But we were at an impasse and grew quiet.

"Mom's not going to check her email until tonight," Claire said first. "I can call her now and tell her to ignore the message I sent."

"It's going to look like I'm ruining Christmas."

"Listen, I don't expect you to reciprocate. I just thought this was something different and fun."

I opened up the calendar on my phone. December was empty except for Joe's podcast schedule and work holiday parties. I had nothing calendar-worthy planned myself.

"Fine, I'll go."

"Really?"

"Yes."

"You're absolutely sure?"

"Yes, it'll be great. Mom will love it—it's a fantastic present."

I hung up and sat down at the small round meeting table. I'd been pacing back and forth the whole time we were speaking. My face felt hot. I texted Joe. *Claire is flying Mom and me to Las Vegas for Christmas?!?!* I wasn't sure if he would know whether I was upset or excited.

I called Mom at her job. "Hello honey," she said, recognizing my number.

"Have you checked your email today?"

"No, should I look on my smart phone?" She still referred to it as that. Her smart phone.

"Claire wants to fly us to Las Vegas at Christmas, and she got us tickets to see Adele. Bart knows. It's a surprise."

"Oh!" Mom was so happy that I got annoyed again. "I love Adele!"

"You do?"

"She has such a beautiful voice."

"You can see Gloria too."

"What a Christmas present! I'll send her a message on Facebook right now."

"I'll tell Claire you know. I was just talking to her."

We hung up, and I burst into tears, frustrated by how I felt. My phone buzzed. Joe. *Amazing!*

I called Claire. "I told Mom. She's excited. She apparently loves Adele."

"I knew it! Are you still excited too?"

"Yes."

"Are you crying?"

"No." I sniffed.

"Are you okay?"

"I just wasn't expecting it."

"Is it really that bad? You love travelling. Do you want Joe to come? He can if you want. I don't think I can get another concert ticket, though."

"No, his mom will kill me if he misses Christmas. It's the only holiday she cares about. She already holds it against me that I skip theirs every single year."

"So why are you mad at me?"

"I'm not mad at you."

"Then why are you crying?"

"I don't know, hormones."

"I'm sorry."

"It's fine!" I noticed two of my co-workers standing outside the meeting room. They smiled at me politely. "I'm truly excited. I have to go. I'll email you."

I hung up, wiped my face, and turned around. "All yours!" I said brightly and waved them in.

The night before my flight to Vegas, Joe and Amit had their annual podcast holiday party. They held it at Bar Hop because they could get good beer there and take over a portion of the bar. The party always had the same format: Joe and Amit would do a preamble at the beginning, a year in review, a quiz, and then they'd all hang out and drink together. There were regulars that came every year, mostly men who enjoyed that particular combination of municipal politics and craft beer. Dads, political science majors, lots of facial hair. I saw the guy from Claire's party, and we acted like we were practically best friends.

When Joe and I got home, we were both drunk. It had been a strange night. Fun, but we'd also found out that Amit and his wife were expecting a baby. Joe hadn't told him about our treatments yet, and maybe if Amit had known he wouldn't have announced it without telling Joe first, but when he said it and we all cheered and toasted them, I recognized a flicker of envy on Joe's face. It choked him a bit. And then we'd both proceeded to get drunker than we had in a long time.

As soon as we closed the door, we shrugged off our coats and started kissing by the ladder. Joe grabbed the bars behind me so I was pinned between it and him. I felt wobbly with desire, our kissing the one thing keeping me standing.

He removed his arms from the ladder to put his hands up my dress and pull down my tights, to feel my underwear and then pull those aside to touch me. I didn't move at first, just enjoyed the feeling of his hands and fingers, but then I reached for his waist and his jeans. We moved over to the couch, by then our clothes mostly off. He started kissing down my body, but I didn't want his mouth, I wanted to feel him inside me. I squirmed away.

"You don't want me to?" he asked.

"Not right now," I kissed his neck and touched him. He was still soft. I kept kissing him. He was breathing heavily but not getting hard.

"Is everything okay?" I asked, trying to be sexy about it. I didn't want to make him feel self-conscious, and I didn't want him to think that I felt self-conscious either.

"Keep going," he said, so I did. But still, nothing.

"You're not in the mood?"

"I am. It's not that."

"What is it?"

"You always just want to go straight to me fucking you."

"I do?"

"Yeah."

"Is there something wrong with that?"

"Laura."

"What?"

I got off of him and sat back on the couch, grabbing one of the throws to drape over my chest. I felt exposed the way I did when waiting for a transvaginal ultrasound, naked from the waist down except for a thin sheet of tissue paper, waiting for the technician to come back in the room.

"I'm not going to get you pregnant."

"What?"

"There's too much pressure."

"I don't expect you to get me pregnant."

The only thing that stung was that deep down, a part of me still hoped we would get pregnant on our own. Despite everything. The internet was full of stories about couples who got pregnant naturally on their off cycles, miracle babies conceived when they'd given up all hope for a pregnancy without intervention, but then a regular everyday romp did the trick. I mean, we weren't having sex like we had at the beginning, when I timed everything and was aware of every minute of my cycle, but I had vague *ideas*, and if sex didn't end with Joe coming inside me, I would feel like an opportunity had been missed.

But it was also true that in that moment, I sincerely had *not* been thinking about potential pregnancy—I was just drunk and horny.

"I just wanted to have sex," I said. "I'm sorry."

He smiled sadly and kissed me on the forehead. "Don't apologize." He stood up and grabbed the other blanket on the couch. "I'm drunker than I thought I was. Did you see that guy who kept buying me and Amit shots?"

"I drank too much too."

"And you have to be at the airport early."

He walked to the bathroom. I waited for him to come back out, but when I heard him turn on the shower I climbed up to our bed. I was tired and drunk and still wanted to have sex, but it was now too late.

At the airport the next morning, I ordered coffee, drank it fast, and then felt restless and hungover. It was barely eight a.m. and the flight wasn't for another hour, but Mom and I had arrived at six thirty to assuage her anxiety over potentially being late. I tried to read a book but couldn't focus. Mom kept shuffling papers around—her boarding pass, the hotel details Claire had forwarded, a printed email from Gloria giving directions to her house. She asked me where my passport was twice and kept her carry-on hugged to her chest, worried that someone might steal it. I put on the headphones Joe had given me for Christmas. They were noise-cancelling, big, intended to replace the cheap earbuds I kept losing and rebuying. I'd never used noise-cancelling headphones before, and in public I realized how well they funnelled away all the surrounding hubbub, channelling my irritation at Mom's paper shuffle toward the action itself and not the sound of it. Small blessings.

On the plane Mom squeezed my hand and then let go to cross herself multiple times during takeoff. She gripped my arm for the first hour of the flight and then fell asleep so deeply that I had to shake her awake when we prepared to land four hours later. Because of the time difference, it was still morning in Vegas, but the time didn't seem to matter.

A row of slot machines greeted us the minute we got off the plane, their lights blinking in an aggressive welcome, everything open for business. You could see the strip from the airport, and it almost looked like we could walk there, but the distance was deceiving. In reality, the city was spread out, all wide boulevards, blocks between adjacent hotels.

I texted Claire from our cab, and when we pulled up in front of the Cosmopolitan, the hotel she'd booked for us, she was waiting outside. Her hair was now light pink. She must have just dyed it. She'd arrived in Vegas the day before to check in, and when I'd talked to her then, her hair had still been the old platinum colour.

Mom hugged Claire and put her hands in her hair. "What happened?" Mom asked.

"It's a magic trick."

"You have so many surprises for us these days."

The Cosmopolitan felt like the inside of a disco ball, the lobby blanketed in a dark glittery shimmer. There were Christmas lights too and a high whine of ambient noise that followed us everywhere we went, a blend of sirens and whirring and clinking and talking and music, Christmas songs interspersed with Top 40 pop and hip hop.

"This is so fancy," Mom said in the mirrored elevator on our way up to our room and again when Claire let us in. It had two queen-size beds, one that I would share with Claire and one for Mom. The beds were three feet off the ground, and there was a small stepstool we could use to climb up if we needed a boost.

Mom opened her purse and removed two plain white envelopes. "I have a present for you from Bart."

"We haven't even met him and he's giving us presents? I like him!" I opened mine and removed five crisp twenty-dollar bills.

"To use at the casino," she explained. "Nowhere else."

"I don't even know how to play anything," I said.

"Anyone can play slots," Claire said. "And you know blackjack."

"What's blackjack again?"

"Twenty-one. You're just adding your cards up. Let's play a round now, ten bucks."

"It's not even lunchtime."

Mom settled into her bed and reached for the remote control. "I'm going to rest. You girls go."

"Come on." Claire tugged my arm.

Our window looked out onto a pool, all dots of people

in the water or lounging poolside, tall palm trees around the perimeter. "I'll gamble with you now if we can go to the pool after."

"I'll do that," Mom chimed in.

"Deal," Claire agreed.

We returned to the lobby. There was a casino connected to it, but Claire wanted to go to a different one, so we bypassed it and went outside. The heat was amazing—dry and powerful. It had only snowed twice in Toronto, but the shortest day of the year had just passed; I'd been feeling like something was shrinking inside me as the darkness came earlier and earlier, some kind of waning shred of vitality. It stirred when I stood outside on the pedestrian bridge Claire had led us to. We walked across, and I didn't bother putting on my sunglasses.

The Strip was packed. People passed us holding bottles of beer. Someone tried to sell us a helicopter tour of the Grand Canyon, discounted tickets to a gun range. We walked toward the calm stretch where the Bellagio fountains stood and then crossed the street to get a closer look at the fake Eiffel Tower. We entered through an archway that said *CASINO* in the same Art Nouveau font used at metro stations in Paris. The entire casino was designed to look like we were actually gambling underneath the tower, the ceiling painted a perfect sky blue dotted with clouds.

"Let's go here," Claire said. She chose a blackjack table and put down a twenty to get us chips. She did all of this in a fluid motion without pausing or asking questions.

Claire wasn't a stranger to gambling; she'd paid for a chunk of grad school with online poker winnings before the US cracked down on playing with real money and diffused the whole industry. I only knew a few details about her gambling because she'd get cagey when I asked her about it. I wasn't sure if she'd ever stepped into a casino or if she'd only played from home. But I knew if she wasn't *good*, she was at least decent.

We were the only two people at the table. Claire put in all her chips; I put in half. The dealer shuffled and handed out our cards. I had a queen, Claire an ace, the dealer an eight.

"I'm winning!" I said even though I knew I wasn't. A queen just seemed like a good card to start with.

"We're both playing against him," Claire said, and the dealer smiled at me. Claire tapped on the table, and he dealt her another card. A king.

"Is that what I'm supposed to do? Tap?"

"You can also say 'Hit me.'"

"Right! I knew that. Hit me." A three.

He dealt himself a seven.

"You can put more chips in if you want," Claire said. "But I don't think you should."

I felt lucky, though. "I'm going for it." I pushed in the rest of my chips.

Claire tapped. A ten! Twenty-one!

"Hit me!" I said. Another queen, and with that I lost all my money.

The dealer flipped a seven and counted out the chips that Claire had won.

"Do you want to play again?" she asked.

I'd landed an hour ago and I was already losing money. "I think I'll save the rest for something else." As we walked away, I asked if she'd visited Vegas since moving.

"Three times. Just for quick weekends." Two more than I expected. Three, even.

"Did you win anything?"

"Nothing much. I'm bad now."

Claire had a good poker face. I had to study her closely to remember her giveaways, the purse of her lips when she was either angry or on the verge of tears, maybe the way she would click her nails when she was nervous—subtle, small movements that I'd picked up on over the years. It occurred to me that she was probably lying when she said she was bad, that she could've fooled me into a game and then taken all my money.

"What's the most you've ever won?"

"Eighteen K, but that was ten years ago."

"Shit, Claire."

"It was just one night. Maybe I should keep playing now. I feel like I'm on a good streak."

I sometimes forgot that Claire could be competitive because she wasn't like that with me. It used to offend me when we went to school together because I wasn't sure if it meant I wasn't worthy of competing with her.

"I don't know how to get back to the hotel alone," I said, which made Claire laugh even though I wasn't joking.

"I'm so glad you're here," she said, and hugged me.

We made our way back to the Cosmopolitan and walked through its casino, which housed a gigantic chandelier, the strings of crystallized LED lights strung from the ceiling in dramatic arcs.

"You're not really going to stay at the casino, are you? We just got here, and we need to eat lunch too."

In the casino it could be any time—two in the afternoon, midnight. There was no change in the volume of the crowd from when we'd checked in that morning. But it was now— one thirty. Only one thirty?

Claire paused. "You're right. Let's get Mom."

Back in our room, I sent Joe a message from the bathroom. *I lost at blackjack.*

Easy there, tiger, he replied.

The next morning, we woke up early and went straight to the hotel buffet. This, I insisted, was my treat, and as we walked over Claire and I planned out our buffet strategy. The first rule was that we wouldn't spoil our appetites on our first plates. Instead we would be mindful about it—and the best way to do that was to give each plate a theme. While Mom ate two plates of sausages, rice, and noodles and gave up, we embarked on our quest. We started off with only fruits and vegetables, so I took a tiny dish of watermelon balls dotted with basil, some dark green kale salad, a few chunks of pineapple, a grapefruit with the top brûléed in a thin crisp lid of brown sugar. Our next plate's theme was "land and sea" (bacon, shrimp, eggs), and then "carbs only." We rounded it out with "breakfast dessert."

This strategy reminded me of how, at Christmas, Dad used to bring us to the country club he belonged to for their holiday buffet. It was always on a weekday, so he would pick us up from school, eat lunch with us, and then bring us back in time for afternoon classes. Claire and I would get identical plates of cold peeled shrimp, devilled eggs, and roast beef from the carvery station. We enjoyed going when we were younger, but in high school we stopped. Dad was busier by then, often travelling abroad for work, and one day when his secretary called us at home to schedule lunch, the first time he'd ever outsourced the task, Claire told her—witheringly—that we were not interested in going. He didn't push it; he sent Christmas money and saved his questions about report cards for when we eventually saw him over the holidays. When I was older, I found out that members of the club had a quota of guests they had to bring in over the holidays. I wondered if that was why he brought us there and who he replaced us with when we stopped going.

After brunch we piled into Claire's rental car and drove to Gloria's house. Mom kept the printed directions smoothed out on the dashboard even though we told her we didn't need them with the built-in GPS, with our phones.

Gloria lived in a subdivision about twenty minutes from the Strip. Her house was pale-pink stucco with a terracotta roof and a pristine front yard filled with pebbles and neat little shrubs. When she saw us, she ran down the path and gathered us all into a big hug.

"It's such a blessing to have you here," she said, her eyes shining, and I remembered the string of religious memes I'd seen on her Facebook profile. Mom was religious too, but not in a meme-sharing way.

I was surprised by how old Gloria looked compared to Mom. I noticed the lines around her eyes and streaks of grey in her hair. Mom was the same age, but our proximity to her had softened our awareness of the progression. That, and Mom had been better preserved by Canadian winters. She also dyed her hair to cover up the grey. But seeing her with Gloria made me aware of how much time had passed.

Mom and Gloria talked non-stop while Claire and I sat there as smiling witnesses. It would've been so easy for the two of them to lose touch. In the past few years, sure, it required less effort, now that they were linked by Facebook and email, but for all those earlier years that they'd lived in different countries, they'd had no common ties. Just phone calls and letters written on the thin red-white-and-blue airmail paper they used for their family in the Philippines even though it didn't affect mailing costs in North America.

"How's your father?" Gloria asked us.

"Fine," I said. "Nothing much to say."

"Is he still so serious?"

"I think so."

Gloria and Mom laughed. "He was never like us," Gloria said.

We took pictures of each other sitting on Gloria's couch, and I posted them on Facebook right away, tagging the two of them. I immediately got a stream of comments and likes from relatives I'd never met or hadn't seen in years, Mom's co-workers at the hospital, Bart.

"What are you doing while you're here?" Gloria asked.

"We're seeing Adele," Claire said, and both Gloria and Mom swooned.

"I love Adele," Gloria said.

Claire gave me a look that seemed to say *I told you*.

"And they're taking a trip today," Mom said. We'd decided to give her some time on her own with Gloria.

"Where?"

I looked at Claire. She'd chosen a destination for us, a national conservation area, a desert. I'd done zero planning for this trip.

"Just to Red Rock Canyon. Not too far."

"Ah, it's hot but beautiful. Go, go, I'll take care of your mother." She went into the kitchen and returned with two Tupperware containers: noodles and lumpia. "For your lunch. I'll give you a cooler."

"Be safe," Mom said when she waved us out the door. "Wear your hats." We could hear them laughing when they closed the door behind us.

Las Vegas felt like a mirage the further we drove away from it, an anomaly rather than the main attraction. Our surroundings quickly turned into desert, dry ground, and tufts of brush. I'd pictured a sandbox, but the landscape looked hard and dry and dusty. When I pressed my hand up against the windshield, I felt the heat beating down from the other side, the physics of it, a force of its own.

Claire and I were quiet in the car, distracted by the drive. I liked the view from the window, the emptiness, the alien terrain. I was generally neutral when it came to nature; I preferred metropolitan to rural areas when I travelled. Of course I was often *moved* by the natural world—and there were places I'd been to that I could barely speak about because they were so beautiful, so unreal—but I didn't actively choose to go out of my way to spend time outdoors.

Perhaps a large part of it was fear. Once, when I was a kid, Dad had paid for Claire and me to go to a two-week sleepaway camp somewhere in the Muskokas. All I remembered of it was a choppy lake, a flipped canoe, a gulp of murky water, the nails-on-chalkboard feeling of grasping for the fibreglass sides of the boat. We, three of us, were fine. Claire wasn't there. I don't remember where she was. We managed to get back into the canoe, and when we got to shore, which was much closer than it had appeared at the time, I vomited, not so much because my insides were spilling over with water but because I was scared and wanted to expel the feeling of fear from my body. Afterwards I tried to mimic the way the others had laughed it off, but I kept having nightmares about the flip, the dark water. After that, something about being far from the amenities of a city freaked me out, the anxiety outweighing the peacefulness of a pristine environment.

I didn't mind wide-open spaces, though, or at least being on the edge of them. Fields. Staring at the ocean rather than *being* in the ocean. Density, like that of forests, overwhelmed me. Maybe in a single moment I could discern details perfectly: the varying shades of green, gold, wet brown;

the myriad textures of leaves, ferns, moss, bark, twigs, and fallen branches; the light filtering through crevices and bouncing off the angles of branches. In an instant I could almost understand it. But one step further and it would dissolve, everything melting together so that I could no longer find my bearings. My brain would compensate by flattening out the scene, painting a green brush for plant matter, brown for dirt, blue for sky, or maybe grey in the winter.

But the desert, I could see now, met all my requirements. There was so much flat space, gentle colour.

I saw the sign that said *PARTHENON* first. We quickly decided to take a detour to check it out. As we got closer, we could see a structure up a slight incline in the distance, the only high point around us, just barely an acropolis, a high city, the Parthenon in the middle of the desert.

Claire pulled into a small parking lot alongside a few other cars. There was a sign warning us that we could be fined five hundred dollars if we fed the burros—donkeys that had escaped their masters and gone feral years ago—but we couldn't see any burros here. There were a few people, though: a woman sitting on a folding chair with a sketch pad open and a neck pillow atop her shoulders, some wandering couples in hiking gear, a family with pre-teen children.

Considering all the replicas of monuments in Las Vegas, it didn't seem unusual for there to be a Parthenon in the middle of the desert. We followed the short path toward the main attraction, dust working its way into my sandals and between my toes. The Parthenon was made of pebbly dusky-rose sandstone, and there were no friezes or engravings, just the main structure of the columns. I ran a fingernail against one and released a small puff of dust. Grit stuck under my nails.

We stood at the edge of the structure looking out onto the stretch of land around us, empty except for a single length of power line drooping between spaced-out towers. There was so much silence; it was is if I were wearing my noise-cancelling headphones. My phone toggled between no service and a single bar of reception. I wondered how we would get back to Gloria's house if for some reason our car couldn't start.

While we walked around, Claire asked, "Have you thought about me donating my eggs to you?"

"I want to get through an IVF cycle first."

"I know, but like I said, a backup plan."

"I guess, but I'm not really ready to start thinking about that yet, and our doctor hasn't brought up me needing donor eggs."

"Is it a genetic thing? Do you only want biological kids? We're close enough, right? And we look similar."

"It's not a genetic thing. I just don't *need* your eggs yet."

"What does Joe think?"

"I haven't said anything to him about it."

"Oh." I could tell she was disappointed.

"You also can't just give me eggs like you can give me a plane ticket."

"That's not what I'm trying to do. I think I want to try freezing my eggs, seriously, and this would be another reason for me to do it."

"Why are you rushing this egg-freezing decision? You'd have to take a ton of hormones. I mean, you've said you've done the research. It's not *fun*."

"I have done the research, and *that's* the rush. Now's the best time to do this."

"Yeah, I guess. I'm almost geriatric."

She didn't laugh at the word the way Joe had. She knew what I meant. "Being away from you and Mom has been making me think about family. Mom moved to Canada without knowing anyone."

"Well, Gloria."

"But she didn't really know Gloria until she got here."

"Right."

"She had to make so many sacrifices. I know she said she dreamed about us, but I don't really know if she had a choice. I feel like both of us have the opportunity to make really conscious decisions about our lives. You're making one now with all the treatments. I don't want to close off a future decision if I can control it now."

The wind started to pick up. In the distance we saw a small funnel cloud, a swirl of heavy wind made visible by dust and sand. A tiny tornado. It looked harmless, and I wanted to walk closer to it, but as if sensing this, Claire lightly touched the back of my arm, a gentle warning to stay where I was. The funnel got taller, not wider, and then a second later it disappeared.

"I'll think about it," I told Claire. "Promise."

On Christmas morning Claire and I both slept in. I woke up to three messages from Joe.

Merry Christmas, my love

Still asleep?

What are you guys doing?

I wrote back, *It was a late night.*

Mom was already awake and dressed, sitting at the desk and putting on lipstick. I poked Claire. "It's Christmas."

"I'm going to call Bart on FaceTime," Mom told us. "Why don't you say hello?"

I got up and pulled back the blackout curtains. The room flooded with light. I half hoped to see snow but was also relieved to see that everything was as dry as it had been the day before. Before we could get properly dressed, Mom took out her iPad, the one she'd gotten exactly a year ago, and called Bart.

"You look beautiful," he said.

"Laura and Claire would like to say hello." She turned the screen toward us before we had the chance to do anything. We waved.

"Nice to meet you," I said. "I hope we can meet in person soon."

"Definitely. My daughter is here too, and my grand-daughter."

He turned his screen, and we saw his family, looking as curious and awkward as Claire and me. But despite the awkwardness, it felt like a breakthrough of sorts. It was a relief to finally see Mom's boyfriend.

When the conversation was over, we got dressed quickly and went down to the lobby. Claire went in search of caffeine while Mom and I staked out a spot by one of the many trees scattered throughout the main floor. There was no indication that this was supposed to be a day of rest. The lobby was packed, not one service closed or unmanned. There was a high proportion of men wearing Santa hats, more than a few ugly Christmas sweaters.

Claire returned with iced coffees and huge cinnamon rolls. I took a sip of the coffee and then a bite of the roll, the icing rich and creamy, the roll pillowy.

In exchange I handed her a box. Being in Las Vegas had thrown off our traditional timing, and we had to exchange gifts on actual Christmas morning for once. She opened it and took out a necklace: a thin gold chain with a small, rough chunk of red garnet.

"It's so beautiful," she said, genuinely touched.

"It's our birthstone."

"Really? I didn't know that."

I'd given Mom a pair of earrings, diamonds that refracted the lights. She and Claire modelled their jewellery, and then we all went to the pool before driving back to Gloria's house for a long Christmas lunch. For once, when Joe and I had our Christmas call, it was my side of the family that was louder.

We'd never spent the holiday with so many people, and it made both Claire and me a little giddy. Gloria's kids were our age, but Claire and I felt like we belonged with the grandchildren more than with the adults and spent most of our time chasing them around. As we sat out in Gloria's pebble-strewn backyard, I thought about what it would've been like if Mom had decided to move us to the United States, to Nevada. We would've had our own stucco bungalow, hung out at baseball diamonds with red clay dirt, everything flat, everything swallowed by the desert. We would've grown up with a different vocabulary, a different lexicon of touchstones, more 7-Elevens or convenience stores with names like Terrible's, more Filipino food and family. Darker skin from the sun, probably. No Joe, no Dad. He surely never would've made the trip to visit us. It was hard to visualize, but it could've happened: this could've been our life and landscape.

It was late when we drove back to the hotel. We got back to the Strip, and I rolled down my window. The garishness made so much more sense at night. It was beautiful. There was something primal about it, the abundance of lights, and I felt drawn to it, as if I were my ancestral self, dazzled by fire.

The Cosmopolitan lobby was still bustling. I took a picture of my surroundings and sent it to Joe, but with the three-hour time difference he was fast asleep and didn't respond, so I sent the same picture to Denny.

Since getting in touch again, we'd been messaging each other back and forth regularly—usually links to articles about food or funny GIFs, but we'd also gotten into the habit of exchanging photos of unusual things we saw. It had begun one night when he'd told me there was a thunderstorm outside his window. I didn't think anything notable was happening where I was, but because there were no windows up where Joe and I slept, who knew? Maybe I was missing something huge.

I wish I had a thunderstorm, I responded.

A minute later I received a video. I watched it first on mute: a window, streaked in raindrops. Ten seconds. I played it again with the sound on and held it close to my ear so I didn't wake Joe. I listened to the sound of the rain.

After that, we'd started doing this regularly, sending each other video clips a few seconds long, not just of rain, but leaves being pushed around by wind, a pug ambling down the sidewalk, a strange-looking storefront. Our faces and voices were rarely in the videos, but sometimes our hands would appear, pointing, waving.

Once he sent me a picture of the inside of his fridge, and I was surprised by how clean and orderly it was. I zoomed in on the organic butter, the carton of oat milk, the pint of strawberries. Joe and I had stopped paying someone to clean our place months ago; it was too large an expense. We kept our place clean enough for a while but then something about the pressures of meds and appointments and Joe working late all the time meant our place was messier than it had ever been, and because it was open concept, it was hard to hide the clutter.

I had opened our fridge, and it was a disaster, everything shoved in haphazardly: a carton of eggs teetering on Tupperware containers of week-old leftovers we would never eat, sawed-off sticks of butter, a small bottle of hot sauce missing its cap. I remembered shoving in a bar of chocolate that had been melting on the counter, and I rummaged around until I found it. I did not take a picture of our fridge, but I did take out all the wilted vegetables that had been languishing for weeks. I threw the leeks and carrots and red pepper and some cherry tomatoes and thyme and broccoli stalks in the big stockpot. That was what I sent to Denny a few hours later—all the soft vegetables in water. I strained them into jars and left them on the counter to cool.

Hey Merry Christmas, he wrote back a few minutes after receiving my photo of the hotel lobby. *Where are you?!*

Las Vegas. I'm here for Christmas with my mom and sister

I thought that's what it was. This is crazy but I'm going to be there tomorrow. A friend of mine is getting married on NYE and a few of us are going a few days early. Will you still be there?

Oh, crazy. Yes, we're leaving the morning of the 28th

Let's meet—are you super busy?

I'm seeing Adele on the 27th, no big plans otherwise. You'll probably be busy??

Would love to see you, though!

Yes! What about tomorrow?

Let's make it work!

When I pressed the button for our floor in the elevator, my hands were a little shaky.

The next morning I told Claire I was going to meet Denny and showed her his Whispr profile.

"He's cute," she said.

"Ha, yeah, sort of. Joe used to call him my blog boyfriend."

"What are you guys going to do—dinner?"

"I guess?"

"Sounds blog-boyfriend appropriate."

I didn't want to be the one making plans, or at least appear too eager, so I waited to hear from Denny instead. The day was quiet—we went to the pool, we walked around, and then Claire and Mom napped in the hotel room while I sat there scrolling on my phone until Denny finally wrote to me in the afternoon.

Just got in. We're at the Bellagio. I have to go to a bachelor dinner thing, but what about if we meet at 8 for drinks?

Sure!

"Have fun on your date," Claire said when I left the hotel room in the evening.

By now I knew my way around the Strip well enough to get to the Bellagio on my own; it wasn't that complicated. I recognized Denny immediately in the lobby, none of that facial blindness stuff I had worried about with my own sister. He was taller than I expected and skinnier too. We hugged, and I felt short and squat. I was nervous and felt silly.

"This is so random," I said. "This whole trip is random."

"I know—we could've planned this better probably."

"It never occurred to me that you might be in Vegas."

"Me neither!"

Our conversation flowed easily. I used to do this all the time—meet strangers who'd read my blog—but I was out of practice now. I'd also spent such little time socializing over the past few months that sometimes when I spoke I felt mealy-mouthed.

Denny knew a place with good cocktails that was just off the Strip. We went outside to get an Uber just as the Bellagio fountains were about to start a light show, and we decided to watch since he'd never seen one. I knew what to expect because Mom, Claire, and I had gone to see it on our first night. We got spots against the railings, smiling at each other when the group of older women next to us practically screamed in ecstasy at the sight of the first arc of water. My arm touched Denny's, bare skin, and I thought of Claire referring to our meeting as a date. When I turned my head toward him to say something, we were smushed so close together because of the gathering crowd that I could've easily tilted my chin up to kiss him, and I was immediately embarrassed by the thought.

At the bar—hipster, neon lights, a jukebox—I drank two strong drinks in a row while we talked as if we'd talked for years, which I guess we had, just over text and email.

His phone buzzed a few times. "I'm so sorry," he said. "We're taking our friend out tonight, and I have to meet them soon. I helped organize."

"Are you going to a strip club?"

He looked embarrassed. "It's a late bachelor party," he explained. If this had been one of our text exchanges, he would've used the grimace emoji, the raising hands emoji. It was cute to see the reaction in real life instead, to see the expression flit across his face.

"Let's head back then," I said, tipsy.

"I insist on paying for your drinks, though. I've used enough of your recipes over the years."

"That's the most money I've ever made from my blog. Thank you."

Outside, before calling an Uber, he took out a pack of cigarettes. "Do you mind if I smoke?"

I shook my head, and when he offered me a cigarette I took it. I hadn't smoked in so long. Years. A decade? I took shallow drags and couldn't help but feel like I had missed this, this mild form of bad behaviour, of not caring what I was doing to my body because it was my body and no one else's, not something that was being judged by doctors, not something that would be growing another human body, requiring a pristine environment.

"This is weird," he said with a smile.

It was a phrase I'd said to Joe so many times over the past several months. I'd said it to him after the last IUI, just the two of us in the room, me shifting and hearing the crinkle of the paper underneath me, my pants and underwear thrown over a chair, the doctor having just injected me with Joe's sperm for the fourth time. *That* was weird, not this.

"How so?"

"Being with you. Here." He gestured around him. "I had such a big crush on you back then."

"Me?" I took another drag of the cigarette and tried to stop myself from sounding giddy.

"I liked your emails."

"I liked your emails too."

"Would it be bad if I wanted to kiss you?"

"Back then or now?"

"Both. I mean, you're right *here* now."

I looked down. I wished he hadn't used the word *bad*. A kiss could just be something innocent and teenagery. I told myself it wouldn't be substantial enough to cause anything more than a tiny hairline fracture in an already sufficiently solid structure. Right? And anyway, if I did kiss Denny, I didn't have to tell Joe. He didn't even know we were meeting—I hadn't bothered to tell him, and it had all come together so quickly that it didn't seem too strange that I hadn't mentioned it. He'd texted me once while we were out, a little *Miss you* message that I'd responded to with a heart, but I hadn't written anything back.

Denny came closer to me. *I can do this*, I thought. I could kiss him and then decide how I felt about it. I stood on my tiptoes next to him. I didn't know if I remembered how to kiss someone other than Joe. I hadn't kissed anyone else since I was in high school, a fact that suddenly embarrassed me, a crucial piece of knowledge that everyone else had that I'd missed out on—How do you kiss *other* people?

I felt disassociated from my body the way I sometimes felt at the clinic, like whatever was happening to me was at a distance. Denny was more aggressive than I'd thought he would be, and when I felt his tongue, I backed away.

"We shouldn't do anything more than this," I said, still trying hard to sound cool.

"I know, you're right. I'm in this weird bachelor-party headspace."

My phone vibrated, and I was worried I'd pocket-dialled Joe for that whole exchange. What if he'd heard what we said, heard the pause when we kissed?

Just making sure Denny isn't a serial killer or anything. It was Claire.

I gave her a thumbs-up emoji and then specified, *Thumbs up as in I'm okay, not that he's a serial killer.*

In the Uber Denny got another text from his friends. "I don't suppose you want to join us?" he asked me.

"I think my scene in Las Vegas is more buffet than strip club."

"That's more my scene too, but it's a bachelor party. When in Rome, right?"

"Is that why you kissed me?"

He laughed. "I guess. I'm sorry."

"It's okay, it's not like I didn't kiss you too."

"I just can't believe we're both here."

"I know."

"Are you going to post about this?"

"No one reads blogs anymore."

"Other than me."

"Thank you for being my only reader." I felt like our night had taken another good turn and that it was the right time to end it.

Outside the Bellagio he held out his arms for a hug. We hugged each other for too long—we both knew it. I backed up and waved. My stomach ached, uncomfortably full from the food, from the cigarettes, from the kiss. We hugged again, which was admittedly weird—I don't know—but at least we didn't kiss again.

I walked back slowly, and when I reached the air-conditioned lobby of the Cosmopolitan I wrote back to Joe—*I miss you too.*

I still had most of Bart's money to spend, and maybe now was the best time to do it—something to clear away the jittery feeling. I also liked the idea of doing it alone, without Claire's hovering presence. I wandered into the casino.

If I was going to blow the rest of my money, it would be on something easy like a slot machine, something that didn't require talking to anyone. I looked at the machines that advertised their highest payouts first—$123.16, $5,603.21, $14,048.84—highly specific numbers, not the round denominations I was expecting. I didn't want to pick based on money, though, so I decided to go with aesthetics. I dismissed the machines that were overtly offensive, ones based on ethnic stereotypes, mainly "oriental," or ones that were especially gendered. I didn't want to play one based on characters from movies or TV shows, so no Willy Wonka, James Bond, Aladdin. I briefly considered animal themes—one called OMG! Puppies, one with cute cartoon pandas—and even sat at a machine called Rhino Charge until I realized it gave off poaching vibes.

I almost settled on the old-school machines with actual handles and vintage images of gold bars and lucky sevens until I noticed all of the mythological machines. I could play one of those, one set somewhere like Atlantis or Valhalla. Finally, finally, I settled on a Mayan one called Sun and Moon. The symbols were snakes, harsh-looking Mayan masks, stony letters, jewels, pyramids, and of course, the sun and moon. It was a little ugly, but I liked the idea of it, and I'd learned about the myth when I'd gone to Mexico: how the sun and moon were twins, split up to guide the sky so that corn could grow, responsible for the ebb and flow of the light. Joe and I had climbed the crumbly steps of a temple dedicated to them in Tulum while gigantic sleepy lizards lounged about us, still as statues.

I fed in my voucher, which had just about eighty dollars remaining, and pushed a button until the entire amount funded the game. On the screen were three rows of five symbols each. I started spinning by pressing a big green button. I couldn't quite follow what was happening, but I figured out that getting a pyramid was best because it bopped around the screen, spun around, and transformed into another symbol, often causing me to win something when I otherwise thought I was losing.

I pushed the green button repeatedly, burning through my credits, but then a scattering of suns and moons caused the machine to sing a digitized Mayan tune and I found myself with fifty free spins. The beeps intensified as I pressed the button, and my tally of credits increased, although I wasn't sure how it corresponded to real money.

On what was my thirty-eighth free spin, I had one row that didn't match at all, another with three suns, and then another with two snakes and a pyramid. I watched the pyramid do its spin and transform itself into another snake. A shower of gold coins started shooting across the screen, and my credit number zipped up again. This had happened before, but this time the gold coin shower kept going and going. Mayan-themed music played in a loop.

I made eye contact with the woman two machines down. "I think something good is happening?"

"You're winning, sweetheart."

"I never win anything," I said.

When the hubbub from the machine died down, I felt my hands tingling with the desire to keep pressing buttons. Instead I hit the cash-out button. The voucher was now $7,634.16.

"Oh my god." I showed it to the woman. "Does this mean I won all this money?"

"Congratulations," she said.

I held the voucher close to me the way Mom had clung to her bag at the airport and marched straight to the cashier station along the far wall. A man behind a counter ran it through his machine.

"Merry belated Christmas." He handed me a stack of hundred-dollar bills in a brown envelope just big enough to fit them.

"Thank you," I said and tried to fit it into my wallet before realizing it was too fat. I couldn't close the latch, even when I squeezed it shut. I tucked the envelope into my purse instead. And then I went to bed.

Finally it was time for the Adele concert. We streamed into the Colosseum at Caesars Palace with the rest of the crowd. Our seats were toward the back, stage left—not the best, but good.

"I'm so excited. Bart and I watched the James Bond movie with her song in it before I left." Mom said.

"Does he like her music?" I asked.

"Of course. Her voice is so beautiful. Maybe when we get married we'll dance to one of her songs."

"*When* you get married?" Claire asked. "How do you know he's going to propose?"

"We've talked about it."

"Do you want to get married?" I asked. "Where would you live?"

Mom kind of shrugged off the questions as if they weren't important.

"Adele's songs are more about breaking up than getting married," Claire said after a moment.

"But look at everyone here," Mom said. "They're all so happy."

The lights dimmed, and the crowd started cheering; it was a mixture of women my mom's age, clusters of gay men, groups of girlfriends. Adele was even more striking in real life, her cheekbones, her dark lips, her hair immaculate, her eyes sultry.

During "Hello," I watched a grown man weep the way I had wept when I was seventeen and watching some indie band whose name I didn't even remember anymore. And then I saw that both Mom and Claire were also wiping away tears. I was jealous; I wanted to experience that level of transcendence inspired by a piece of art.

Instead I felt heavy. I was bogged down by the past twelve months, by the miscarriage and four failed IUIs, by the morning appointments. But I had the money from the slot machine in my bag. It was so much, and so little, but it felt like a talisman of sorts. I didn't need a patron saint or Claire's eggs or good luck: I just needed money to keep me safe and give me hope for whatever happened next. I sent both Joe and Denny the same picture of Adele on stage, and while Joe responded immediately (*Whoa, good seats*), Denny didn't respond until the next day, after I'd arrived at the airport (*Nice!*).

Maybe the fundamental way to feel in Las Vegas is like a failure. Even if you win, you never win enough. If something scandalous happens, what does it matter if it has no impact on your real life? Dreams have no bearing the morning after they happen, and this trip felt like it might be the same. A blip in an otherwise engulfing desert, a moment that briefly shimmered and was then extinguished.

PART SIX: SPRING

In January it snowed often, and the drifts butting up against the buildings slowed me down. I was in hibernation and felt the need to fatten up. I made us big pots of Bolognese. When Joe worked or recorded late, I used our biggest knife to hack squash into chunks that I would roast and eat directly off the sheet pan while the pieces were still blistered and steaming.

I would only willingly go outside to go to work. My office was ugly—low ceilings, bristly brownish carpet, and fluorescent lighting—but it was housed in a beautiful old stone building downtown. There was a good cafe next door where I sometimes bought lattes. If I needed an extra pick-me-up, I'd buy a berry scone and eat it on a bench in the small courtyard partially hidden behind the building. It had a small Henry Moore sculpture, a curved, teardrop-shaped female figure that you could wrap in a hug if you wanted. Not many people knew about the sculpture, although it would sometimes show up on lists of hidden gems in the city. With my latte balanced next to me, I'd eat the crunchy, craggy outer parts of the scone first and then the soft dough inside; even if I was running late, I'd sit until the scone was done and my butt was cold.

How are you? Claire would text me, and I'd always give the same answer: *The same.* I'd never felt so stuck in a loop as I did that winter, the grey sameness of everything, the same body and same feelings and same ways of passing the hours in a day. Both Claire and Joe seemed to have lives more variable than mine. Claire was working constantly—first her regular job and then with Shannon on Whispr. They were looking to expand on the idea since Whispr's focus was too narrow and increasingly controversial in a way that neither of them wanted. They were in the process of raising funds for it, and she'd asked me to copyedit their investor deck. *I'll give you equity for the work you're doing*, she'd texted me, and I wasn't sure if she was joking or not.

With time, their mission had become clearer: women's lives were difficult, and they wanted to make them easier. Minimize the stress associated with dating on apps. Clarify the steps required to have a baby when there were roadblocks in your way, and give women the help they needed once they had a baby—a network to find daycares, babysitters, nannies. They called it the Lookout.

This was one of the first slides I reviewed:

The Lookout, as in looking out for other women.

The Lookout, as in a high-up place to look out onto the world and get a sense of perspective.

Join us. At the Lookout.

Their ability to think so broadly about the world was enviable when I instead felt so focused on myself on a *cellular* level, so low down, so unable to see beyond the constraints of my body. In order to start IVF, I had to spend the first month of the year redoing tests. They checked for things that wouldn't have occurred to me, like whether or not I was immune to chicken pox.

Because of all these tests, I perceived my body as a collection of organs, cells, hormone levels. To describe it was to focus internally: my uterus, I read on one of my ultrasound reports, was inhomogeneous. Not smooth, not like when you run your tongue over the inside of your cheek, but bumpy, like—the moon surface, cratered? When I would crane my neck to look at the ultrasound screens next to me, it was the closest I got to looking up at the sky through a telescope on a cloudy night. There was activity—there was something happening—but no real signs of life. Shooting stars that were just satellites.

Blood tests, I insisted, didn't hurt. But I still flinched.

For a one-week period, Mom and Bart were broken up, and she called me crying. "I can't do this," she said, something I'd never heard her say before. If she couldn't do something, she simply wouldn't and she'd move on.

"Do what?"

"Dating. I don't want to date."

"You don't have to date if you don't want to, Mom."

"I just want to be married."

"Maybe it's too soon for him. It's a big commitment."

"He said he wanted to get married."

"Can I meet him first before you make that decision?"

It was officially weird that I still hadn't met him in real life, that she'd been keeping this important thing so hidden away from me and Claire, despite Claire emailing him about Las Vegas, despite seeing him on FaceTime, despite the Christmas present. I lived so close; I could drive over anytime and meet him.

"I told him not to call me anymore."

"Why?"

"I just did."

"Did he do something wrong, other than not propose to you immediately?"

"No."

"Did you have a fight?"

"No."

"Has he been calling you?"

"Yes."

"But have you been answering?"

"No."

"Mom, if you want to marry him, I don't think you should just *ghost* him."

"I'm not a ghost!"

I wondered how I could fix this for Mom the way she would fix things for me when I was younger. But then, I realized, there were so many things she couldn't fix. I couldn't fix this either.

Anyway, she didn't need me. A few days later she called me back and invited me to dinner to meet Bart and his daughter, Olivia. There was an unspoken agreement that this first meeting should be just us kids—minus Claire—without our spouses or children.

~~~

What's he like in person? How does Mom behave around him? Does she seem happy? Does he seem nice, like genuinely nice, or is he phony nice? Does he genuinely like Mom? Does he display any signs of aggression, like subtle ones, or does he unconsciously expect Mom to be his servant, to take his dishes, to serve him food? Does he objectify her? What's his daughter like? Did she speak to you directly or through him? Did she give you and Mom the once-over? Did you sense any sort of competition or protectiveness in her father, not in a genuine loving way but in a way that could cause us pain in the future?

~~~

He seems nice. Like herself. Yes. Yes. Yes. No lol. No, gross! Nice. Directly? (Weird Q but no, I don't get the

feeling she's like Lisa/Julie.) Lol no. No! She talked
a lot about her kid, but not in an annoying way.
Apparently her husband listens to Joe's podcast.
I liked them both. If anything Bart seemed more
smitten by Mom than the other way around.

⁓

In February, while putting some final touches on an article for the summer issue, I accessed my boss's folder on our shared server to get a file he'd forgotten to email me. Sean had already left for the day, and I didn't want to bother him. I knew where he saved his files and retrieved them often without a second thought. His files were immaculately organized—by publication and date, drafts neatly numbered and final copies clearly distinguishable. It was soothing to click down layer by layer and witness the consistency, one that made my own system of folders and drafts seem like an embarrassingly tangled mess.

I noticed a folder called *Job Descriptions*. Benign enough, but I clicked on it and saw a list of Word documents whose file names corresponded to positions, including one that looked like mine. *Senior Editor, Food and Drink.* I right-clicked and copied it to my hard drive, off the server, and then opened it. The document was a bullet-point list of everything I did, and I felt a sense of pride when I saw it laid out like that—I did a lot!—but I was quickly distracted by the fact that the description was colour-coded, certain tasks highlighted in either green or yellow. I went back into Sean's folder and copied over a few other job descriptions. It didn't take long to figure out the colour-coding: tasks that overlapped with those of other roles were highlighted in yellow, tasks unique to the role in green.

Sean was a good boss, I thought. He was in his mid-fifties, a lifer. He was fair and patient, and was not swayed by office politics the way I saw others get embroiled in them, all the disagreements and gossip. He knew I had a medical situation of some kind, but he never pressed for details or made any comments about my frequent morning appointments. I liked that he trusted me, and I felt protected by him, I guess. We hadn't had many interactions recently, but I'd assumed my independence was a good thing, that it meant I was an employee who didn't need hand-holding, who didn't ask for much, who was consistent. There *had* been more talk than usual about cutting costs around the office. We needed a new printer in our department, but no one was replacing it even though we kept complaining. Also, the magazine had just changed paper stock to something thinner and supposedly more environmentally friendly, but also cheaper. I felt dumb when I realized that this talk of cost savings could be applied to us, the staff. I had just assumed we were less affected because the magazine was a branch of a corporate entity, not dependent on advertising dollars.

I'd been at this job for three years, and I'd assumed I'd be here for more. Not forever, but at least until I had a baby. My salary wasn't great, but it was a good supplement to Joe's. More importantly, the health benefits were great and covered a large chunk of my fertility treatment drugs.

I think I might be getting fired, I texted Joe from my desk.

Why would you think that? he responded right away.

I found some documents when I was looking for another file

I forwarded him the job descriptions and waited for him to read them and write back.

It does look odd

"Should I be worried?" I asked back at home, the minute Joe walked in the door.

"I mean, it's probably a good idea to update your CV."

"I guess."

"But Sean seems to depend on you more than others."

Joe was right. I was the first one Sean called if he had a problem or a question. He'd gone on vacation recently and his out-of-office email had directed recipients to me, not to anyone else. I went through a list of my co-workers and thought of reasons why each would be laid off before me, for reasons ranging from seniority level to flakiness. Still, it was enough to make me realize that if there was a time to have a baby, it was now, while I still had benefits.

Later that night I sent Denny a video of my scone, featuring the Henry Moore sculpture in the background. We still wrote back and forth to each other, but we never referenced the fact that we'd kissed, just went back to the same jokey banter as before. If I couldn't sleep, I would check to see if there was a glowing green dot next to his name in my chat list, and usually—because of the time difference between him in California and me in Toronto—there was. Claire would maybe be available too, but she wouldn't write me back in the middle of the night the way he would.

I want to give her a hug, he wrote about the sculpture.

Omg, I responded. *Me too.*

While looking for some paperwork, I found the information package Dr. Sutton had given Joe and me on our first visit. The folder had remained on the counter in a pile with bills and flyers. I sorted through the papers, all the various FAQs and statistical charts and storage plans for frozen embryos. I'd ignored this information at the beginning because we weren't doing IVF and I was hopeful we never would.

At the back of the folder was a pamphlet featuring a picture of a hotel room with a bay window that looked onto a beach. It reminded me of where we'd stayed in Barbados, and I wondered why our clinic was giving us ads for resorts. It turned out they had partnerships with four different clinics around the world, in Palm Springs, Denver, Athens, and Buenos Aires. A couple could do preparation for a round of IVF in Toronto and then, closer to the egg retrieval and embryo transfer, travel to one of the partner clinics for the final steps.

I took out my phone to see if this was an actual thing people did—I hadn't come across it on the message board, but I also hadn't known to look. Sure enough, I found a few threads about it, and then a whole section devoted to it that I'd never paid attention to. The point of doing the treatment abroad was so that it could feel more like a vacation than a surgical procedure, and although there was no scientific claim to the effect of relaxation on successful conception, it couldn't hurt to be outside of your regular day-to-day life in a different, calming environment.

I put down my phone and set up my laptop on the counter to get a better look at my clinic's options. Their partner clinics in Buenos Aires and Denver seemed nice, but I didn't feel particularly drawn to them. Palm Springs was appealing because it was closer to Claire. Athens was the most interesting because it reminded me of the time Joe and I once found a flight to Santorini for three hundred dollars each through one of those sites that trawls airlines for online ticket fare glitches. I'd found the deal when I was at work, and I had only ten minutes to make the decision to go. I called Joe from my desk, and we talked it over for one minute ("Should we?" "Um…" "Should we?!" "Yes!"). After it was booked, we expected it to be cancelled—airlines usually figure out a way to renege on these mistakes—but this one actually stuck. We flew out a week later. The trip was just seven days, too short for such a long flight, and it was impossible for us to adjust to the time difference, but we didn't care—nor did we know enough at the time to be concerned about our carbon footprints.

We stayed in Oia, a town built along the steep edges of the island and famous for its sunset views. Every evening tourists would descend to sit on the low walls lining the streets to take pictures or film it. I'd never seen a sunset like that, so textbook it seemed like a simulation. The colour change from bright yellow to burning orange, streaky purple to deep pink was perfectly timed, as was the graceful arc of the sun moving from the top of the sky down to the darkening sea. It was incredible, but watching it in Oia was also maybe the worst way to witness this type of sublime scene. There was so much commotion, all the gasping and clapping, as if no one had ever seen a sunset in their life.

What I liked best about our stay in Oia was the hotel. Our room was tiny, just big enough for a bed and a small desk. Our suitcase took up all the floor space. The room had cool stone floors and dark blue shutters that opened up to a view of the sea and the street below. There was no screen on the window, and I would stick my head out to watch people walk by. When I was in bed, the din of tourists and a language I couldn't understand seeped into the room—not in an annoying, disruptive way, just enough to remind me that we were somewhere foreign. The sunsets seemed fake, but life in our room was real.

I wanted to go back. Out of curiosity, I emailed the nurse at the clinic to get more information on how the program worked, if we were eligible for it. I wanted to know how they timed everything correctly to coincide with travelling. She wrote back first thing the next morning: *Because your hormones are so regulated throughout the IVF process, your travel time is based around that schedule. I've attached a publication that shows success rates across clinics.*

That evening I showed Joe the brochure from the clinic. Maybe this would be our chance to revisit Greece.

"You can do IVF in another country?" he said, thumbing through it.

"Yeah, so it's like you're on vacation."

"Are you sure it's not a scam?"

"Definitely not."

"Which clinic is the best one?"

"They're supposedly equally qualified."

"Really? The one in Greece is as good as the one in California?"

"Apparently, or else the clinic wouldn't be partnered with them."

"It seems expensive."

When we used to travel, we planned our trips together, determining the budget we needed and ways we could be frugal, but I was always the one who paid closer attention to actual dollars. When we'd bought our place and secured the mortgage, I'd been the one to figure out a way to split the amount so that it was fair to both of us, given the difference in our salaries.

If we chose to do this, it would alter some of our timelines. There would be more planning involved. However, I felt suddenly okay with the wait. Something about the idea of it all seemed worthwhile. But the other issue was that going abroad was also, obviously, more expensive than doing IVF at home—travel and accommodations alone were a lot, even if the clinic offered discounts at nearby hotels. I had the slot machine money, though, still in US dollars in the same envelope. It was tucked into my underwear drawer for safekeeping. I took out the envelope and showed Joe the stack of American hundred-dollar bills.

"Where did you get *that?*"

"I won it in Vegas."

"Why didn't you tell me about it?"

I shrugged. "I wanted it to be a surprise."

"You want to use this to do IVF in Greece?"

"Why not?" Looking back, the Parthenon in the Nevada desert suddenly seemed like a sign. How many gods and goddesses had been born outside of regular conception? All of them. Why couldn't our baby be the same? Why not be close to the original source?

"Maybe we can figure it out," he said. It wasn't quite the *Yes!* from the Santorini trip, but it was enough.

What if you used the opportunity to do research for me and Shannon, Claire replied when I texted her. *We could pay for part of it. Reimburse your flights at least.* While I bristled at the thought of it, I accepted. I felt the way I felt when Dad transferred us money, relieved but also slightly ashamed as I deposited it into our account.

One day in March, I got to work and saw that Sean had sent me an invite for a meeting at nine thirty a.m. He'd sent it late the day before, which was unusual for him—he didn't typically work late, and our morning touchpoints were usually after ten. I didn't think much of it until I got the calendar reminder ten minutes before the meeting and noticed it was booked in a boardroom located on the other side of the office, near HR. It occurred to me that this meeting could be related to those documents I'd found: maybe Sean was going to tell me about the layoff plans and didn't want us to be near the rest of my co-workers. I walked over a bit early, carrying my notebook.

The door was closed. I opened it and found Sean sitting with Robyn, the head of HR.

"Sorry, am I interrupting?" I asked. "I'm a little early."

"No, come in, Laura."

I sat in front of them, and there was a beat of silence that caused a pit to form in my stomach. Something wasn't right—the vibes were all off. Robyn was holding a folder. I thought about the recent direct references to cost cutting I'd heard about since I'd found the job descriptions. The previous week someone had taken an early retirement, but there was gossip that she'd been asked to leave.

"I have to tell you something," Sean started.

"Is this about...cost cutting?" I asked, sounding more incredulous than I meant to.

Robyn and Sean exchanged glances, and he kept going. "Right, as you know, there has been a lot of pressure to cut costs. We also have to scale back on our staffing requirements. Your role is being terminated, effective immediately."

"Immediately as in right now?"

"I'm sorry."

"Like, today? Not the end of the week?"

"Effective immediately." Robyn took over. "Thanks, Sean. I'll go over the package with Laura now."

Sean got up from his seat and held out his hand. "I'm happy to give you references for any future jobs. I've always enjoyed working with you."

He looked so sad, like he was going to tear up. I bit my tongue and willed myself not to cry.

"Thanks."

After Sean left, Robyn passed the folder over to me. "Here are the details of your exit package. You don't have to read it now. Go home, look it over on your own time. You just have to sign off by the end of the week."

"My husband is a lawyer. I want him to read it to make sure it's fair."

"Wonderful," she said, and I hated her for doing her job.

Robyn walked with me to my desk, where I collected whatever made sense: some used notebooks, a framed photobooth strip of me and Joe. I looked at my laptop. "I have some personal files on my computer," I said. "Will I lose them?" I felt foolish for keeping anything personal on something that was clearly never mine.

"We can coordinate that with IT."

I saw one of my work friends look up from his desk and watch me leave. *Bye*, I mouthed, and he looked confused for a second before a wave of recognition took over.

I shook Robyn's hand before walking out the main door. I hadn't bought a fruit scone that morning, and I wished I'd had one more chance to sit with the Henry Moore in the courtyard. I thought about going now, but the territory was no longer mine. It would've been humiliating to stay. I'd been cut loose, and the only thing left to do was leave.

Robyn had given me an Uber voucher to get me home, but I started walking. I pulled out my phone. *I was laid off*, I wrote Joe, though I knew he was in court this morning and likely wouldn't be checking. I sent the same message to Claire. It was early for her, but maybe she would be awake.

What??? she wrote back immediately. I hadn't told her about my fears from before.

Cost cutting, etc.

I'm so sorry! Aren't you leaving for Greece soon?

For one brief hour I hadn't been thinking about Greece or my fertility. At least, I thought, I would get some vacation payout from saving those days. I didn't want to think about the implications of getting pregnant and having to look for a job at the same time. I didn't want to think about *not* getting pregnant and having to look for a job at the same time. We wouldn't be able to sink money into fertility treatments if I was unemployed. How would it work?

Finally I got an Uber, sat in the back, and cried silently until I was almost home. As I let myself in, Joe called. I answered, and he said, "Baby, what happened?" and I started crying again. I hated crying over this stupid job.

Two other editors and three designers were laid off at the same time as me, as well as a handful of people in marketing and a few other departments. Someone arranged an impromptu meet-up two days later for those of us who'd been laid off plus the survivors. We met at the same bar we always went to for work events. It was an awkward dynamic until the employed bought the unemployed drinks. I hadn't started my meds for this cycle yet, so I figured this would be my last chance to get a little tipsy.

I came home that evening feeling marginally better: my package gave me three months of salary continuance. I'd get employment insurance. I would be fine for the next little while at least. But I woke up the next morning, after Joe had left for work, feeling nervous. What was I going to do? Despite Joe's advice, I'd never gotten around to updating my CV. I didn't even know where it was. I finally found a copy attached to an email from years ago. I read it over and wondered how I could bulk it up. It was so flimsy.

For a brief period of time I'd made jewellery. I'd collected beads from our trips: some wooden earth tones from Thailand, a small selection of clear blue glass from Mexico. Back at home I ordered the right kind of floss and a packet of clasps from an online wholesale jewellery store. I made some bracelets and necklaces, gave some to friends and Claire and Mom. If I had been more enterprising I could've turned it into a solid side hustle, an Etsy shop, a dedicated

Instagram account, but I'd let it slide. My food blog, which I'd started around the same time, was easier in that it didn't require any upfront capital or manual labour.

One of the bracelets I'd made and loved had recently become so worn out that the floss had snapped and the beads had scattered around the kitchen as I got ready for work one morning. I hated the metaphor of it, and I didn't bother retrieving the stray beads that had rolled into various crevices. Even if I started making jewellery again, the thought of it, of stringing beads on a thread, seemed ridiculous, like I was one of those birds that collected shiny bits of garbage and little twigs to construct their nest. Maybe it could build up to something eventually, but in the meantime it was a mess. I felt so useless sometimes, so unable to sustain something meaningful, something solid.

Have you thought about getting a job in tech? Claire texted a few mornings later.

That's so vague. What do you mean exactly?

There are so many jobs that need your writing skills, your editorial skills

Like what kind of jobs?

Let me talk to some people

You don't have to talk to people for me. I know how to talk to people

Soon after that I checked my email and found that my dad had sent me a transfer for $2,750. *I heard about your job problems,* he wrote. *Just in case you need some help.* I wondered how he'd settled on that amount. Did he think it was equivalent to a mortgage payment? A certain monthly amount of living expenses? Was it a lot or a little to him? I truly had no idea how to interpret it, but of course I was grateful for it, of course I needed it, of course I felt embarrassed with both him and Claire *helping* me.

I left the house so I could feel like a functioning member of society rather than someone sitting at home waiting for handouts from her family. I ended up at a new cafe nearby that I hadn't tried yet and ordered a scone. I knew the minute I saw it on the plate that it wouldn't be very good. It was a uniform rectangular shape, dusty with flour, not as complex and texturally varied as the ones I used to get at work. I took a picture of it and sent it to Denny. *This is a very sad scone :(.*

Did the cafe change their recipe?

This isn't from the good place. I lost my job. Laid off!!! No more good scones

Oh shit. That sucks. Are you okay?

Yeah, it will be fine. This scone is not helping the situation, though

I walked back home, texting back and forth with Denny, then lounging on the couch and doing the same, like we were catching up after months apart, suddenly with so much to say to each other. Las Vegas energy.

Joe was going to record that night, so I was on my own.

What should I do for dinner? I texted Denny.

I have to figure out the same for myself. I was thinking sushi

I could do that

Should we order the same thing and pretend we're sharing?

I sent him the link to the place Joe and I normally ordered from. He sent me his. When Joe got home, I'd fallen asleep on the couch, my phone on my chest, the delivery containers on the coffee table.

"Hey," he said gently.

I watched him eat one of the leftover spicy tuna rolls. I'd ordered too much. "Did you not eat? I assumed you would at Amit's."

"It's okay. You got a hand roll? You never order those."

"Just felt like something different. I'm sorry, I should've texted you when I was ordering to see if you'd want anything."

"It's fine. Go to bed. I'm too wound up to sleep. We ended up having this huge debate with a councillor about the process around bike lanes. I haven't seen Amit that worked up in a long time."

"Sounds fun."

"I think we'll stockpile a few episodes before we go to Greece. We have to plan for when he's off for his baby too."

"Yeah. That's coming soon."

"Did you do any job things today?"

"A little," I lied.

"How do you feel?"

"Good, actually." Another lie.

He leaned over and kissed my head, picked up the take-out boxes, and brought them to the kitchen. I fell back asleep on the couch.

One evening, on the way home from buying groceries, I was listening to CBC on the radio and heard a documentary about the Syrian refugee crisis and how it impacted Greece. Greece, it turned out, was an attractive country for refugees because there were so many different island entry points and because it was part of the EU. Maybe *attractive* was the wrong word—the journeys were treacherous and deadly, the boats barely making their way through rough seas, but if you made it, you were out. If you were arrested in Greece, you had to stay within the EU, which wasn't necessarily a bad thing—it meant you would have to stay in the country. But of course Greece was still reeling from its own economic crisis and didn't have the social services to spare. It was different than Toronto, where I knew groups of people who devoted time to welcoming refugees. Not just formal organizations, but regular citizens, neighbours coming together to sponsor families or organize clothing drives so that newcomers would have warm clothes for their first Canadian winter. That time and energy was harder to come by in Greece.

The journalist in the documentary recited her closing monologue over a background recording of the sounds of a makeshift refugee camp in Athens. Amidst the noise I could pick out the high shrieks of children and babies crying, and I was suddenly filled with self-loathing: not only was I trying so hard to conceive a child when there were real people in need, but I was paying money for it and doing it in Greece, the location of this documentary. I was going there for *leisure*. I wept in the car where I'd sat listening, rapt.

"You couldn't adopt any of those children, right?" Joe said at home when I couldn't stop crying. "They're with their families. They want better lives, not different parents. Us going there is not an affront to them."

"But isn't it? We could use all our money to sponsor a family."

"You say *all our money* as if we wouldn't have anything else to spend it on. We're also putting a lot on credit."

"Right."

"You're currently unemployed."

"I know."

"Would you sponsor a family using our line of credit?"

"Maybe I should."

"Maybe everyone should then. Claire should. What about your dad? He could sponsor a dozen families—Why did he send money to us and not them?"

"I should've donated the money."

"That's not why he gave it to you, and it's not your individual responsibility."

"But this is how terrible things happen! When we shirk individual responsibility because we think others should take care of things."

"Laura. In terms of this specific thing, we've paid. It's non-refundable. We won't get our money back if we ask for it."

"We would only lose a portion of it." It was the majority of the amount, but still.

"You're not a bad person for doing this," he said.

I suppose, ultimately, that was what I wanted to hear—some kind of reassurance that what we were doing wasn't *bad*.

I continued to do little on the job front for the rest of the week. What I did do was bake my own scones, tweak the recipe, bake another batch and then a third. I sent Denny pictures of the dough, of the finished product. The best batch had been brushed with heavy cream, which gave the top the same crispy edges as the cafe scones.

And then I received an email from a recruiter at a startup that made meal delivery boxes and sponsored Joe's podcast. *Your sister Claire recommended that I reach out to you. Are you available for a call to talk about a potential opportunity?*

I forwarded the email to Claire. *Who is this?*

I don't know, but I'm friends with the founder. She must have given her your name. Call!

You don't have to tell me how to look for a job, I wrote, then deleted it and replaced it with *Thanks!*

The truth was that I needed a job as soon as possible. The sooner I got one, the more time I'd have on the job before I'd have to go on maternity leave—if I got pregnant from the IVF in Greece—and the less guilty I'd feel about it.

I talked to the recruiter on the phone, and she invited me for an in-person meeting the following week. On the day of the interview, I arrived forty minutes early. I waited in the car. The office wasn't far from the party I'd been to with Claire months earlier. When it seemed like a decent time to get to the office, I walked to the building and took the elevator up to the third floor. There was no reception desk, so I typed my name into the iPad at the front and waited.

A young woman, maybe twenty-five, opened the glass door and let me in. She gave me a tour before the interview. The space was like my own home, like where Claire worked—all open concept. I checked off everything you'd expect to see at a startup: a Ping-Pong table, a beanbag chair, a dog, guys wearing headphones and hoodies. What bothered me, though, was the way I suddenly felt—like I wanted to work there, among twenty-somethings and dogs and a Ping-Pong table. The natural lighting was so much better than the track lighting at my old office. It was so nice to see hardwood instead of commercial carpet. I passed a basket of snacks. Clif Bars, Halloween-size chocolate bars. Could I just take something if I wanted it?

I was interviewing for a website content editor position. Their site featured stories about their customers and food suppliers, and they needed someone to guide their overall content strategy beyond just their blog. They wanted to beef up their Instagram presence, other social media channels. The marketing director interviewing me was older than the recruiter but likely still younger than me. We chatted for long enough that for a while it didn't feel like an interview.

"Can you tell me how you would whiteboard an idea?" she asked as we moved out of the chit-chat phase.

I hated the word *whiteboard* as a verb. I hated the non-specificity of *idea*. "Sure. What kind of idea?"

She gave me a scenario, something about a farmer who grew pesticide-free strawberries, and I got up and flailed around on the whiteboard. Finally she asked me if I had any questions.

"What are your parental benefits like?" It was the stupidest question I could ask; I realized this the minute it came out of my mouth. I might as well have just worn a T-shirt that said *I'M WITH BABY* in black Helvetica.

She narrowed her eyes for the briefest second. "They're competitive: eighty percent top-up for the first six months. Meal delivery, of course."

"That's great. I'm not pregnant," I said. "I'm just curious how companies deal with it."

"You don't have to explain yourself." She smiled at me, and I couldn't tell if it was a smile of sympathy or pity. She took a sip of the iced coffee she'd walked in with, its paper straw damp and bending over. "Our founder really likes your older sister. She said Claire is a genius. We've all heard about the Lookout and think it sounds so cool."

"Yeah, it's such a good idea. And Claire *is* so smart. She's my baby sister, though."

"Oh, I assumed she was older." I couldn't tell if it was a dig at me, but the marketing director looked at me with wide eyes and I knew she felt like she'd had her turn saying the wrong thing. We chatted a bit longer, and then she walked me to the door. A dog ran up to us, hers. "This is Wally."

"Nice to meet you, Wally." I held out my hand, and he actually shook it.

I took the elevator back down and walked to the car. I didn't feel like texting Claire about how it had gone since I didn't expect to hear from them again. I was out of practice with interviewing.

What were my *strengths?* Lately I'd felt like my biggest one was my ability to give myself needles. I was an expert at mixing vials of medication and injecting them without hesitation. "It's kind of sexy," Joe had said once when he watched me flick some air bubbles out of the syringe, my first round of IVF meds. For a brief second, I had basked in the way I felt: competent and productive.

I knew something was up from the way Mom called and invited me and Joe over for dinner. Bart was also inviting his whole family—Olivia, plus her husband, Thomas, and their six-year-old daughter, Rosalie. After meeting Olivia the first time, I'd met her family too, but this felt more formal, more like there was an official reason for it.

"I told Claire to be at home so we can FaceTime her," Mom added.

"What's the occasion?

"You'll see!"

I texted Claire. *What do you think's going on?*

Isn't it obvious?

I felt dumb for not finding it obvious. *She's going to move in with Bart?*

I think they're going to tell us they're getting married

Hmm, maybe!

When Joe and I arrived, Bart went into the kitchen and returned with a bottle of champagne. We moved to the living room where Olivia, Rosalie, and Thomas were already settled on the couch. I called Claire and panned my phone around the room so that she could see us all. Rosalie hid behind her father, shy for a moment, and then popped her head up and stuck out her tongue.

"Does Bart have champagne?" Claire asked.

Mom stood next to Bart. "Can Claire see me?"

"I can see you," Claire said.

"Can she?"

I turned the volume up all the way so they could hear her better. "I can see you!" Claire said again.

Mom nodded at Bart. He smiled at her before she spoke. "Bart and I are getting married."

"Dad!" Olivia exclaimed.

At the same time, I said, "Mom!"

I was moved by the sight of Bart holding the still-closed champagne bottle with one hand and Mom's hand with the other, by Mom's happiness. On screen, Claire wiped away a tear. Joe put his arm around me, and then I gave him my phone so I could hug Mom, then Bart, then Olivia, who was also weeping. Mom was getting married—this was not what Claire and I had expected when we'd set up her dating profile.

"Do you have a ring, Mom?" Claire asked.

She took out a small box and put on the ring inside. I held the phone up close so Claire could see it.

"That diamond is huge."

"Thank you."

"When do you think you'll have the wedding?" I asked.

"We're going to pick a date that works with Claire's schedule."

"I'm deciding your wedding date?"

Mom spoke to the phone in my hand. "I have to make sure you can come. We only want to celebrate with our children."

"But when do you *want* to get married? I'll make anything work."

"We don't really care, as long as you can be there."

"Mom, this is a lot of pressure. Are you sure you don't have a preference?"

"Any date is fine with us," Bart added.

"What about at Christmas? I have time off then. We all do, right?"

"That's perfect!" Bart said.

"Christmas!" Rosalie squealed.

Mom smiled in a way that I couldn't quite place until I realized that it was simply youthful, the smile of a teenager, of a blushing bride.

"Let's celebrate," Bart said. "We have a lot of food." He'd ordered a huge tray of takeout from a Filipino restaurant—pork skewers and shrimp and rice and lumpia.

I turned Claire toward me. "You don't have to watch us eat, but I can prop the phone up on the table if you want."

"It's okay, I'm actually still at work."

Mom came over next to me. "I wish you were here, Claire."

"Me too, Mom. I'm so happy for you and Bart."

"I love you."

"I love you too."

Claire hung up, and I excused myself to the bathroom. I sat on the edge of the bathtub and sobbed for a minute, a quick burst that felt almost like throwing up. I just had to get it out of my system, the rising cloud of emotion in my chest. I wished Claire was here too.

"Hello?" I heard a small voice from the other side of the door. It was Rosalie. "I have to pee."

I opened the door and let her in.

"Don't forget to wipe!" Olivia yelled from the dining room table.

"I *know*." She exaggerated the word the way a teenager would.

I was still emotional when I got home. At dinner we'd discussed Mom selling her house. It made sense—Bart's house was nicer, bigger. I'd volunteered to help with the logistics, but it also made me sad, the house we'd grown up in belonging to someone else. Mom had always been self-conscious about what she could provide for me and Claire compared to what Dad could, but the house had been a source of pride: a place we could return to whenever necessary.

Everyone was on the verge of something new. Now that Claire had settled on the Lookout, it felt even more viable, a real part of her future. Mom was going to start a whole new chapter of her life too.

"Maybe we should move into Mom's house," I said when Joe and I were in bed.

"Do you really want to live there?" he asked. I'd always been adamant about not living in the suburbs and had told him specifically that I didn't want to settle in the kind of neighbourhood we grew up in, let alone the exact same neighbourhood.

"It's practical. There aren't any ladders."

"But what would we do with all the extra rooms? We barely need doors."

"We hate doors."

"Except for the bathroom."

"Obviously."

Mom's house was the kind of starter home many couples wanted: the right amount of bedrooms, a basement, a driveway, a backyard. Just outside the city, a reasonable commute to work downtown, not far from where Mom would be living with Bart, not far from Joe's parents.

"I'm not sure it's what I want, though." I admitted. "What do you want?"

Joe looked at me for a second longer than I thought he would. "You know I want whatever you want," he replied.

PART SEVEN: SUMMER

When Joe and I landed in Athens, my ovaries were swollen. I was aware of them in a way I'd never been before: actual growths in my midsection, plumped up by the injections I'd been giving myself. We had one last consultation with Dr. Sutton before leaving, with the Greek doctor we'd be meeting shortly sitting in via video chat, and they were both enthusiastic about my ultrasounds.

A man holding a sign with our names on it greeted us at the airport exit after we'd collected our luggage. "Welcome! I am Pericles. I will be your driver for your stay."

A driver was included in the clinic travel package, but I'd imagined the driver would be an older Greek man, more Zorba-like, someone wise and warm. Instead this man, Pericles, was young, maybe younger than us, lanky, with short brown hair, wearing a short-sleeved button-down shirt. He spoke with an English accent.

"How was your flight?" he asked. "Do you have to go to the loo? Would you like some water?" He held out two bottles for us.

We bypassed the crowd and walked to his car, a small van that could fit up to six people but would be empty except for us. It was eleven in the morning, and the sun gave everything a bleached, bright-white hue. I rummaged through my bag for my sunglasses but couldn't find them and felt disoriented and woozy. We climbed in, and I kept my seat belt unbuckled. I didn't like the idea of straining a seat belt over my expanding ovaries. I'd done the same when we landed, just draping the belt loosely over my waist. Pericles didn't say anything about the seat belt. Things seemed both safer and more dangerous here.

Athens looked nothing like Santorini. We weren't surrounded by water, just a tangle of highways. When we left the airport, big box stores lined the road. There was an IKEA. A car dealership. Sometimes there were stretches of open fields dotted with olive trees.

"Are we going far?" I asked Pericles. Our hotel and clinic were by the sea, outside of Central Athens.

"Far enough. It's a nice suburb." He proceeded to tell us about the daily excursions the hotel organized—to beaches, to ruins.

"That sounds fun," Joe said, but it reminded me of the sea turtles in Barbados.

"Do you travel a lot?"

"Not as much these days," Joe answered. "We used to."

"Why did you stop?"

"Oh, you know." I waved my hand. My gesture meant *Life, money, fertility issues*.

"What do you do for a living?"

"Joe's a lawyer," I said. "I'm unemployed."

"Laura's an editor," Joe said.

"Intellectuals! You will have a smart baby."

We laughed, but it felt too soon to evoke the word *baby*.

Pericles dropped us off at the hotel to check in and freshen up. Once we were done he was going to bring us straight to the clinic for our first in-person appointment. We had no time to waste.

The hotel room had simple white tile floors. There was a small balcony with a wrought-iron fence. Our room looked out onto a courtyard filled with lemon trees, the fruit still green and small. The bathtub didn't have a shower curtain, and when I took a quick shower I managed to spray water all over the floor with the hand-held nozzle. I left the bathroom to find Joe passed out on the cool white sheets, and I nudged him awake for our appointment.

Back downstairs we met with Pericles, who was chatting with the woman working at the front desk.

"It's so hot," he said to us in the car. "It's not normally this hot in May."

"How long is the heat wave supposed to last?" I asked. I hadn't looked at the weather forecast before arriving.

He shrugged. "Who knows?"

"Where do you live?" Joe asked.

"In a nearby suburb."

"Do you have a family?"

"I do! Twins. They are three years old."

"From the clinic?"

He laughed. "It would be good marketing! It runs in my wife's family. Three sets of twins between five siblings."

"Is it really hereditary?" I wished he'd lied and told us it was because they'd gone to the clinic.

"I think so."

"Laura's practically a twin," Joe said.

"Not really." I reached into my bag and finally found my sunglasses.

The clinic was an unassuming white three-storey building. It looked exactly like the pictures, down to the pots of leafy green plants lining the front entrance. In fact, everything looked like the pictures: the lobby, the waiting rooms, the artwork. I felt a twinge of disappointment even though it met our expectations. I'd hoped the clinic would look better in real life: more glamourous, more vibrant, not so sun bleached.

A nurse took my blood; a technician gave me an ultrasound. Everyone spoke English; everyone was kind. Joe sat in the waiting room for most of it, but everything happened quickly. Soon we were in the doctor's office. He kissed both our cheeks when he walked in, and I realized I couldn't remember if we'd ever even shaken Dr. Sutton's hand.

"It's a pleasure to meet you. I reviewed your recent ultrasound and blood work, and everything looks excellent. We'll stay the course with your medications."

"Oh, great," I said, and Joe squeezed my hand.

"And when will you visit the Acropolis?"

"Excuse me?"

"Tomorrow will be cooler, but I suggest waiting another day or two for this heat wave to end."

"We don't have to stay close to the clinic?"

"After your morning appointment you're free. We want you to enjoy yourselves."

Our doctor folded his arms and smiled at us before giving us more details. I liked him more than Dr. Sutton, his warmth and chattiness. Coming to Greece was a good idea; I felt confident sitting in this office with him.

When we were done, Pericles wasn't in the waiting room, so I fished out the number he'd given us to text him.

Hi, it's Laura! We're done with our appointment!

Okey, he texted back a moment later. I would later learn that this is how he'd respond to all our texts.

Good morning! We're ready to leave. Should we meet you in the lobby?

Okey

Can you drive us to the beach?

Okey

Thank you!

Okey

He must have typed it once and now it autocompleted. I didn't read it as an incomplete *okey-dokey* but more like an aspirated, more guttural *okay*, one with a Greek accent. *Okhay.* While most of Pericles's English was spoken with an English accent—which he explained he'd picked up from years of tutoring from a woman who'd moved to Athens from London—his Greek accent often poked through in little words that peppered his sentences. *Okey?*

"You are at a very good clinic," he said on the drive back. "Every year I get sent so many pictures of the babies. Look." He opened his glovebox, and a stack of photos fell out. With one hand on the steering wheel, he leaned over, picked up the photos, and handed them back to me. I flipped through the pictures like they were trading cards. All these babies— chubby, pinkish, bald or with full heads of hair, naked, wrapped up like tiny burritos. There was a Baby Hall of Fame in one of the hallways at our clinic in Toronto, but I usually avoided it. Pericles's photos were different, though. They were comforting.

Before we left Joe had talked about our upcoming treatment on his podcast. The night he recorded it, he came home buzzing, almost skipping through the door.

"I talked about us on the show," he said, leaning over to give me a kiss.

"I thought you were interviewing someone about property taxes. What did you say?"

"We were talking about our hiatus, and it came out from there."

"Oh. You talked about...IVF?"

"Yeah."

"How did Amit react?"

"He didn't expect me to talk about it on the air, so he was surprised, but he was good. And I feel good too. Lighter."

"Oh, that's great." I got up to get a glass of water. Something about the meds made me thirsty, and I was constantly getting up to drink and then to pee and then to drink more again. As I let the water run colder, I thought more about Joe's podcast revelation. They often spoke about their personal lives, and listeners knew my name, but I was more like a character in their lives than a real person. Laura was usually bemused, tolerant of whatever their latest obsession or rant was, but Laura was supportive too. Laura was on their side.

"Can I listen to the episode?" I called out to Joe.

"Why wouldn't you be able to?"

"I mean, ahead of time." Not since the first few episodes, when they were self-conscious and wanted feedback, had I listened to an episode before it was posted.

"Sure, why?"

"I'm curious about what you said."

"You're not worried about it, are you?"

"I just want to know what you say about us before everyone else hears it."

"I didn't say anything too personal."

"That's fine. I just want to listen first."

"I don't want you to think I would say anything you wouldn't agree with."

"I don't think that, I promise." We looked at each other in a way that acknowledged that I *did* think that, but neither of us wanted to turn it into a fight.

The next day Joe emailed me an audio snippet:

AMIT: So we're taking a bit of hiatus for the next few weeks.

JOE: A formal one, not just us being lazy about recording like we were last summer. Or the summer before.

AMIT: We've grown up a little. We have important things to attend to.

JOE: Just like politicians, we have some important cottaging to do.

AMIT: I wish I had a cottage. I wish you had a cottage. I need more friends with cottages.

JOE: This is why one of us has to run for office. I think you get a cottage as part of the package. What are you doing if you aren't going to a cottage?

AMIT: Having a baby. Taking paternity leave.

JOE: I can't wait to bring the baby on as a guest. Do babies have opinions on bike lanes?

AMIT: My baby most definitely will. What are you doing on your break?

JOE: Oh, hmm. Well, speaking of babies, Laura and I are taking some time off to... This sounds funny in comparison to your plans...

AMIT: Oh?

JOE: We're doing IVF in a few weeks. I'm taking time to be there with Laura.

AMIT: I'm sorry. I knew you were doing this and I just talked about having a baby.

JOE: It's okay. I'm so happy for you, dude! I'm just in a different situation.

AMIT: Are you feeling okay about it all?

JOE: Not really! *[They both laugh.]* I mean, I'm grateful that we have options.

AMIT: Me too. It's amazing what you can do these days.

JOE: Definitely. Laura has been going through a lot, though. I'm really grateful to her. She's done all the research, goes to the doctor all the time. I'm just along for the ride.

AMIT: We all know you do more than that. Thanks for sharing, Joe. I know you've been really preoccupied with all of this.

JOE: You've been really helpful too.

AMIT: Oh, jeez. Thanks.

JOE: Why don't I make this the segue into asking for donations to our Patreon? Pay for my IVF?

AMIT: You're saying it, not me. *[More laughing.]*

After the show aired, Joe received emails from listeners, some with fertility issues and some who just wanted to send encouragement, variations of *You're so brave* and *We're rooting for you*. He forwarded me the messages, and they were heartening to read, but I deleted them right away so they wouldn't linger in my inbox.

"I felt much better after talking about it on the podcast," he said. "Maybe you would too if you wrote about it publicly."

"Where would I write about it?"

"Your blog?"

"It's a *food* blog. And I don't have any readers anymore."

"Maybe Claire has a suggestion. I think you would feel better if you weren't keeping all your feelings inside."

"You said, like, a sentence on the air. I could publish a sentence, sure." I hated that no one understood why I wanted some privacy. I'd even stopped posting on the message boards; I didn't see the point. There was a quote from M. F. K. Fisher, the food writer, that said, *Probably one of the most private things in the world is an egg until it is broken*. I was still in that phase.

Joe kept quiet, and I realized I'd hurt him.

"I know I didn't say a lot, but I feel like I exposed myself more than usual by saying it on the podcast for everyone to hear. I could've edited it out, but I didn't."

"I didn't mean to belittle it. I'm sorry. And you said you were grateful to me. That was really sweet."

As if Claire had eavesdropped on the conversation, she asked me the next day if I wanted to help with some research for the Lookout. They were thinking of adding content to their landing page—not just your typical sporadically updated corporate blog, but something with real women's stories. *I know it's not groundbreaking*, she said, *but it's something*. She wanted me to write about Greece. Maybe, I told her.

~~

Day 1: I'm in Athens and my stomach is swollen and I imagine the drugs are making my ovaries swell up like bunches of grapes. I'm afraid they might get too big and pop.

~~

The next day Pericles drove us to the clinic with another couple in the van, Katie and Peter. On the drive over we learned that they were also on their first round of IVF, that they were from Toronto and went to our clinic, and coincidentally, that they lived close to us. Maybe it wasn't such a coincidence, given the clinic partnership, but it did seem auspicious as we spoke.

Katie had thick dirty-blonde hair, and Peter was tall and fit. He was Greek too, and when he chatted with Pericles in Greek I felt a surge of jealousy that we couldn't communicate like that.

"I'm so happy you're friends!" Pericles said when he dropped us off. "Your babies will be friends too." I was

starting to get used to Pericles talking about these hypo-
thetical babies.

Katie and I were called in for our exams at the same time.
Our rooms were side by side, and we passed each other in
the hallway again when we left our ultrasound rooms for
our respective doctors' offices. Whenever she saw me, she
would cross her fingers and smile.

On the drive back, they invited us to have lunch at one
of the tavernas near the hotel. Part of me didn't want to go,
but we didn't really have a reason to say no. We grabbed a
table, and Peter ordered for us in Greek. A waiter brought
us a basket of yellow bread, cutlery, a bottle of water, and a
plate of thick tzatziki. Joe and Peter had beers.

Like us, Katie and Peter thought going abroad for IVF
would make the experience more enjoyable. A vacation. At
this moment, sharing small plates of food on a shady patio,
it did.

"When I had my first ultrasound in Toronto," Katie said,
"I closed my eyes and visualized myself at the beach. Now I
can actually go—it makes it so much better. Not that I like
the way I look in a bathing suit these days."

I looked at her midsection, but it was hard to tell if it was
bloated like mine. I was back to wearing seat belts again,
but my stomach ballooned out as if I were three months
pregnant.

"Are you planning on doing anything special while you're
here?" I asked.

After the egg retrieval, there were five days when we'd be
free to do what we wanted: no further injections, no clinic
visits. It was just a matter of waiting for the embryos to de-
velop before they were implanted. The clinic recommended
that we use that time to travel to a nearby island.

Katie and Peter were slightly ahead of us and already had plans lined up for the next three days. "We're going with Peter's family to Spetses. You?"

"We're either going to Hydra or renting a car for a road trip," I said.

"I don't think I could drive here," Peter said. "The drivers are crazy! Pericles is a madman."

"It doesn't seem any worse than places where we've rented cars in the past," Joe said. "Thailand was riskier, I think."

"Yeah, I wouldn't drive there either! You guys are brave."

I liked being called brave in this context, and I felt a warm, sweeping fondness for Joe in that moment, for us.

Joe and I stayed for coffee when we finished, but Katie and Peter wanted to head back. Katie leaned over and hugged me. "I'm so glad we met. We can be mat leave friends."

When they were out of sight, Joe said, "They're nice."

"Really nice."

"I can see you and Katie as best friends."

"You and Peter too."

"Definitely."

I said everything sarcastically, but I didn't really have a good reason to be snarky about them. They were sincerely nice. They were easy to talk to. During lunch, when I'd returned from the bathroom and mentioned that the tap inside wouldn't stop running, Peter had gone out of his way to tell someone at the restaurant, in Greek. He was eager to help like that. Also, something about them made our own situation seem less strange. If these two completely normal and well-adjusted people were doing IVF at a clinic in Greece, then what we were doing couldn't be that unusual, right? But I guess I also felt threatened by them. They looked like they had better odds than us. They looked fertile. I felt haggish compared to Katie; Joe was slight compared to Peter. Peter had the hairiest chest, which I knew even before seeing him shirtless at the beach because the hair stuck out through his shirt. Katie had alluded to their problem being on her side, and all I could think of when I looked at Peter's hairy chest were the millions of motile sperm he could produce in a single shot.

"I really don't want to picture that," Joe said.

~

Day 2: I've avoided bruising in the past, but with these daily needles my stomach is purple and yellow. So much of motherhood is presented as a kind of masochism, all these sacrifices you make for your child, and I am ready for that, I really am, but seeing these bruises now, before there is a child to sacrifice myself for, is depressing.

~

Joe had to do some last-minute work, so when we went to the pool back at the hotel he brought his laptop and we claimed lounge chairs on the shaded side under some trees. There were a few other couples outside, probably also patients of the clinic, but I'd depleted my capacity for socializing and kept my distance. The pool was small and empty. I figured with the heat people would at least splash around, but we all just sat around it instead. Eventually I put my legs in for a few minutes to cool down, and the water was nice, the hot sun luxurious on my skin. I was relaxing. I couldn't remember the last time I'd done that.

I paid attention to the rumblings in my lower abdomen. It was sensitive from the shots, but I had the distinct feeling of something growing within me, something happening, a stronger feeling than when I was on Clomid for the IUIs. I could almost trick myself into believing I was already pregnant. Wasn't I, though? Pre-pregnant? I remembered being surprised to learn that you were supposed to count the weeks of pregnancy starting from the day of your last period, before the egg was even fertilized, so the first two weeks before actual conception counted toward your overall pregnancy. Why couldn't I push it earlier? I was pregnant; my body just didn't know it yet.

〜〜

Day 3: I bought a pomegranate from the small grocery store around the corner from the hotel. I thought of it as an offering to the goddess of fertility, Demeter, but then I learned that pomegranates are actually responsible for the barren part of the year, not the other way around. In the myth explaining the seasons, Hades kidnapped Demeter's daughter, Persephone, and while she was held hostage in the underworld, she ate six pomegranate seeds. It turned out that consuming anything in the underworld was grounds for eternal damnation, and because of those six seeds she was fated to stay forever. Demeter, mad with grief, still managed to strike up a deal that allowed her daughter to leave the underworld for half the year. When Persephone was free, Demeter happily allowed the Earth to flourish and flower. The other half of the year, when she mourned her absent daughter, winter descended. Nothing grew.

〜〜

Over the next two days, my ultrasounds were just, as Pericles would say, *okey*. Things had kind of stalled out after the promising start. I had seven follicles in my left Fallopian tube and five in the other. Twelve wasn't a bad number, but the problem was that three of the five on the right side were growing faster than the others. This was a familiar scenario. If the three follicles kept growing at the same rate, we'd have to do the retrieval before the others could completely mature, and three was a bad number for IVF; we were aiming for double digits.

"This is not ideal," our doctor said, looking at my most recent ultrasound. Every time we met him, I noticed a new, luxe detail about him. His beautiful thick black hair, his Gucci loafers.

"Is there anything I can do?"

"Just wait and see."

This seemed unscientific and not worth the money we were spending. When I got back to our hotel room, I wrote to our nurse in Toronto for a second opinion. Dr. Sutton had said we could do this if we wanted to, even though she'd said she had the "utmost trust in our partner clinics" and that it was "likely unnecessary." I felt a pang of guilt tattling on our Greek doctor.

In our prior travels, Joe and I rarely did group activities. We liked figuring things out on our own, creating our own itineraries without relying on guides, but that afternoon we'd planned on visiting the Acropolis with Katie and Peter as part of one of the excursions organized by the hotel.

"We don't have to go if you don't want to," Joe said, sitting next to me on the edge of the bed where I sat with the laptop, refreshing my inbox to see if the Toronto nurse had written me back yet.

"What would we do instead?"

"We can hang out by the pool. Whatever you want."

"What's the point of being here if we don't even go to the Acropolis?"

"We can go tomorrow."

"Peter and Katie are doing their retrieval tomorrow."

"We don't have to go with them."

"I want to."

"Listen, I'm just giving you an out if you want it."

"I don't." Refreshed again. Still nothing.

"Then we have to go now—they're already waiting downstairs."

I hauled myself up, and we met the rest of the group in the lobby, six of us in total. The other two were an older couple from New Jersey with no connection to the clinic. Pericles was at the wheel. He looked happy when he saw me; he'd sensed our tension when he'd driven us back from the clinic that morning and had remained quieter than usual, but now that he saw us in the van he was chatty again.

It was our first foray into downtown Athens, and once we were off the highway the streets got narrower. The buildings were the same as the ones around the hotel, no taller than six or seven storeys, all with the same dark green pergolas pulled down to protect balconies from the midday heat. Traffic was more intense, and the heat seemed stronger as well. Pericles dropped us off in Plaka, near the Acropolis, and arranged a pickup time.

Joe and I hiked up the path toward the Acropolis with Peter and Katie. There were a few different ways to get to the top, and we chose the less busy path. The ground was dry with clumps of brush, and the air smelled sweet, a kind of heady pineyness. There were thin, gnarled olive trees, and leaping insects bounced against my ankles. At the entrance we were pushed into a funnel thick with large groups of tourists, but once we bypassed them we were free to wander around the summit.

The real Parthenon was surrounded by scaffolding. From afar you could almost pretend it wasn't there, but up close it was like a construction site. We walked along the wall around the perimeter of the summit. Up there you were aware that you were on a mountain, that this was where the gods stood to survey their kingdom. Athens spread out around us, a colour study of rusts and off-white. It was a mess of urban planning, and none of the streets looked like they made sense. I had no idea where our clinic was. By the water somewhere.

I took photos from various angles and thought about sending them to people. Denny, for instance, would've liked all these photos from Athens—but I'd pulled back on our messaging as the trip approached. It didn't feel right to be talking to him from here. But I also hardly reached out to Claire or Mom either. I felt like I had that time I stood in the Humber—on my own, far away. Hopefully Joe and I would emerge with stories to tell. In the meantime there was something comforting about the chaos of this city, that despite it Athens survived, grew, took people in, chugged along.

When we were done, we had another hour and a half before we had to meet Pericles to bring us back to the hotel. We thought about visiting the Acropolis Museum, but Katie felt uncomfortable and wanted to sit down, so we went to a nearby taverna instead. As always, we let Peter order in Greek. I used the taverna's Wi-Fi to look up a store I wanted to visit in Plaka. I followed the store online and liked the jewellery they sold. It wasn't far from the restaurant.

"I'm just going to pop by this place," I said. "It's not far. I won't be long. Don't wait for me if the food gets here."

"You want to go alone?" Joe asked. The waiter had just given him his beer.

"Yeah, I'm fine."

I made my way through Plaka, soaking it in. It was a touristy area—the streets lined with shops selling novelty T-shirts, leather sandals, replicas of ancient vessels—but still charming. I took a turn and ended up on a street that led to a busy thoroughfare. I kept walking. Twenty minutes had now passed, and I still hadn't found the store, which was apparently a seven-minute walk from the taverna. I could see some ruins across the busy street and, since I couldn't find the store, decided to have a peek. The street was broad enough that I had to cross in two stages, and while I stood in the middle, trolleys and cars and motorcycles zipped in front of me. I felt swallowed by the city in a way I hadn't realized I'd been craving. I was no longer my body—I was nobody, just a regular tourist. It was a relief to have a break from myself.

I felt my phone vibrate in my pocket. *Everything okay?* Joe asked.

Heading back soon

We'll have to leave soon. You need to eat! Where are you?

I'm not exactly sure

Are you lost?

Maybe? I took a picture of where I was and sent it, despite how much data it would use up.

I have no idea where that is

Me neither

Just walk back toward the Acropolis

Okey, I wrote back, and I kept walking toward the ruins. I touched the fence around them, peered in, and then turned back. I took pictures of the buildings and street signs as I walked. Petted a cat.

ETA? Joe wrote.

Soon

When I found Joe, Katie, and Peter, they were still at the table, mostly empty plates around them. Katie squeezed my arm. "We were worried about you!"

"Were you?" I asked Joe.

"A little." He sounded sheepish.

"I was just down the street."

"How are you feeling?" he asked as we left to find Pericles.

"Fine."

~

Day 4: The follicles in my Fallopian tubes look like tentacles. Or dandelion puffs you can blow on to make a wish.

~

By the time we got to our egg retrieval two days later, the state of my follicles had improved. Dr. Sutton confirmed what our Greek doctor had said, *Just wait and see*, and in the end they were both right. The eager-beaver follicles had slowed down, and of the twelve original ones, nine were at similar sizes and maturities. The other three were passable, and in the meantime another three had sprung up. The eggs attached to those were probably too immature, but you never knew.

I took the trigger shot at eleven the night before the extraction, and from then on everything was tightly choreographed. Pericles picked us up exactly at eight. At the clinic Joe was whisked away to give his sperm sample. He'd downloaded porn on his phone in case the clinic's Wi-Fi or selection was lacking. "Just in case you see it," he told me, "I want you to know that I don't usually save it."

A nurse brought me to another room to get hooked up to an IV so they could administer a twilight anaesthetic for the procedure. She draped a heavy sheet across my bare legs while she tapped the veins on my arm. "Good luck," she said.

Joe joined me a minute later. "How was it?" I asked. He gave me an awkward thumbs up.

When it came time for the procedure, I walked to another room and settled onto a hospital bed. I put my feet in the stirrups, and they administered the anaesthetic. I quickly slipped into a fuzzy, hazy state. I felt dreamy and happy. Joe looked down at me and said, "You're doing great." He wore scrubs and a cap that pushed his hair down over his forehead and ears and made him look like a child. I laughed. I laughed again when the doctor walked in because for the first time he actually looked like a doctor, with scrubs over his expensive shirt.

"I am so excited," he said, sitting between my splayed legs. "You look wonderful."

I wanted to make a joke about whether he was referring to my eggs or my vagina, but the words drifted away from me.

He described each step of the procedure, but I didn't pay much attention until he said, "There are many eggs here," and I laughed again.

The drugs tapered off almost as soon as the procedure was done, and then we were free. I walked gingerly to Pericles's car, suddenly tender and vulnerable. I'd been stuffed full just an hour before, and I was now scraped clean. It was gross if I thought about it too much, the way my body had been manipulated by medications completely dictated by a stranger's whims. I knew it had all happened with my own agency, with my own money, but sometimes I felt like a kind of husk.

"Did it hurt?" Joe asked, watching me walk.

He asked me this question so frequently these days: when I gave myself injections, after an ultrasound, during sex—although we were definitely not having sex now that I felt so uncomfortable and bloated. I was ready for another question. I wanted to be asked if I felt good.

"Sort of."

"I can't believe they got sixteen eggs."

"Let's just implant all of the embryos and start a reality show."

"I don't know how else we're going to afford all those children."

Pericles opened the door for me. "Efaristo," I said to him.

"You learned Greek!"

"Just for you."

I don't know if I was imagining it, but he seemed to drive more slowly than usual back to the hotel, and I was grateful.

Katie and Peter were now off travelling. By the time they'd be back for their transfer, we would be away and would therefore miss them. When we saw them in the lobby after their retrieval, they didn't give us many details, and I didn't want to ask them how many eggs they'd extracted; it felt like asking them their salaries. They said everything was "awesome" and gave us hopeful smiles. Katie looked tired, though. We hugged and promised to keep in touch, even though I already knew I would never talk to them again. Like all our other travel friends, maybe we'd stay in touch on Facebook, occasionally post birthday greetings, but that was it—the most intense period of our friendship was done.

The night after our extraction, Joe and I were still at the hotel. We were going to leave for Hydra the next morning. We thought about going into Athens, but I was still tired and our ferry was early, so we checked out another nearby taverna that Katie and Peter had recommended. It seemed to be geared toward tourists and was full of English-speaking people—expats, not many Greeks—all ordering beers and frothy pink and peach cocktails that came in big round coupes. I wanted one of the frothy drinks. My body was now independent of the situation; Joe and I could hang out at a tourist bar, and I could drink something alcoholic.

"Date night!" Joe said when I told him that it felt weird to be so separate from something so important to us, petrie dishes with our names on them in a lab somewhere in Athens. "Think of it like a babysitting service."

"I want that," I told the waiter, pointing to one of the pink drinks.

He left us a bowl of chips, a carafe of water. We ordered lamb and ate the small pieces with our hands. Shared a big plate of fried potatoes. I speared all the tomatoes from the salad. I was still hungry and ordered a chocolate crepe for dessert, which had LOVE written on it in cursive with chocolate sauce. As we were eating, karaoke night started at the bar, and we stayed to watch. A man with white hair got up first to do "My Way." He rested his arm on a bar table while he sang. Next, a group of women did "Girls Just Want to Have Fun."

"Do you want to do a song?" Joe asked.

"No way." I normally loved karaoke. It was an activity that made me feel connected to my Filipino roots—Filipinos are known for their love of singing along to instrumental tracks of pop songs—but my stomach was still tender, and I didn't have the protective coating necessary for public singing.

"It might be fun." He leaned over and grabbed a song binder from the next table.

I looked over his shoulder. The selection was minimal, last updated in the early 2000s.

"I'm going to do a song for you," he said. I didn't believe him, but he got up and talked to someone. When his name was called, he stood up holding his beer. The music started, and two women in the front started enthusiastically clapping.

"I love this song!" one of them yelled.

Joe had chosen "I Will Always Love You." We'd once spent an afternoon in a hotel in Portugal watching *The Bodyguard* on television while felled by food poisoning. The bathroom was the size of a closet and disgusting, and we took turns running to it or sprawling out on the small double bed. But at least there'd been a TV and at least this movie was on, and we watched it hungrily, a distraction from everything else.

Joe sang terribly and missed most of the words, but the crowd cheered and clapped. The mistake people often make in karaoke is giving up too early—you need conviction, an almost embarrassing persistence to make it to the end, to not get dissuaded by garbled lyrics, vocal mistakes, off-tempo phrasings—and despite his lack of talent, Joe had that conviction. He was comfortable with performing because of his podcast. He knew how to hold a mic with confidence. He pointed to me while he sang, and I did a fake blush hand movement and a woman next to me smiled. *Young love*, her smile said.

When he sat down, I leaned over and kissed him, pulled back, hugged him, and then kissed him again. I remembered kissing Denny and felt guilty. Since it happened I'd tried to absolve myself of the guilt because I knew it didn't mean anything, and if I didn't talk about it or even think about it, it was as if it never happened. Sitting with Joe, in Athens, I was especially deeply relieved that he didn't know.

The next person who went up chose "So Long, Marianne." It felt appropriate since we were going to Hydra, where Leonard Cohen had written the song. Some people at the front put their arms around each other and sang along. I cried watching it all, and Joe put his arm around me too. I buried my face in his shirt, smelled his smell.

"Are you okay?" he asked when he noticed that the wet spot on his shirt was getting bigger.

"I don't know," I said.

"Let's go back."

I nodded. The song still wasn't over. He put down cash, and we got up, me still clinging to him as we walked away.

~~~

Day 8: An embryo is not a living thing; it is a clump of cells that may or may not divide into the number of cells necessary to become a viable pregnancy. An embryo does not die, it arrests. Our nurse calls with daily updates on the status of the embryos. When she tells us that three of our sixteen embryos arrested overnight, I feel a pang from the loss, from a diminished chance. Thirteen embryos still sounds good. The math works. When she calls the next day and says another three are gone, we think: Okay, still in the double digits. Then when she calls the third day and there are another two down, I want to throw up. Instead we hike up a path to an empty church and look down at the island and the sea. The sea is big; life is big. We still have eight embryos.

~~~

No cars are allowed on Hydra, so we'd wake up in the morning to the sound of donkeys clomping past our window. We went to remote beaches, jumped in cold water, walked up long stone paths, ate sweets coated in honey.

On our last full day before returning to Athens for the implantation, I found a kitten sprawled out in the sun on the windowsill, a skinny thing with dirty white fur and ginger-tipped ears and paws. When I opened the window, she woke up and tried to squeeze her way in. Instead of stopping her, I opened the window further. She crawled in and flopped on our bed. I scratched her head, and she closed her eyes in unbridled ecstasy.

"We should get her some milk," Joe said. "She's so little."

"I bet she doesn't have any problem finding food. You can tell she's smart just by looking at her."

We knew someone who'd brought home a stray dog they'd befriended in Thailand through a company that arranged the adoption; it was part of a program to save dogs off the street. Maybe we could do the same with this kitten.

I rubbed her exposed belly and noticed little pieces of what felt like grit in my fingernails. I looked more closely at my hands. The grit wiggled. It was, Joe and I realized simultaneously, a bug of some sort. Fleas? We looked at her again and noticed she had tiny black, moving spots all over her. This beautiful creature was crawling with bugs. There was one on our bedspread.

"Sorry, little buddy," Joe said as he picked her up and carefully put her back on the other side of the window. The kitten looked at us, suddenly haughty, and sauntered away. For the rest of the day, we kept an eye out for the kitten, but we never saw her. She probably found some other sucker to take her in.

In the end we had four embryos left, two to transfer and two to freeze. The morning of the transfer, I texted Pericles and then chugged a litre of water. Instead of the dreamy state

I'd been in for the retrieval, I would be one hundred percent sober for this one, with the added bonus of a full bladder. I felt strangely relaxed as I walked into the room in my gown and placed my feet in the stirrups. They were tanned from the sandals I'd worn for the past few days in Hydra.

"And they're in," the Greek doctor said when he was done. "Best of luck to all of you." He kissed us both on the cheek again before he left.

"All good?" Pericles asked afterwards. It was just us in the van. We'd requested to be dropped off at the beach. Katie and Peter had done this, and it seemed like a good idea when she'd told me.

"Yes," I said. I think I believed it.

"Have you seen my children yet?" he asked.

"No, can I see them?"

He turned his phone toward me. The screen was cracked, but two perfect faces stared back at us, little boys with chubby cheeks and tiny pearly teeth, both with black curly hair.

"They're adorable," I said sincerely and without envy. They looked pure. They were a good luck charm.

At the beach Joe and I staked out a spot. We hadn't changed into our bathing suits at the clinic, so we shimmied into them behind towels and then decided to pay extra for lounge chairs. I stretched out. My suit was a two-piece, but the top was more like a T-shirt than a bikini top so that my midriff wasn't always exposed. I hiked it up and tilted my stomach toward the sun.

From the lounge chair, I could see a small rocky island not too far away. *Island* was maybe too generous a word for what it was—more like a small cluster of flattish rocks. Someone had built a tiny white church on it, and the brightness of the white indicated that it was still maintained. I wanted to swim to the island, haul myself up, and say a little prayer. I could see others doing so and then diving off the rocks back into the water. At any other time in my life, I would've done it. Maybe I would've even done it when we were in Hydra. But today wasn't the right day.

Joe looked over and noticed my exposed belly, rounded and bruised from the dozens of needles. He reached over and patted it, and even though I'd been feeling so self-conscious about the way it looked, I put my hand on top of his so that he would keep it there.

I wanted so badly to believe we'd done everything we could: we'd done our procedures surrounded by mythology, even. We'd made our sacrifices. I said a prayer in my head from my lounge chair.

PART EIGHT: FALL

I kept having the same recurring dream. It was nighttime and I was driving Claire's car through unfamiliar city streets, anxious and unsure of where I was going. I turned down a narrow alleyway that opened up to an outdoor fruit market. I stopped the car, worried that the market owners would yell at me for blocking the entrance, but instead they beckoned me out. Street lights flooded the market in a way that reminded me of suburban baseball diamonds or backyard swimming pools at twilight. The market owners urged me to pick any fruit I wanted, and I racked my brain trying to think of the perfect one. I'd tried pineapple, mangosteen, pomegranates. *What could be next?* I thought. I woke up before I could figure it out.

Upon our return from Greece, I became obsessed with figs, which hadn't been ripe when we were there, but soon came into season and were shipped in big flat containers across the sea to our grocery stores. Sometimes they would be as expensive as buck-a-shuck oysters, and sometimes, when they were a little squishy, a steal for the lot. I kept my eye out for those deals and would eat them stirred into yogourt, baked in a tart, reduced to a jammy juice to eat with pork chops. I still didn't have a job, so I had time for all of this.

I needed a better project, though. One morning after Joe left for work, I drove across town to a fancy grocery store in the hope that I'd be inspired to make something I could write about on my blog. It occurred to me as I wandered the aisles that I should make Mom and Bart's wedding cake. They both had a sweet tooth; I would make them their dream cake.

I put the largest sack of flour into my cart. I grabbed a new bottle of pure vanilla extract and a beaker of vanilla pods. I bought a bag of sugar and one of confectioners' sugar, a roll of marzipan, fondant, some food colouring, baking powder, baking soda. We didn't have many baking ingredients at home since I hadn't baked in months. In the dairy aisle, unsalted butter was on sale so I bought a few boxes.

At home I unwrapped the marzipan and rolled some between my palms. It was like Play-Doh. I squeezed out a drop of the red food colouring and kneaded the marzipan it in until it turned a light pink. I shook some confectioners' sugar onto a cutting board so that it wouldn't stick and used a small sharp knife to cut out little petals. Pink teardrops. Once I had a few, I rolled another piece into a stem and glued some petals on the side, dipping my finger into a cup of water for adhesive. Little roses. They weren't perfect, but they were still beautiful—or at least they could be beautiful if I practised more, and even if I didn't get any better, they were beautiful the way flowers were out in the wild, even when their leaves were wilted or ripped or rotting. I left the roses out on the counter overnight, and in the morning they were dried out into delicate pieces I could use to decorate a cake. The first cake I made was plain vanilla with chocolate frosting. It was good, but it felt too much like a toddler's birthday cake—I could do better. I emailed everyone, *I'm making the wedding cake!*

What do you know about wedding cakes? I texted Denny.

Ever since Greece I hadn't had much to say to him. Sometimes I'd type something out with my thumbs only to immediately delete, delete, delete. But then another old blog friend posted an Instagram story asking for recommendations for a business trip she had to take to Toronto, and I'd responded, and we'd met for lunch. It had been a lovely, out-of-the-ordinary experience, and it reminded me that, just like in the old days, my blogging relationships were fulfilling and interesting and, ultimately, harmless. I'd let things get a little weird with Denny, but I thought I could achieve that balance with him again too.

For someone who has never been married, he wrote back, *I know a lot.*

I knew he'd worked at a bakery, and it turned out his time there had been at the height of wedding season. I tried a different vanilla recipe he suggested, this one less cloying, with raspberry filling and a white buttercream. It was better.

Joe and I started eating cake for breakfast. I'd leave him a slice on a napkin on the counter so he could eat it as he walked to the subway.

I sent Denny pictures from the aisles of the grocery stores. He liked seeing the Canadian brands the way I liked seeing the American ones. We also worked out cake math together. Even though the wedding was going to be small, I wanted to make sure there was more than enough for everyone—and most importantly, it had to be perfect. We scaled up recipes together in a shared Google Sheet. Once we were accessing it at the same time and I watched the numbers change before my eyes as he typed.

Hi, I typed in a cell.

Whoa so weird, he wrote below.

I still wasn't pregnant. Shortly after Joe and I had returned from Greece, I went back to our regular clinic for a blood test to see if either or both of the embryos had implanted.

My nurse had called with the results one day just before lunchtime. I was on the couch with my eyes closed, not sleeping, still jet-lagged. Normally I kicked jet lag quickly, but I couldn't shake it this time around. I hoped it was a pregnancy symptom.

"Hi!" I answered too brightly and loudly.

I was pretty sure I knew what she was going to say. Ever since we'd returned I'd been feeling the familiar turning in my abdomen that I associated with my period.

"Is this Laura?"

"Yes."

"I'm sorry. The blood test was negative."

This was the fifth time I'd had this conversation with her. "Are you sure?"

"I'm so sorry."

"It's fine." I tried to maintain my brightness.

The nurse told me Dr. Sutton wanted to see us after I had my period and then said a few more things that didn't register, something about a frozen transfer for the two remaining embryos that had been shipped over and were being kept in storage for an additional thousand dollars a year that we hadn't figured into our original budget. When I hung up, I texted Joe. *Negative.* He called me a few minutes later, but I ignored it. *I don't feel like talking*, I typed.

He called me two more times, and I swiped the calls away. *Don't worry, I'm okey*

I'd really like to talk to you. He included a period at the end of the sentence, which meant he was serious.

I need a minute

Please

I finally called and burst into tears the minute he answered. I don't remember what he said, just that he listened to me cry and then I didn't cry again for the rest of the day until he got home and hugged me. As he held me, I could feel his body shudder. It was the first time he'd cried since the miscarriage, when he'd walked into the bathroom and found me sitting on the floor with my head in my hands.

"I was so sure it worked this time," he said.

I knew this process was hard for him too, but he'd told me frequently that it was okay if we didn't have a baby, and while that sometimes annoyed me, it also made things easier. It meant that if it didn't work out, he would be able to convince me of the advantages of that. I assumed he felt similarly—that if I got pregnant, any ambivalence he might feel would be eclipsed by my enthusiasm. We balanced each other out. Now, with both of us on the same side, it threw off the teeter-totter arrangement. We were just a sinking thud in the sand, the other end impossibly up in the air.

"You said it was fine if it didn't work out," I said, almost as if I were chastising him.

"Of course it will be fine, but I really wanted *this* to work. We had such a good trip. It felt right."

"We still have two embryos left," I said. I clung to the number, which was bigger than both zero and one.

"Yeah."

"And it only takes one. That's what they always say." In this moment I enjoyed being the one doing the comforting. "Should we get pizza for dinner?"

It was our ritual now. Negative test meant pizza and wine.

"That would be good."

Day 14: Negative.

When my period started, I called to make the clinic appointment. Dr. Sutton sat across from us and said that the two frozen embryos weren't in great shape. I was surprised because I assumed that as long as they hadn't arrested, they were fine. The Greek doctor hadn't said anything bad about them either, but it turned out that embryos were graded with letters, like a report card, and ours were a C.

"Just because these aren't As doesn't mean they're bad," Dr. Sutton said.

"But a C is a shitty grade," Joe said. I liked that he used the word *shitty*. I liked the way he said it too, spitting it out like a scornful teenager.

"Think of it more as staging than grading then. A C embryo is a tiny bit behind a B and A at the moment they're frozen. They keep developing, though—many C embryos go on to implant like normal."

"So should we be worried?"

"I can't make any guarantees, but don't be worried yet."

Yet? I looked at Joe. The look meant *I am worried*.

"Isn't it a bad sign that the first two embryos didn't implant?"

"Not all embryos implant; that's just the way it goes. It could be a number of things."

We left the office discouraged. I'd been so *relaxed* in Athens. I could still conjure a hot night, the pink-and-purple skies of the sunset in Hydra or from our balcony in Athens—not as dramatic as Oia, but still beautiful. What more could we have done to encourage a hospitable environment for a baby? I should've gone to that jewellery store for a proper good luck charm.

"Fuck all of this," Joe said when we got back into the car.

"Yep," I replied.

I brought some cake for Mom to try the next time I went over. She and Bart had decided not to sell her house right away, to wait till after the wedding at least, but until then we were slowly getting ready for it to go on the market. First we had to clear out the excess, make a dent in the lifetime of artifacts, from both my youth and Claire's, that had to be purged before the house could be sold. Claire's room had been converted to a guest room, so a lot had already been cleared out, but there were still boxes shoved into my room and in the basement. I sifted through them, occasionally taking pictures of what I found to send Claire. *Keep?*

No, she responded every time until she eventually told me to stop asking. *Just burn it all.*

I didn't want to, though. I liked this history, the high school essays and photos of friends we didn't speak to anymore and clothes that didn't fit. Mom had a trove of our childhood clothes, and I set it aside. Maybe one day there would be a child to wear them.

"I think Rosalie might fit into some of those," Mom said.

"Yeah, maybe," I said, taping the box shut.

"So Claire thinks the wedding should be in Niagara-on-the-Lake."

"She does?"

"She suggested it last night on the phone. Bart likes wine; it's close. She offered to buy a ticket for Gloria and her husband to come."

"That could be nice."

I called Claire when I returned to the basement to do more cleaning. "When were you going to tell me about your wedding idea?" I asked when she picked up.

"Oh, did Mom tell you? I just thought of it yesterday."

"You never tell me anything."

"I was going to tell you today, I've just been busy. It's a good idea, no?"

"Olivia has a kid. It makes travelling more complicated."

"Driving an hour and a half to Niagara-on-the-Lake hardly counts as travelling. I was already looking at Airbnbs and found a huge one we could stay in. Enough rooms for all of us. Also a hot tub."

"Sounds like you've got it all figured out."

"Are you annoyed?"

"I thought we would plan as a group, I guess."

"I'm not saying we have to do this—it was an idea, and Mom was into it right away. Also, we need to plan something quickly."

Maybe this was now part of our Christmas ritual: Claire doing something that bothered me, me having to get over myself. I was just tired of *going places*. Even a quick road trip seemed like so much effort. I wanted to stay in one spot for a while, experience the consistent quotidian rhythm of a life at home, but somehow in the past two years I'd been to Barbados, Las Vegas, Greece, and now I had this wedding trip. I wondered if I'd ever get an excuse to just stay home instead of being a loose ball in a pinball machine.

The clinic wanted us to wait another two cycles before the frozen transfer. I was still unemployed, still looking for jobs half-heartedly while I received EI. Dad started taking an interest in my job search and would sometimes call me in the morning to check in.

"Have I told you how I got my first job?" he asked me.

"Yes," I replied, but he kept going.

"I walked into the lobby of the engineering firm I wanted to work for and asked if they had any open positions. They gave me an interview a few days later, and I was hired at the end of it."

"Jobs don't work like that anymore. I can't just walk in."

"Maybe it's worth trying. It might set you apart from other applicants."

"I think it would work *against* me."

I could tell he was frustrated, but I wasn't sure why. He'd

never been involved in my career in the past. I wasn't asking him for money.

"Claire doesn't have anything you can help with?"

"I'm maybe going to write for her," I said.

"That's something."

"It's not a job."

"I'm going to invest in the Lookout."

"Well, that's great for both of you."

I hung up and immediately went to bed to take a nap. I didn't even bother sending a message to Claire about Dad's investment—I didn't want to know. I was constantly exhausted even though I had no real reason to be tired: I wasn't working; I wasn't pregnant.

"You don't think you can work with Claire?" Joe asked when I told him about the conversation with my Dad.

"She doesn't have a job for me!" I hadn't asked her outright, but she also hadn't offered anything. She had asked me for the writing I'd done in Greece, which I'd sent over with the caveat that I wasn't actually ready for her to publish it anywhere. Now, even worse, I was starting to feel defensive that she hadn't asked me for more.

Once everyone agreed that yes, Niagara-on-the-Lake at Christmas would be a beautiful place for Mom and Bart to get married, Olivia asked me to lunch. We'd only seen each other at family gatherings, never one-on-one, and I hadn't thought to seek out a relationship with her. I was nervous when I accepted the lunch date.

We met at an Italian place near her office. I ordered a glass of wine; she got sparkling water. When the waiter set the glasses down, Olivia took the straw out of her glass and started fiddling with it. She looked down at the table.

"I know it's early, but since we're going to be, you know,

celebrating things together, I don't want any of you speculating about why I'm not drinking."

"Oh, we would never," I said, even though I knew we probably would.

"I'm pregnant. It's only seven weeks, but I thought I would tell you now."

"Congratulations!"

I hadn't expected this at lunch, or at all. She'd had champagne at Mom's house. I thought she had, anyway. I'd filled her glass at one point. Also, Rosalie was six years old—it would be a fairly sizable gap between the two kids. I'd assumed she and Thomas were done having kids.

"And cheers!" I took a gulp of my wine. I'd gotten good at congratulating people about their pregnancies, but usually I found out at a comfortable remove, like through a text message or a Facebook announcement, rarely in person.

"Listen, I know you've been struggling." Olivia leaned over and touched my hand. I flinched for a second, but she looked sincerely anguished. "My dad told me about your trip to Greece."

"It's totally okay. IVF doesn't usually work the first time anyway."

"At least you got a good vacation from it?"

"We did. Greece is beautiful. I have another embryo transfer coming up." I was eager to turn the conversation away from me. "Anyway, Rosalie must be so excited to have a sibling."

"She is! I couldn't help it; I told her right away."

"And you're feeling okay?"

"The nausea is pretty bad, and I'm tired." Unlike me, she had the right reasons to be tired. "Did you know that when I was pregnant with Rosa, my mom was sick?"

I knew Bart's wife had died six years ago, but I hadn't placed Rosalie's birth in that context. For the most part, I didn't think about Bart's life or Olivia's, unless it coincided with my mom's. "Did your mother meet Rosalie?"

"No. She was diagnosed a month after I found out I was pregnant, and then I gave birth two weeks after her funeral."

"Oh, that's so sad."

"I was at the hospital with her all the time even though Thomas and Dad told me not to go. They were worried I would be too exposed to viruses or whatever, but I never got sick."

"That must have been so stressful for all of you."

"I was happy to be with her. Once an ultrasound technician did my stomach after my mom's appointment so we could see Rosalie. It totally wasn't allowed, but they felt sorry for us."

"Rosalie is so cute," I said, not sure how to respond.

"She really is. I'm hoping to feel more connected to this pregnancy, almost like I have to make it up to her too. I was so distracted the first time."

"I can imagine." Olivia obviously wanted to talk about this, so I tried to remain present in the conversation. "It must have been hard to be happy when you were worried about your mother."

"Yeah. And Dad too. He didn't deal with it well either."

"I'm not surprised."

"I *was* surprised, though. I wasn't used to him being emotional then. He's changed since." I didn't know Bart well enough to comment, and as I tried to formulate a response, she kept going. "Enough about me, though. I wanted you to know that I'm really so sorry you and Joe are having trouble. I'm glad you're going to have another transfer. I didn't know."

"I appreciate it." I felt embarrassed when someone felt sorry for us. Joe was still sometimes getting emails from listeners curious about what was happening, but I'd asked him not to give an update just yet. Anyway, Amit's baby was born, and there had been an announcement for that, a cute picture of the newborn—a girl!—wearing a custom-made onesie with their podcast logo printed on it.

Sometimes I felt like I'd lost perspective on the scope of my problem: What did it mean to not be able to have kids? In my bones it felt like nothing short of a tragedy, an immense grief. But was it? It was a loss of something that didn't exist and that many people didn't even want, so how could it be *that* bad? Was I exaggerating? People got over their personal griefs all the time—Olivia had lost her mother and Bart his wife, for instance, and look at them now. I should've been able to deal with my own problems too.

The waiter came by with our food, and Olivia and I looked at him for a second like we had no idea why he was interrupting our important conversation.

"If there's anything I can do to help, please ask," Olivia said, and she sounded so sincere that I felt sheepish about how little I'd thought about her life until now.

I figured, though, that I might as well be completely honest with her if she was being honest with me. "The hardest part is that it feels like everyone in the world is getting pregnant these days."

"Like me?"

"Yeah, exactly!"

"That's why I was nervous to tell you."

"We're just at the age where it happens all the time. I'm trying not to be upset by it, but it's tricky."

"That must be hard. Are you okay, though?"

"I hate how everyone always asks me if I'm okay."

"Me too, actually. Thomas asks me constantly. I've been puking a lot; I didn't have morning sickness with Rosa, and I'm trying to hide this from work. I'm afraid if too many people know, something will go wrong."

"That sucks."

"Yeah. But, I'm sorry, I do have to ask...*are* you okay?"

I felt tears in my eyes. Sometimes I wondered how much water I had in my body, how I could cry so frequently, so immediately, without being a desert by this point. "It's just a shitty situation."

"Does IVF hurt?"

"Well, it doesn't feel good."

"Does it mess up your hormones?"

"Unfortunately."

It would've been easy for me to hate Olivia for her pregnancy. Not just for the fact of being pregnant, but for being pregnant and in such close proximity to me. I couldn't mute her the way I could a Facebook friend; I couldn't reschedule dinner plans because they involved our parents, who were getting married.

"I'm sorry. I don't know what else to say."

"You don't have to apologize. And don't feel guilty about being pregnant. I'm really happy for you, I promise! I'm so excited that Claire and I will get the chance to be aunts to your kids."

Olivia's eyes welled up too. "It's amazing that we'll be stepsisters. I always wanted siblings."

"Claire and I have two half-sisters from our dad's second marriage. We don't get along very well."

"I hope we get along."

"I think we will."

We ended up sharing dessert before leaving.

The next morning, I got a text from Olivia. *BARF.*

Damn, sorry. Did anyone see?

No, I think I'm good at hiding my puking. An important skill?

From then on Olivia and I started texting more regularly. Sometimes she'd send little videos of Rosalie, who wanted to say hi to her auntie. I'd respond with a selfie of me making a face at her. My phone, which had been mostly dedicated to short logistical texts with Joe, clinic follow-ups, and touchpoints with Claire and Mom, on top of the uptick in messages from Denny, was now a more exciting and varied place with these messages from Olivia.

You didn't tell me Olivia was pregnant?? Claire texted me a few days later.

Did Mom tell you?

Yeah. Are you okay with her news?

Totally, I responded.

When the embryo transfer date came, I woke up feeling a sense of dread rather than excitement. I climbed down the loft ladder and grabbed a bottle of water from the fridge to chug. Then I got dressed and chugged more water while Joe was in the shower. I needed a full bladder, and I was determined to have the fullest bladder a person could have, the fullest bladder in the entire clinic. On the drive over, I realized how badly I had to pee, but I didn't complain. I walked with short, painful steps from the car to the elevator.

"I thought by now you'd know the exact amount of water you need for these procedures," Joe said.

"Don't say anything else and don't make me laugh," I said through clenched teeth. "If I laugh, I will pee."

The paperwork and preparation of changing into a gown at the clinic distracted me, but when the ultrasound technician looked at my abdomen and remarked on how much water I'd drunk, I couldn't help myself. I didn't want the insertion of my potential child to be marred by the memory of me pissing myself. "I really have to pee."

"You can go if you want while we're waiting for the doctor. You have enough liquid in there."

"Really?"

"Yes, it's not all going to get flushed away immediately."

"I think you underestimate how much I have to go."

This made him laugh, and Joe too, and I relaxed, which made it even harder to hold in my pee. I shuffled to the nearby bathroom and went, just enough to stop me from feeling like I was going to explode.

Dr. Sutton arrived, her hair perfect under her cap, as always.

"How are the embryos?" Joe asked.

"Unfortunately one didn't survive the thaw."

I hated how many of our interactions with our doctor started off with the word *unfortunately*.

"It only takes one, right?" Joe said before I could open my mouth and say anything back.

How many times did a person need to receive bad news before becoming numb to it? Did I just expect bad news because I had no prior history of good news? Was it a self-fulfilling prophecy? Maybe I wasn't getting pregnant because I didn't believe deep down that I could get pregnant. Were my negative thoughts creating antibodies against good ones? Of course I knew none of this was true, but I had a nagging feeling that maybe, somehow, the universe *did* work like that.

The monitor hooked up to the ultrasound wand was tilted toward all of us so that we could watch what Dr. Sutton was doing. When the wand and speculum were inserted inside of me, we looked at my uterus, the big empty space of it. The procedure felt separate from me, as if it were being done in another room that we happened to have viewing access to. She used a catheter to guide the single remaining embryo inside me.

"There it is," she said. A dot in the void. And then she removed the catheter, the speculum. "I'll see you in two weeks."

The room cleared out quickly. Joe helped me off the bed, and we went back to the prep room, where I could sit in a reclining chair with a blanket for as long as I wanted. The blankets were hospital-issued, that light blue colour I knew so well from Mom's job.

"How do you feel?" Joe asked.

"I have to pee again." The thought of peeing scared me—what if it jostled the embryo? I knew by now that this was impossible, but I sat still for a few more minutes and thought about our little underachiever, the dot, the potential of a human life.

On the drive home, I noticed the leaves on the trees were starting to change colour. Time just kept passing. "I don't feel good about this." I wept into my hands. Joe didn't have anything to add.

And then I was right: negative, two weeks later.

Olivia invited me out to look for dresses. Mom and Bart's ceremony wasn't going to be formal, but we all wanted something new and pretty for the occasion. We walked into a store and started browsing the racks, holding up dresses.

"What kind of dress are you looking for?" I asked. I didn't know Olivia's style well enough to suggest outfits to her.

"I'll be about sixteen weeks then, so I won't need a maternity dress, but it should be...forgiving. What about you?"

"I probably won't need a maternity dress either."

"You never know."

Joe and I didn't have any treatments on the horizon. "I'm pretty sure."

We chose a few dresses to try on. My last one was pale pink, silky, with loose three-quarter length sleeves and a deep V-neck. I couldn't quite reach around to zip myself up in the change room.

"Are you still there?" I called to Olivia.

"Yeah. These dresses are terrible. What about yours?"

"Can you help me with this zipper?" I opened the change room door and peeked out. A second later she came out of hers wearing a black sleeveless shift that was far too big.

"I look like I'm in mourning."

"Except with glitter."

"Ugh." She came over and zipped me up. "That dress is perfect on you."

I looked in the three-way mirror. It *was* nice. "I don't usually wear pink."

"You should get it. It's beautiful."

"Did you try on everything?"

"Yes, this was the best one, if that tells you anything."

Before changing back I took pictures of myself in the mirror from a few different angles. On a whim, I sent the best one to Denny, who was still at the top of my messages history after we had chatted that morning. *I'm wearing this to my mom's wedding. Good baking outfit?*

I'd never sent him a picture like this. Up until now, the most suggestive message I'd sent him was a video of me picking meat off a roast chicken. I'd tucked the leftovers in the fridge after dinner one night, and when I removed the chicken the next day to make soup, it was half congealed in fat. I started tearing off chunks of meat, spreading the bones and rescuing every last piece so that nothing would be wasted. I wiped my hands off on a dishtowel and pressed record on my phone, and in the clip he could see my fingers slick with chicken fat, the meat in a pile next to me, the rough bones pinkish and white and greasy. The chicken was seemingly a creature I'd killed for food with my own bare hands.

I shoved my phone into my bag, feeling silly. When I pulled it out later to tell Joe I was on my way home, Denny had responded with a series of fire and heart eyes emojis. I giggled before I could stop myself.

That weekend I tried another cake recipe, popped the pans into the oven, and then went to take a shower. When I got out, Joe was looking at my phone, which I'd left out on the counter.

He looked up at me. "Who's Denny?"

I felt weak for a second. "An old blog friend of mine."

"Oh, *Denny*, your blog boyfriend?"

I was embarrassed that he remembered the term. "I forgot we referred to dudes like that," I lied.

"He was the one you were closest to. I mostly remember him because his name was Denny."

"Yeah, that's him."

"You're still in touch?"

"He has experience baking wedding cakes, so he's giving me some tips on what to do for Mom." I took my phone back and quickly looked down to see what Joe had seen.

"Oh, that's random," he said.

"I guess a little?"

"Have you ever met him?"

"Just a bit, when I was in Vegas."

"Last Christmas?"

"I think I told you about Vegas."

"You totally didn't."

I almost believed myself that I'd told him. "Oh my god, you never remember anything. Anyway, it's not a big deal."

The main reason the blog boyfriends had not been a perceived threat in the past was because there was no secrecy around them. The fact that I hadn't brought up Denny this round made it weird, and I knew that, but I'd been telling myself that it didn't matter.

Joe's concerned face, however, told me that it did matter.

"Okay." He disappeared into the bathroom and came out in gym clothes. "I'm going for a run."

"But there's cake." I pulled the pans out and set them on the stovetop to cool. I'd made these cakes with the most expensive cocoa I could find, from a gourmet shop on the west side of the city, and I was planning on sandwiching raspberry jam between the layers. I wanted to give Joe an entire layer plain, just hand him a huge slab of chocolate cake, still warm, so that he could eat it and tell me it was perfect the way it was. I wanted him to ask why I didn't just stop obsessing over what cake to make Mom and Bart because they would love it no matter what.

"I don't want any cake right now, Laura."

I didn't like that he said my name.

When he came home an hour later, he was quiet at first and refused my offer for cake again. "Do you want to have a baby with me, or do you just want a baby?" he asked eventually. He was still in his neon-green running tank, and his hair was all sweaty.

"What? I want to have a baby with you."

I wondered how many of the messages to Denny he'd seen. He knew the password to my phone. I knew the password to his, and even if I didn't, I could answer all of the security questions to figure it out: the first street he lived on, his mother's maiden name, his first pet.

I cringed at the thought of Joe reading the exchanges, my attempts at flirting or being charming. I didn't want him to have those sentences in his head, to jump to conclusions.

"Things get harder with a baby. Amit isn't getting any sleep and still has to go to work every day. What if they get harder for us in other ways? What if you want to see other people? It's a lot harder to split up with a kid in the picture."

"Why are you even talking about splitting up?" I started crying. "If this is about those texts you saw, there's nothing to it."

"I didn't see multiple texts. Would it have been worse if I'd seen them all?"

"No, not at all."

"Can you show them to me then?"

"Show you what? The texts?"

"Yes."

"You really want to see my message history?"

"Why didn't you tell me you saw Denny in Vegas?"

"We had one drink together."

"You had a drink with your blog boyfriend and you didn't think I should know?"

"I'm sorry," I said, still crying. "It was dumb. It was before we did IVF and I was depressed and we were in Vegas and it was just a coincidence that he was there for a bachelor party."

"His bachelor party?!"

"No, for one of his friends."

"Right. So everyone was on their best behaviour."

"It wasn't like that at all." I was digging in my heels about the kiss. Joe did not have to know about it. "Claire even met him."

"Seriously?"

I felt stupid for lying about that and reminded myself to tell Claire in case it ever came up, but it seemed to make it less of a big deal if Joe thought Denny didn't meet me alone.

"Laura, this whole thing is just really weird to me. I don't know what to think."

"It's fine. Let's just forget about it."

Maybe this was all a sign that Joe and I should give up on having a baby, on us. If a baby was considered a miracle, was I cursed because I couldn't have one? When had it been decided? Before I was conceived? Or was it written into the egg that had come from my mother's body, or the sperm from my father that had crashed into it?

Or maybe Joe and I just weren't fated to have a baby together. At this point it was hard to separate fate from science. The doctors had failed us so many times, and now we were failing each other too. I wondered if the relationships of all couples who wanted kids would survive if the process had to be drawn out like ours. I suspected the answer was no.

Joe and I had started dating when I was sixteen and he was seventeen, just like in *The Sound of Music*. That single year made a difference; I was awed by him being an older man, so much more intriguing and mysterious than the boys in my own grade. All I knew about him—Joey—was that the soccer coach had yelled at him for wearing black nail polish and that he'd quit in protest.

I couldn't believe he chose me, but he did, me, out of all the girls who hung out with the skateboarder boys after school at the skate park by the river. You could find me there at least three days a week. Claire came occasionally, and after the first time she joined me, she asked on our walk home, "So, you just watch them?"

Now, as an adult, I felt like it was some kind of intellectual failing in my younger self that yes, that was exactly what I did: just watched. I'd never skated, never tried. It felt like more than just passive observation, though. Those skateboarding older boys with their floppy hair and jeans and grimy All Stars: they were freshly unearthed marble statues of Roman gods, all litheness and clean lines, utterly deserving of unquestioning worship and deep study. And shouldn't everyone have that phase in their life, of uncomplicated adoration for something or someone? You need it so that you can practise how to love optimistically, generously, how to open your heart to something with no guarantee that it will love you back.

When the boys stopped skating, they would sit with us under the shade of the trees. Some would smoke, share cigarettes. We took swigs from each other's Cokes or water bottles, and these exchanges of vessels that touched our various mouths felt so intimate, so mature. This is what grown-ups did, we believed—shared beverages.

Sometimes the boys lay down, stretched out on the grass. Sometimes one would put his head in your lap! Sometimes it didn't mean anything, but sometimes it did. One day in early May, an afternoon that felt like the middle of August because it was so hot, Joey took off his baseball cap and shook his head to loosen his chin-length hair. He leaned back on his elbows close to me and then scooted backwards a bit so that the top of his head was on my thigh. I felt the tendons on the back of his neck against my jean shorts. I stayed casual, but snuck looks at his hair, his forehead. He always had good skin, not zit-covered teenage boy skin, but smooth, olive skin—maybe a bit oily, but that was its only flaw. I wanted to absent-mindedly stroke his hair, run my fingers through it.

Claire hadn't been there, but I told her about it that evening. "Do you even like him?"

I buried my head in a pillow and shouted, "Yes!"

"I didn't hear you."

"Yes!"

"Ugh," she said. "Calm down."

This blur of adolescent love. The phone calls. The notes passed back and forth between me and my friends, me and Joey, me and Joey's friends. More afternoons sharing Cokes, his head in my lap. Finally him walking me home. Finally us sitting on my front stoop and him kissing me. My first real kiss. Not like the kissing games from middle school. We kissed and kissed. I was so in love, so wholly in love, that it was stupefying.

I wonder how I would've turned out if I hadn't had the experience of love at sixteen, a love that was not only innocent, but reciprocated. Of course there was drama, but it was ordinary drama that I recognized from television, from movies, drama that I enjoyed despite the heartache it also caused. It stretched out over the endless months of the last half of our time at high school. Some tearful fights, my mother telling me to slow down, Claire saying, "Laur, I'm worried about you," lots of discussion about virginity and the pros and cons of its maintenance, poetry written for my English class that I ceremoniously burned when I announced that Joey and I were over for real this time. For our formal he asked another girl to be his date. We were broken up, but *come on*. Then one of the other skater boys asked me, and I said yes. But of course by the end of the night, Joey and I were back together again. Forever, I said to myself. Who could've predicted that I was right?

Because imagine that I was. Imagine that we lost our virginity to each other in his bedroom in the house that his parents still lived in and would live in until they died. I was seventeen when it happened; it was a new millennium, and Coldplay's "Yellow" was on the radio all the time. The song was too commercial for us and our friends, and we made fun of it so much that we all obviously secretly loved it.

This is how a pop song sticks—it needles into you at these specific moments in your life when you're teetering on the edge of something, on the cusp of surrender. These songs with these perfectly timed tonal shifts. I barely remembered us dancing to the first song at our wedding ("God Only Knows"), but when I heard "Yellow" I remembered being a teenager convinced she was an adult.

Now I'd hear it somewhere—in a waiting room, sung by a busker in the subway, in some tourist bar in Thailand while Joe (he dropped the *y* sometime in university) was getting me another beer—and my heart would do that old familiar lurch. It happened again in the car the other day, and I'd turned off the radio, unable to deal with the feeling. Instead I tried to channel what Claire had told me that first night: *Ugh, calm down.*

Olivia forwarded me a job posting from where she worked, a health and wellness company that made all kinds of vitamins and supplements and powders. They needed someone on their content team, and she'd thought of me. *You would be perfect*, she wrote, even though she knew nothing about my work. I applied, and they called to arrange an interview a week later.

Over the next two weeks I had one interview, then two. They sent me an offer soon after the second. Olivia and I wouldn't be working together directly, but we would be in the same office. We were both excited by this, and I went over for dinner the day I found out. Joe was working late again.

I'm so happy for you! Claire wrote me a few hours later. Olivia and I were chatting in her kitchen while Thomas put Rosalie to bed. *I want details. Call me.*

I'm at Olivia's right now, I'll call later

I put Claire on speakerphone when I drove home. "Olivia helped me get the job," I explained.

"Wow, you'll be stepsisters *and* co-workers."

I could detect a strange tone in Claire's voice. She hadn't said anything outright about being jealous, but she occasionally made this kind of offhand comment. I never knew how to respond, so I'd ignored it. I barely saw other people these days; I spent most of my free time with Olivia, and even when I would see friends, I'd invite her to join us. We also had regular family dinners with Mom and Bart, not weekly, but almost biweekly. Olivia, Rosalie, and I would meet Mom at Bart's house. Sometimes Joe and Thomas would join, but we tended to congregate on the female side. Even Bart would eventually retreat so it would just be us left at the dinner table, talking and planning. Occasionally Claire would call while we were meeting, and she would talk to Mom or me but not Olivia because they didn't know each other well enough.

I pulled into my parking spot and was about to end the call, but Claire kept talking.

"I have a job announcement too, actually," she said.

"Really?"

"I'm going to work on the Lookout full time." Over the past few months, they'd accumulated more funding, most crucially from a business incubator that focused on health startups, enough for her to take the plunge and join Shannon. "Dad invested some money in the company. It's kind of weird, but nice."

"He's always believed in you." I didn't mention that I'd already known about his investment.

"Yeah."

"So does this mean you'll be busier now?"

"We have a team of five, and Shannon and I are talking to more investors."

"You should have flexibility, though, right? Like, you could probably come to Toronto before Mom's wedding."

"Maybe, we'll see how things go."

"I'm sure she would love to have you around sooner."

"I'll try my best. What's the timing of your frozen transfer?"

I hadn't told anyone that the transfer had already come and gone. I figured that either it would work and we'd have good news, or it wouldn't work and we would have another plan that I could share. The problem was that there was no plan. Joe and I were still delicate around each other—we didn't talk about babies or embryos. However, he had told people: all of his podcast listeners.

I feel like I owe all of you an update, he'd started before launching into the previous few months. The trip to Greece, the failed transfer. He sounded choked up when he got to the end, and Amit asked what we were doing next. *We don't know.* I'd always suspected that my family didn't listen to the podcast—it wasn't really of particular interest to them, although I thought maybe Claire would like the updates. But the episode aired, and none of them said anything to me.

"I'm not sure when we'll do it," I said to Claire on the phone, noncommittal. "I should probably start this job first."

"That makes sense. Well, congratulations on the job. I'm glad it worked out."

"You too," I replied. "It's so exciting that you're able to quit."

We hung up, and I felt far away from Claire, like we were colleagues instead of sisters.

PART NINE: WINTER

Travelling was sometimes so stupid, the unnecessary effort of it. It was December 23, and we were already behind schedule getting to the Airbnb we would all be sharing for Mom and Bart's wedding. Joe and I had left later than planned, and when we went to get Claire from Mom's house, we realized we couldn't fit everything in the trunk. It wasn't that we had too much stuff—we'd just put everything in carelessly and couldn't get the trunk closed. We had to remove it all and reload, making sure my cake supplies were carefully nestled so that nothing would be jostled on the way over. This meant playing Tetris in the trunk while we shivered, cranky and in need of coffee. I used to be better at this, at going somewhere and being amused by the mishaps.

Claire had only arrived in Toronto the evening before; she had been too busy to come any sooner. I hadn't seen her since last Christmas—our longest time apart from each other ever—and she felt skinnier when I hugged her. She smelled of sandalwood and cigarettes even though I didn't think she was smoking anymore. We were quiet in the car, Claire's car that I no longer thought of as hers, and this time Joe drove. It started to sleet, and we got into a brief fight over who should've remembered to take the car in for winter tires (me, probably, but I didn't want to admit it.)

Bart and Mom had already left, and Olivia had texted me that she, Thomas, and Rosalie were also on the road.

We were the last to arrive at the Airbnb. Mom and Bart had already come and gone; they'd left to go look at their wedding venue. Rosalie was on the couch with her parents, her head in Olivia's lap, her socked feet on Thomas, kicking the air absent-mindedly. She wore a pair of headphones to listen to the tablet she had propped up on her stomach, and every so often she took swigs of water from a sippy cup. For all our struggle to have a baby, Joe and I knew very little about children. I'd spent a lot of time with Rosalie in the past few months, but just for short bursts, usually revolving around a meal. Sometimes I could feel myself studying her, almost anthropologically.

"I would get up and give you guys a hug, but I can't move at the moment," Olivia said and gestured toward Rosalie.

"Are you my aunt yet, Laura?" Rosalie asked.

"Almost."

She smiled. "I love you."

I was moved and looked at Olivia, who smiled but also rolled her eyes. "She means it, but she's also really into telling everyone she loves them these days. She told the clerk at the gas station today."

"Claire is going to be your aunt too," I said. "Do you remember Claire?"

"No," she said, barely glancing up again.

"She's only seen me on phone screens," Claire said. "I'm not offended."

"This Airbnb you chose is beautiful," Olivia said to Claire, as if apologizing for Rosalie.

I'd seen the listing for the home, and Claire had told me to ignore the exorbitant price because she had some kind of steep discount from an acquaintance who worked at the company. It was a large split-level ranch-style house located on a sprawling multi-acre piece of land surrounded by vineyards. The branches were bare and spindly in December, but the sleet from the morning had frozen into delicate droplets. There was forest toward the back of the property, and the trail leading up to it had an accumulation of snow despite the dampness.

I went to the kitchen to unpack my cake stuff. I'd brought all my own appliances and pots because I didn't want to rely on the Airbnb kitchen. It was a good decision because, while I'd been impressed by the gorgeous gas burners and stainless steel appliances pictured in the listing, every other utensil was terrible: a glass cutting board, a single old wooden spoon, but, for some reason, four huge soup ladles. The set of knives on the counter was passable since I wasn't going to be chopping much, but of the random assortment of mixing bowls under the sink, all were small.

I'd finally settled on a vanilla cake sandwiched with mango curd, decorated with lush buttercream and marzipan roses and edible gold dust. Before we left, I'd printed out my baking schedule: curd that evening, then icing the next day, then roses the morning of the wedding on Christmas Day. I'd baked the layers and kept them in the freezer. Everything was already made except for the curd, which I thought might be fun to make with everyone around.

Mom and Bart soon returned, and the house turned celebratory. Gloria was in town too, and she came over with her husband and one of her kids, who'd brought their children as well. Olivia had had a meal catered from a nearby restaurant so no one had to leave or cook, and the kids all played with each other.

When dinner was over and Gloria's family finally left, we were all exhausted. But I still had to make the curd.

Claire was sprawled out on one of couches in the living room, near the kitchen. Mom and Bart were in bed. Joe's parents had also arrived and were staying at the inn where the wedding was being held. He'd gone over to see them.

"Can you move a bit?" I asked Claire so I could sit with her.

"Go sit on that other chair."

"I want to sit here. Just for a minute before I start."

"There's not enough space."

I lifted her feet, and she kicked her legs out straight, just enough to hit my thigh. "Ow!"

"This house has like, ten different comfy chairs. Find your own."

"I want to be close to you."

"Fine." She moved another inch. I didn't know why this was so irritating to both of us, but it made me feel like a teenager again, our Christmas dynamic maintained despite us being surrounded by more people.

I pulled up the recipe on my phone. I noticed I had a message from Denny.

How's the cake going?

Ever since Joe had seen the messages from him, I'd mostly stopped writing, only responding when he wrote first. When I'd settled on the final flavours for the cake, I'd asked Joe to taste it. He liked it, but he also asked me if the recipe had come from Denny. When I told him the truth, which was no, I was pretty sure he didn't believe me.

I picked up my phone and typed quickly even though Joe wasn't here to see me. *About to make the curd.*

Good luck!

I responded as if he were a co-worker. *Thanks!*

I took the eggs and butter off the ledge where I'd put them to bring them to room temperature.

"Can I help?" Rosalie asked when she wandered in. She was in pyjamas, and her hair was wet from a quick bath.

"You can help me cut the butter, maybe." She reached for a knife from the wooden block on the counter until I stopped her. "I mean with this." I handed her a butter knife that could easily cut through the room-temperature stick. It just needed to be cut into chunks, so it didn't really matter how it looked. She stepped up on a stool near the counter and grasped the knife awkwardly. Olivia walked in as Rosalie muddled through the task.

"I'm glad you're helping, but it's your bedtime. It's very late."

"I'm busy!"

"You've done a lot today. Let's leave Laura alone. She has to concentrate."

Rosalie immediately burst into tears. "I'm not even tired."

"I can tell you're very tired."

"It's *not* my bedtime. I am *not* tired."

"Rosalie."

"Stop being *stupid*."

"Hey. You're going to bed now. Don't use that word. It's not nice."

Rosalie started sobbing in earnest. As she flailed her arms around, I was happy that I'd made sure to only give her the butter knife.

Olivia dragged her off, and Claire looked at me and shrugged. Anyway, I did have to concentrate on cooking.

"Is it hard to make?" Claire asked from the couch.

"Curd can be tricky." I separated the egg yolks, cut the remaining butter, and then grated lemon peel and squeezed juice. I had a Tupperware of thawed puréed mango flesh ready.

Olivia emerged again as I was about to start melting the butter. "Can I join you both?" she asked. She was now sixteen weeks pregnant and starting to show, but she wasn't throwing up anymore. She looked flushed when she sat next to Claire.

I was too focused on my curd to help ease any tension, but I could tell the two of them were awkward with each other.

"You're so lucky to live in San Francisco," Olivia said to her.

"How come?"

"It just seems...nice." Olivia looked a little flustered by the question.

"It's fine."

"Sheesh, Claire," I said as I stirred the chunks of butter with the wooden spoon. "It's better than fine." Her behaviour reminded me of conversations with our half-sisters— the way they never elaborated, the way they quietly shut us out.

"It has a lot of problems."

I turned the gas down on the burner and slowly started pouring in yolks. The curd needed low heat, just enough for the eggs to cook without curdling into scrambled eggs. Stir, stir, stir. Whenever I made curd, there would always be a point when I was sure it wasn't going to work; I would turn up the heat just a smidge, and the mixture would either suddenly thicken, or, every so often, break. I'd used a dozen eggs in this mixture and didn't have extra purée with me, so I didn't want to fuck it up, but I also wasn't familiar with the stove and wasn't sure how hot it would get if I turned it up a notch. I took my chances and kept stirring. I regretted thinking this would be fun.

Claire stood up and came over. "How's it going?"

"Okay."

"You look so serious."

I knew she was joking, but it still bothered me. I was making our mother's wedding cake. I had practised this and prepared; I hadn't just opened a web browser, asked my rich friends for help and typed in a credit card number. I wanted to say this to her, but I didn't. Stir, stir, stir. I noticed a speck in the curd and swore.

"What's wrong?"

"Can you just give me some space for a minute?" I lowered the heat, lifted the pot, and stirred madly before the rest could get ruined. It seemed to work. I took a deep breath, lowered the pot again, and soon the concoction had transformed into something thicker. I coated the back of the spoon and cooled it for a second before touching it to my tongue. The acidity was a slight jolt, like crossing an invisible electric fence, and there was no egginess that would've indicated it had broken. "Is there a strainer some-where?" I asked—the one thing I'd forgotten. I'd brought my own big Mason jar from Toronto to store the curd, but I wanted to strain it to remove the flecks of zest and any stray eggy bits.

Olivia got up first and started opening the dozens of drawers in the kitchen. She found a strainer and ran it under the faucet. I was so grateful when she handed it to me.

The finished product was a plush pale orange, thick and smooth, something you could eat by the spoonful in the middle of the night if you woke up hungry. I screwed the top on the jar, and the glass in my hands was soothing, warm. I took a photo of the jar held up against a light. I sent it to Denny. It felt like closure, somehow. The cake components were done; I had no more questions for him. I muted the app so that I wouldn't see his response.

Claire had gone back to sitting on the couch and was doing something on her laptop.

"I'm finished," I said.

"Congratulations. Now go to bed, you look exhausted."

But we all were. The three of us remained in place with-out talking. I felt like I should say something, about our parents' union and how the three of us would be connected, but the vibe was off.

It was Olivia who finally spoke. "Rosalie is going to be up at dawn. I should get some sleep." She left, but Claire and I lingered.

Eventually Joe returned from seeing his parents. I tensed up thinking about the message to Denny, but there was nothing to see, really. Still, I made a mental note to delete it.

"Do you want to try the mango curd?" I jumped up to show him the jar in the kitchen, but he shook his head and returned to the bedroom.

"Is he okay?" Claire asked.

"What do you mean?"

"He seems cranky."

"He's just tired."

"I guess we all are."

"Yeah." I finally got up first, put the gorgeous jar in the fridge, and left Claire there alone.

The next day we had multiple plans: a visit to a winery, wedding prep, general Christmas Eve activities. And I had to finish the cake, which was why I woke up early, thinking I would be the first one up. Instead I found Rosalie sitting at the kitchen counter poking at a bowl of yogourt. I didn't know where Olivia was.

"I have something that might make it better," I said to her and removed the jar of mango curd from the fridge and dolloped a small amount into the yogourt. "Try this."

She looked suspicious of the yellow-orange goo, but licked her spoon tentatively. Her face wrinkled up. "It's sour!" She immediately started eating more. "I like sour things."

"Me too."

"Look," she gestured toward something on the floor: a

line of bugs. Ants, but wispier, smaller. They looked like they would smudge at the slightest breath. How were they alive in winter? I must have spilled sugar the night before. "Do you think they look like ghost ants?"

"They do!"

"I know how to say *ghost* in Spanish."

It was fun talking to Rosalie, the twists the conversations took. She'd been watching some Spanish cartoons on her tablet the day before. "How?"

"*Fantasma!*"

Olivia walked into the kitchen and looked at the full yogourt bowl. "You have to eat more than that."

"I'm sharing with her," she said defensively and pointed to me.

"Eat, Rosalie." Olivia opened the fridge and took out the eggs.

"Can I crack them?" Rosalie hopped off the stool and stood on her tiptoes next to Olivia.

"Careful, careful."

I left them to make breakfast and went back to my room. Joe was awake, looking at his phone. He pulled the blanket over his head when he saw me.

"How are you feeling?" I asked.

"Tired. Hungry."

"Olivia is making us breakfast."

"I kind of want to go somewhere, just the two of us."

"Like where?"

"Anywhere."

I didn't really want to, but I hoped it would improve his mood. We changed quickly, and when we left the room, everyone was gathered in the living room and kitchen. There was a platter of scrambled eggs on the table, a pot of coffee and some mugs on the counter.

"Joe and I are going out to get something instead."

"Alone?" Claire asked.

"Why are you spending money on breakfast when we have so much food here?" Mom asked.

"Will you be long? We were planning on going to visit that winery right away," Bart said.

"You're right," I said. "We'll eat with you here. It smells good." I looked at Joe. A nod of his head, a shrug of agreement. That seemed to appease the group. I couldn't tell if he was annoyed or not, and then I was mad at him for suggesting we do something alone when we were clearly here to be together as a group. It was a *wedding*.

We took two cars to the winery: me, Claire, Mom, and Joe in ours; Bart, Olivia, Thomas, and Rosalie in the other. Joe's parents met us there as well, and Gloria's crew. After the tour we sat at a heated picnic table under a pergola wound with lights that sparkled in the grey day.

"Hello, family," the waitress said to greet us. She kept addressing us as that throughout the meal, as if it were our collective name, *Family. Are you ready to order, Family? Here are your drinks, Family.*

"To Family," Thomas said as a toast when we had our glasses of icewine.

The picnic area was next to a big field that had been cleared of trees. In December it was desolate, the ground hard and cold from recent snowfalls, but that didn't stop Rosalie from running around like a puppy.

"Can someone play with me?" she called out.

"I can," Joe volunteered.

"Are you sure?" Thomas asked.

"I'm getting cold sitting here."

He got up and ran out to the field like a football player being called into a game. I watched him pick up Rosalie and swing her around, over and over, until suddenly she started crying. Olivia, Thomas, and I ran toward them.

"What's wrong?" Olivia asked.

"My arm," Rosalie sobbed. "My arm hurts."

"What did you do to her?" I asked Joe.

"Did I break it?" He looked terrified.

"This has happened before," Thomas said. "Sometimes kids' joints aren't quite fused and they pop out if they're being swung around. Honey, can you stretch out your arm?"

"No."

"Give me your arm."

"No." But she tried anyway, and then kept crying. Her cheeks were red from the cold, and snot was smeared all over her face.

"Daddy's going to get you a popsicle, okay? Do you want a popsicle?"

"I don't think they have popsicles here," I tried to say quietly. "I saw ice cream on the menu, though."

"I want a popsicle," Rosalie whimpered.

"We'll get you ice cream." Thomas carried her inside.

Olivia left and came back with a small bowl of the only ice cream on the menu: lavender honey. It would have to do. Thomas held out the bowl, and Rosalie tried reaching for it with her arm. Suddenly we all heard a slight pop. It was gross, but also a relief. She sobbed harder than ever, but kept stretching, then grabbed the bowl and started to eat. "This tastes like soap," she said.

"Is it back in?" I asked Thomas.

"Yeah. The same thing happened to us last time—it went back in on its own. We had to go to the hospital the first time."

"I thought I broke her arm," Joe said. "I'm so sorry."

"Kids are pretty hard to break," Olivia said. "Don't feel bad."

On the drive back home, Joe was still mortified about the incident. "I didn't know their bones were so loose."

"It's so gross," Claire said.

"You should've heard it pop back in."

"I can't."

I was too jumpy to relax afterwards. When we pulled into the driveway of the Airbnb, I asked Joe and Claire if they wanted to go out for coffee, something better than what we had there.

"I feel like I need a nap like Rosalie," Joe said.

"Me too, but I just need more caffeine," Claire said.

Mom, Bart, and Joe went inside. Claire moved to the front seat, and I took the car keys.

"Where should we go?" I asked. "Everything's going to close soon probably."

"I'm kind of craving McDonald's."

"Really?"

"I go about once a year. I think it's time."

Claire looked at a map on her phone and found the closest one—off the side of a highway about twenty minutes away—and directed me as I drove.

Neither of us wanted to eat inside. At the drive-thru I ordered a McChicken combo, Claire a Filet-O-Fish. We'd been ordering the same thing since we were children. I pulled over to a corner of the parking lot and lowered the windows so cool air blew through while we ate. The fries were hot, almost scalding, and when Claire dumped a pack of salt on hers, I did the same. We chatted for a while, like we were warming up to each other. It was easier to speak there than it had been in the house. Maybe it was because we weren't facing each other. Maybe we'd become accustomed to talking without being close.

"I caught up on Joe's podcast," she said. "I didn't know you'd done the frozen transfer in the fall."

"Oh." I threw my McChicken box back into the paper bag and started fiddling with it a bit. "The whole thing was a huge bummer. I didn't want to talk about it."

"He sounded really disappointed."

"We both were."

"I'm sure you were. I'm sorry." The conversation had more gaps in it than we were used to, but we just sat through them, feeling our bodies, our physical presences in the car, fill in those spaces. When Claire said she was sorry, I knew she really meant it. "I did something too," she added.

"What did you do?"

"I froze my eggs."

"Why didn't you tell me?"

"Same reason you didn't tell me about your transfer."

"I guess. Still. It's different."

"Is it?"

"I don't know anymore. What made you decide to go ahead with it?"

Claire continued looking straight ahead and not at me. The McDonald's parking lot looked out toward the road we'd driven on, two lanes, farmland or a winery on the other side. Some Christmas lights had been wrapped around the McDonald's pole. "It's been such a strange year. I've been feeling lost, I guess. It was something concrete I could do."

"You've gotten into meditation. You launched a startup. It sounds like you're doing a pretty good job of finding concrete things to do. Why not, like, get a tattoo instead?"

"Are you making fun of me?" Claire looked at me, and for a second I saw her kid self so clearly, the flash of her eyes, a look of anger that she would give to other people, to Dad, to our stepsisters. Never me.

I felt my eyes well up. "No, I'm sorry. I'm not. It's just hard to understand why you're putting yourself through something that I know is so hard on your body."

"Your experience is different than mine, I think. I feel like I've been throwing strands of spaghetti at the wall to see what sticks."

We used to do that, Claire and I. We'd make spaghetti for dinner when Mom was working late, and we would fight over who got to fish out a noodle from the pot of boiling water and toss it at the wall to see if it was ready, this being the test of doneness we'd heard about. If it remained glued, we knew it was ready to eat. One night we just kept throwing the strands for fun, laughing hysterically at the shapes they made, and then forgot to clean up. Then Mom came home and saw the gluey mess on the wall and floor. She didn't yell, just sat in a chair and rubbed her eyes for a long time.

"Unlike you I don't know what I want out of my life," Claire continued. "I have to make sure I keep my options open. You're lucky that you're so sure of everything."

"How do you know I'm so sure?"

"I don't I guess, but, look—you married your high school sweetheart and you're still in love. That's statistically impossible. You're about to start your family. You have a nice, clear path ahead of you."

"But I don't?" I was so confused by her statements. "I can't have a baby."

"Not yet, but you will."

"Considering the amount of research you've done, you should know that it's not certain. Also, Joe found out about Denny in Las Vegas."

"The dude you met that one night?"

"Yeah. He saw some texts on my phone."

"What kind of texts?"

"Nothing scandalous. Selfies. Stuff about Mom's cake."

"You send him selfies?"

"I mean, you send selfies to your friends, right?"

"I guess. But wait, Mom's wedding cake? I don't get it."

"He's a chef."

"Okay. That's weird, though."

"I *know*. Also I kissed him in Vegas, but it was nothing. Joe doesn't know that part."

It felt so silly saying it out loud. We kissed. I should've had sex with him for the moral weight it seemed to impart, like the consequences would've been the same, and at least it wouldn't have felt as juvenile, at least it would've felt like something adults did and not high school drama. But I also knew that if the situation were reversed, if Joe had kissed someone, it would be absolutely devastating. The brief physical intimacy of a kiss was one thing, but everything else it implied was another.

I'd been thinking a lot about what it could imply. A crossing of a threshold of closeness, for one thing, a clear translation of the intangibly emotional into physical, with weight to it. A kiss was, what—first base? Even if first base was kid stuff, it was still the first step toward whatever happened next. But to me the kiss hadn't implied that at all. It had been a moment for myself, an experiment that I'd known immediately was not successful, and it didn't change how I felt about Joe. I could've maybe even explained this properly to him at the time, but because I hadn't, my argument was obviously weakened.

Claire gave me a look unlike any she'd given me before. A once-over, almost, like she was somehow impressed with me. "You *kissed* him?"

"It's embarrassing."

"You're just the last person I would imagine cheating."

And suddenly, all my arguments about why it didn't matter evaporated.

"It was hardly cheating. It was like, nothing."

"Would you do it again?"

"Of course not."

"Seriously, though. Would you?"

I actually did take a beat to think about it. To really think about her question and give an honest answer. If I couldn't be honest with Claire, then I didn't know if I could be honest with Joe either.

"I wouldn't."

"I can imagine Joe would be hurt, though. Is he mad?"

"He's mad I didn't tell him I met Denny. Like, the principle of it."

"Of course he would be. But he'll come around."

"It doesn't seem that easy." I paused. "If you think my life looks figured out, yours does too."

"Laura. I still have roommates."

"That's your decision. You can afford your own space. I thought you liked the idea of communal living."

"I do, I just think the bathroom part ends up being fundamentally untenable after a certain point."

"Fair."

Claire drank what remained of her Diet Coke. "Did you know that I don't even know if I like men?"

"Oh. No. I mean, it doesn't surprise me, I guess?"

She laughed. "Why?"

"I don't know exactly?"

"I've been dating women recently. I think it feels right."

"Maybe you will need your eggs frozen then."

"Can you let the eggs go for a second?" She didn't say anything else for a while, and we just sat there. "I don't know, maybe that's all I have to say. I have no big revelations. I can't even properly come out because I don't even know."

"I mean, sexuality is a, um, spectrum, right?"

She rolled her eyes. "I live in San Francisco now. I know. That's not what I mean."

"Well I support you in whatever you do. Always."

She smiled at me like she was about to make a joke, but she didn't. "I have twenty-two eggs frozen."

I choked. "*Twenty-two?*"

"Apparently. How many did you have when you did IVF?"

"Sixteen, but they only resulted in four embryos, and then in the end only three of them could be implanted."

"Oh."

"I have a feeling your eggs will make more embryos."

"How come?"

"I don't know, I just do."

"Well, it's hard to say. I just want you to know that there's so much I'm trying to figure out, and it's hard sometimes, especially when I'm away from you and Mom. You have each other to talk to, and now you have Olivia too. That's all."

"I'm here to help you too, though. I just need you to tell me."

"I think I know that. And it's the same for you too."

"I think I know that too."

We drove back in silence, but we weren't angry at each other. It was the opposite—I felt closer to Claire now than I had felt since she moved. The idea of her wanting me to use her eggs didn't feel as fraught as it had when she'd first mentioned it. I began to see it as what she'd intended: a gift.

Over the past few months I'd been mulling over the theory that I didn't know my sister as well as I thought. If someone like Olivia asked me a question about her—*Is she dating anyone?* for example—and I didn't know the answer, it would reinforce my theory. It confused me because one of my core beliefs was that I knew Claire—and Joe—better than anyone in the world, but somehow over the past few months I'd lost my connection with both of them. What would I do if my theory was right?

"I still haven't talked to Joe about using your eggs yet," I said to her. It felt like a confession.

"I figured. I don't know if it helps, but I read something recently about how scientists are trying to prove that genetic material gets passed to the baby in utero, which is why sometimes babies from donor eggs still sometimes look like their mothers."

"Really?"

"Apparently. I like the thought of it."

"Yeah," I said. "Me too."

We drove the rest of the way back in silence, past the bare-branched vineyards and apple orchards, past the farm stands closed for the winter.

There was a flurry of activity back at the Airbnb. Mom needed help pinning the back of her dress and figuring out Bart's boutonniere. We wanted to do face masks. Olivia, Thomas, and Rosalie got dressed for a walk, and then Rosalie made a big deal about me and Joe going with them, but not Claire, and that was awkward for a split second. Joe kept retreating to our room and everyone kept asking after him, which was also awkward in a different way. Olivia had bought two rolls of Pillsbury sugar cookie dough so we could make cookies for Santa, and I helped ice them with leftovers from the wedding cake. It was six, then seven, then eight, and then suddenly almost eleven, and Mom and Bart were already in bed so they'd be rested for the wedding, but I still had to get some things ready for the cake. One by one people started disappearing until I was the only one left in the kitchen. I hadn't expected that even with a house full of people—so many more than I normally had around me on Christmas Eve—I could still end up alone with my thoughts, with myself.

Are you already asleep? I texted Joe.

Then I texted Claire. *When you froze your eggs, did you give yourself your own shots?*

And then in subsequent messages: *Did you feel bloated and uncomfortable? Who drove you to the clinic the day of the retrieval? Did you take an Uber home? Why didn't you tell me again?*

When we were finally all in bed, I nuzzled Joe's neck.

"Claire told me something," I said, emboldened by the fact that he hadn't turned away from me.

"What?"

"She got a bunch of eggs frozen."

"Oh my god, is Claire pregnant?"

"No! But she wants to donate some to us. She has *twenty-two*."

He didn't say anything for a good minute. "Do we need them? We don't know if the problem is your eggs."

"I never responded well to Clomid or the IVF drugs. And the embryos were Cs."

"That still doesn't mean you're the problem."

"We would have to do another round of IVF again to see—that's what Dr. Sutton said. It doesn't seem like you want to."

"I don't know what I want to do."

"We should make a decision."

"I agree, but I don't want to be forced into one right now."

"I swear I'm not trying to force you into anything. I just have no idea what you want. It sounds like you want to give up, but if we're doing the IVF thing it's not considered excessive to try more than once. It's more common, probably."

"We've just tried so hard, Laura."

"So why not try harder?"

"It's so much work."

I couldn't tell if we were talking about having a baby or our whole relationship. "It's worth it, though," I said. "I think so, anyway."

Joe sighed and closed his eyes. "What if we decide to do another round and it doesn't work—then what? That's when we use Claire's eggs? Or are you asking me if we should just use them right away?"

"Maybe we can think of them as an insurance policy."

"What if after everything Claire decides she wants the baby?"

"Come on, Joe."

"What?"

"Now you're just being mean. Claire wouldn't do that."

"You haven't seen the cases I've seen."

"You work in corporate law. You don't ever see family law cases, and I'm sure you've never seen a case where someone donates an egg to her sister and then wants to keep the baby for herself."

"I have!"

"That's not going to happen to us."

"We would need a contract either way."

"I don't want to talk about *logistics* right now. I just wanted to tell you what she told me." It was hard discussing this in the rental. Everyone's rooms were so close together. The previous night I'd woken up to the sound of Bart snoring next door. "Can we just agree that Claire is offering us something nice?"

"Well, I'll thank her then."

If I'd just gotten pregnant right away, or at least the normal way, we wouldn't be having these conversations, squished together and whispering in an unfamiliar bed. Mom and Bart would be getting married, and we'd have a kid with us, and maybe our kid would be sharing a bed with Rosalie, and it would all be so adorable. *Hello, Family.*

What was it like to simply sleep with someone and get pregnant? It sounded impossible, like a magic trick. Imagine just fucking and getting a baby out of it. I thought of all the movies I'd seen in my life about accidental pregnancies. Entire plot lines built around one single, sloppy night with so many ensuing decisions to be made. The movies were always about those decisions, not the night you got pregnant, which was just the jumping-off point for the rest of the story. In my case, I was stuck in an interminable pause, the sexiest part drawn out so long that it was just clinical and repetitive. *Get on with things*, I silently yelled at the imaginary movie reel of my life. I wanted the luxury of decision-making. I saw so much online about how hard motherhood was, and I believed it, I really did, but I wanted to experience it myself too. Maybe I would hate it and regret it, but I wanted to make that decision myself.

"I'm afraid I would be a terrible father," Joe said. I thought he'd already fallen asleep.

"Why would you think that?"

"I almost broke Rosalie's arm. I don't know what I'm doing."

"That was an accident. Thomas said it happened to them too."

"Maybe this is natural selection. We're not supposed to have kids."

"I don't think there's anything wrong with me," I said quietly.

"That's not what I mean. I know there's nothing wrong with you."

"But that's not what you just said."

"You know I wish there were a million mini-yous in this world."

"I don't want a mini-me, though. I want a mini-us. And I don't need a million, just one is fine."

We were both weeping.

"So, what are we going to do?" he asked.

"We'll just have to keep doing this."

"I'm not sure what this is."

"Talking to each other at least."

Despite everything, I knew how I felt about Joe: I wanted us to be that family eating dinner at midnight at a restaurant in Rome. Our version of it. Maybe life was pinning yourself to stupid visions. It wasn't philosophy and ethics; it was manifesting these little dreams and then dealing with whatever happened next.

On Christmas morning, Mom and Bart's wedding day, I woke up first to finish assembling the cake. It was one of the best things I'd ever made. Three layers of vanilla cake made with browned butter to give it some depth and then brushed with a sugar syrup to keep it moist. The mango curd in between each layer. I'd covered it in a creamy vanilla buttercream, and was about to dot it with the marzipan roses I'd made, pale yellow, a few deep red, and then finish it off with a dusting of gold leaf I'd brought in a vial.

Mom woke up even before Rosalie. "Oh, honey," she said when she saw the cake. "It's so beautiful."

"It's not finished yet. And Mom, it's so early. You should be resting." The ceremony was at one, and then everyone was going to have a late lunch at the inn's restaurant.

"I'm hungry! I didn't eat much yesterday because I was nervous. Bart is still sleeping. How can he sleep? We're getting married. Eat with me." She took out a banana, cut it in half, and put one of the halves on the counter next to me.

"You must be so excited."

"I am." She ate her half of the banana. "I was thinking about something. Are you sure you and Joe don't want my house? It's a good home for a young family."

"We don't have a young family. I'm not pregnant."

"You will be pregnant, though, soon."

"Mom."

"I have a feeling. It's your turn."

"It doesn't work like that." I'd said that to her so many times now. "How did you get pregnant so easily? I should have your genetics. And Dad has a million kids too."

"We never get what we want, but if you're lucky, you like what you get."

"That's deep, Mom."

"And you know I already love your baby so much."

"It doesn't exist, though."

"It doesn't matter." Mom's phone buzzed. It was weird seeing her comfortably accept and respond to a text. "Bart is awake."

She got up and went to see her almost-husband, and I opened the Tupperware of pre-made marzipan roses, some better than others.

Rosalie was up next, a pyjama-clad sprite rushing to the fireplace and squealing with joy over Santa's visit. She saw my finished cake. "Did Santa bring that too? For breakfast?"

Olivia came out and also gasped at the cake. "Santa did not bring that. Laura made it!"

"I'm going to wake up Daddy so we can open presents." She ran off.

Olivia and I were alone for the first time this trip. For all our closeness beforehand, we'd barely had the chance to speak since we'd arrived, her wrapped up in caring for Rosalie, and me preoccupied with Claire and Joe.

"I can tell something is going on between all of you," she said as she made us coffee. "You, Joe, Claire. Is something wrong?"

"The usual dumb family things."

"It's so interesting watching all of you."

"What do you mean?"

"I can just tell you know each other so well."

"That's debatable."

"I can see it, though. It's sweet."

The rest of the morning went by in a blur. I put on my pink dress, Joe a linen suit that he'd bought because it reminded him of *The Great Gatsby*. Claire wore a jumpsuit. Olivia was in a beautiful flowery peasant dress. Mom wore a cream sleeveless dress and gold flats, and Bart wore a navy suit and gold cufflinks. Olivia had organized flower crowns for Rosalie and for Gloria's grandchildren.

The wedding was in a small greenhouse attached to an inn at another winery, and it was humid, bursting with foliage and tropical plants. There were even butterflies. The ceremony was short, and Mom and Bart's vows traditional, including the officiant asking if there was anyone in the room who objected to their union. We all looked around, at each other, the plants, and laughed at the absurdity of the question. Claire wept; Olivia wept. Rosalie fidgeted. Joe squeezed my hand, and I thought that I would be the only one who didn't cry, but then of course I did.

I took a breath and tried to take it all in, but how was it even possible to capture all of it? The cream dress; the marzipan roses; the conversations we'd all had over the past few days; the unknown future that stretched out far before all of us, before Mom and Bart, and myself and Claire, and me and Joe, and Olivia and Thomas and Rosalie.

When Joe and I had gotten married, we'd been children, and so naive, but I had believed in love then, and I was pretty sure I still believed in it now, even if it felt muddled sometimes. Its tenor changed over the years, and I was still getting accustomed to the new sounds, the new tones. What if at Mom's age I married someone else? It seemed unfathomable, but then again, all of this was unfathomable. So I stuck to the moment we were in: the wedding and the bursting love that existed now, straining the walls of the greenhouse. If someone opened their mouth and said something, it would be like an opera singer shattering a glass with their voice. We were all so attuned and in harmony for the ceremony.

I looked up at Joe, and his eyes were shining. We kissed. For a perfect shimmery minute I had everything I ever wanted.

The cake was delicious. I was worried that it would be too dry, but the sugar syrup worked. Rosalie ate two bites before asking if there was chocolate cake too, but then she finished her slice anyway. We drank champagne and ice water, and everyone toasted each other multiple times. We were suddenly a family, and it felt strange. I mean, it felt natural.

Dad called in the afternoon to wish us a merry Christmas. He even spoke to Mom for a minute to say congratulations. When I watched her on the phone with him, I felt so proud of her, for the life that she'd built for herself.

We returned to the house by seven. Mom and Bart were going to stay at the inn overnight. Now that their wedding anniversary would be December 25, Claire, Mom, and I might never have a Christmas alone again. I didn't mind, though. Christmas Day was a miracle of physics; it spanned years, generations. On Christmas Day time could be pulled apart and crawled into; it was like a Polaroid, revealing itself to you slowly and looking like a relic of the past only a minute after being taken. It was a day for Claire and me as children, for Joe and me as high school sweethearts separated tragically by a few blocks and family obligations, and now it was a day for a wedding anniversary. So if we had to share it, what was the problem? There was room.

Rosalie was strung out on sugar and hyped up from the wedding. Olivia and Thomas let her run around a bit more and then swooped her off to bed. Joe settled into one of the comfy chairs with a glass of Scotch. Claire and I decided to get into the hot tub, which we, amazingly, had not yet used this whole trip. We changed out of our outfits and into swimsuits and met outside in the backyard. We lifted the cover off the hot tub, and then Claire pressed a button and the water started churning, the lights glowing lavender beneath it. We lowered ourselves in.

The water was hot, the air cool. I felt like rising dough in the steamy air hovering around the hot tub, like I was a dumpling, my pores opening up, my shoulders softened. I rested my head on the ledge behind me and looked up. Beyond the skeletal tree branches, there were so many stars.

"I haven't been in a hot tub in years," I said.

"I went a few weeks ago in Tahoe. Shannon's parents have a cabin there. Well, a house. Maybe a mansion?"

"Oh yeah. You told me her family was rich."

"How do you think she can afford to have so many business ideas?"

"So that's the secret."

"She's not an asshole about it, at least."

"Well I'm glad the two of you are going to disrupt the fertility industry. Please consult with me if you have questions."

"You're not mad at me about it, right?"

"I'm just confused that you didn't ask me for help, or just advice."

"I will in the future." She kicked her feet up. "There's been this distance between us."

"I know."

"Joe told me you told him about the eggs."

"He did?"

"This afternoon. He thanked me and said you were still deciding what you were going to do next, but that it meant a lot to him."

"It does," I said. "It means so much to both of us. I don't know if I've made that clear enough."

"I just want you to be happy."

"I wish I could explain it, but I don't even understand it. I keep thinking that by now I should have a better rationale for the effort we're going through, but whenever I think I know, it kind of evaporates and I'm left with this feeling of just wanting a baby."

"I think I get it. Sometimes I'll get, like, a glimmer of that feeling. But then it goes away."

"It just won't go away for me. I hate it. It doesn't feel normal."

"I think I'm more abnormal."

"Maybe we both are then."

Our faces were flushed pink, sweaty. We had the same skin, the same shape of nose. Claire's face was narrower. She had better bone structure, I thought, in the cheeks.

"I'm sad knowing I'm leaving in two days," she said.

"You have work to do. And you enjoy it." Ever since Claire

had left, something about the move had made it feel like a move that would stick. This would be it, our separation, a lifetime of texts and phone calls and visits like these.

"I guess."

"You could come home, though, whenever you want. Or just visit. Stay with me and Joe."

"You barely have a nursery, let alone a guest room."

"You can camp out. Also, we're thinking about buying Mom's house.

"I could do that. I'll come when you have a baby then."

"Who knows when that will be?"

"I can't read the future, but soon." She reminded me of Mom, the certainty in her voice.

"There aren't any guarantees, Claire. Even if we use your eggs."

"Can you just believe me on this one?"

"I'll try."

Belief could be dangerous, but it was a form of hope, and maybe that's what I needed now—a way to shift my hope onto others. Because what if Claire was right? What if it turned out that a year from now I finally had the Christmas in Toronto I wanted, but instead of at home we were in a hospital?

Imagine a baby had just been born, and it was mine and Joe's, and maybe it was Claire's too. It would be early morning, and the sky would look the same as it did after Mom and Bart's wedding, bright blue, a child's rendering of a sky, with just enough billowy clouds.

Mom and Bart would be there too, and Olivia and Thomas and Rosalie and Rosalie's new sibling, born a few months earlier. Bart would suggest going down to get us breakfast.

A colleague of Mom's would come by, someone who had known her since she'd joined the hospital and cleaned the linens, who had seen Claire and me as children visiting when school was closed. She would insist on bringing up food so that Bart could stay.

When she returned Joe would reach for our baby so I could have some coffee. But I would shake my head, wanting to hold on to the image in front of me for a little longer instead: everyone crowded into the small room around me, our baby cradled in my arms. And anyway, I wouldn't need coffee right then.

I would be, suddenly, so awake.

ACKNOWLEDGEMENTS

This book has been in progress for a long time.

I had the incredible privilege of working with the wonderful team at Invisible Publishing again. Thank you, Norm Nehmetallah, Kimberley Griffiths, and Megan Fildes. Your commitment to independent publishing is a gift.

Thank you to my editor, Bryan Ibeas, for your willingness to break Google Docs with me.

Thank you to the Canada Council for the Arts and the Ontario Arts Council's Recommender Grants for Writers program for financial support. Thank you to Meg Storey for your essential editorial suggestions.

This book would not exist without the writing advice and moral support from Samantha Garner, Julia Zarankin, and Lindsay Zier-Vogel. Long live the Semi-Retired Hens!

Thank you Andrew Emond for your support. You lived through a few scenes from this book too.

Thank you Emily Robertson-Riggio for absolutely everything, including a steady supply of karaoke. Team Emily/Teri forever. Thank you also to Adam Riggio, and of course, Ginger and Phinneas Turcotte, the cornerstones of CPG!

Thank you so much to the people who offered up cheerleading, encouragement, cheese, or playdates for our kids when I needed to work on writing: Jessica Westhead, Charlotte Schwartz, Vanessa Lamb, Amanda Presutti, Sheeza Sarfraz, Jeff Dupuis, Laurent Grant, Alexie Landry, Caroline Pelletier, Lesley Trites, and Chitra Unnikrishnan.

Thank you to my family all over the world: Panagiotis Zervogiannis, Angeliki Stamatakou, Serge Papatakis, Olga Rankin, and especially my loving parents, Tony and Lita Vlassopoulos.

Thank you to Mark Altosaar for your love.

And thank you to Clara Emond. To paraphrase the poet Sharon Olds, whose poem "The Planned Child" I referenced frequently during early drafts of this book, the world was not enough for me without you in it. Every day I am grateful you are here.

Invisible Publishing produces fine Canadian literature for those who enjoy such things. As an independent, not-for-profit publisher, we work to build communities that sustain and encourage engaging, literary, and current writing.

Invisible Publishing has been in operation for nearly two decades. We released our first fiction titles in the spring of 2007, and our catalogue has come to include works of graphic fiction and nonfiction, pop culture biographies, experimental poetry, and prose.

We are committed to publishing writers with diverse perspectives. In acknowledging historical and systemic barriers, and the limits of our existing catalogue, we emphatically encourage writers from LGBTQ2SIA+ communities, Indigenous writers, and writers of colour to submit their work.

Invisible Publishing is also home to the Bibliophonic series of music books and the Throwback series of CanLit reissues.